ROOM TO DREAM

ALSO BY KELLY YANG

FRONT DESK

THREE KEYS

ROOM TO DREAM

A **FRONT DESK** NOVEL

KELLY YANG

SCHOLASTIC INC.

TO MY LAO YE, WHO TAUGHT
ME TO DREAM BIG. I MISS YOU
EVERY DAY.

ISBN 978-1-338-80320-4

10 9 8 7 6   22 23 24 25

Printed in the U.S.A.   40
First printing 2021
Book design by Maeve Norton

CHAPTER I

Silver strands of tinsel hung from our classroom Christmas tree, swaying slightly under the ceiling fan. Even though it was nearly December, it was still fairly warm in Anaheim—not enough for air conditioning but enough to keep the fan on. As our seventh-grade math teacher, Mrs. Beadle, handed out problem sets for us to do, I sat at my desk staring at the shimmery strands, wondering if I should get some for our little tree at the front desk of the Calivista Motel.

"Hey, Lupe, do you think we should get some tinsel—" I turned to my right and asked, then remembered. Lupe wasn't in math with me this year. I kept forgetting. Thanks to all the studying she did with my mom over the summer, Lupe was now in Algebra 1, while Jason and I were in regular seventh-grade math. In fact, Lupe wasn't in any of my classes at Anaheim Junior High this year.

I sighed, and Jason lifted his head. "You want some tinsel?" he asked. Before I could answer, he jumped out of his seat and lunged for the Christmas tree, nearly falling on top of it. All the kids shrieked and laughed.

"Take your seat!" Mrs. Beadle ordered him.

Jason muttered, "Sorry," and went back to his desk, but not before making off with a fistful of tinsel. When Mrs. Beadle's back was turned, he passed it to me. I giggled.

At least I had Jason in my classes this year.

Jason squished his legs under his desk. He had shot up like a bean sprout over the summer and now towered over me. His smile disappeared when he looked down at the problem sets Mrs. Beadle placed in front of him. "Not a quiz again," he moaned.

"Jason, you're in middle school now," Mrs. Beadle said. "And you've known about this quiz all week."

"But I've been busy cooking!" Jason replied.

Twice a week after school, Jason went to a cooking academy in nearby Orange. Sometimes after class, he came by the motel and let us taste his creations — Hawaiian peach mousse, tomato ricotta with sesame, barbecued butternut squash and choy sum. Every dish he made was *delicious*. His cooking teacher said he was one of the most talented junior chefs she'd ever taught. At the rate he was going, he'd be promoted to the elite cooking academy any day now!

But Mrs. Beadle shook her head. "Your extracurricular activities are just that. *Extra*curricular. They're not supposed to get in the way of your real subjects."

"Yeah, Jason," Bethany Brett chimed in. She was sitting in the row in front of us, wearing five necklaces and twirling them with her fingers. "Cooking's not a real subject. It's for old ladies."

Jason's face turned beet red as the class started snickering. Most of our classmates came from other elementary schools; they hadn't been to last year's cookout at Dale Elementary, where Jason's chef skills had impressed everyone. Bethany had been there, though.

"That's funny," I said to her. "I distinctly remember you gobbling up Jason's delicious braised pork belly and asking for seconds. . . ."

"Let's get back to math," Mrs. Beadle urged.

I put a hand on Jason's arm, and we shared a look. Then, as Mrs. Beadle went back to her desk and started the timer on her clock, I got to work. Maybe if I did well on these quizzes, I'd get promoted to Algebra 1 too.

After class, Jason and I put our books back in our lockers and raced over to the eighth-grade side of campus, where Lupe's math class was. We found a spot over by the trees. I looked up at the tree roof. It made me miss the Kids for Kids club we had in elementary school.

Unfortunately, most of those kids had gone to different middle schools. Some had moved away. The ones who stayed suddenly had other interests, like computer club and hanging out by the bleachers with the cool girls.

Lupe and I tried hanging out with the cool girls too. But they had taken one look at us and scooted over to the other side of the bleachers. Lupe wasn't so bothered. But I wondered: What made them popular and not us?

"So how's algebra?" I asked Lupe.

Lupe reached into her bag of chicharrones.

"Good," she said, munching on a chip. She handed some to me. Chicharrones were these spicy chips from Tijuana that melted and exploded in your mouth at the same time. Now that Lupe's dad had received his papers from the immigration judge and Proposition 187 was overturned, Lupe's family got to go back and forth freely from the US and Mexico — and bring all sorts of delicious snacks with them!

"Some of the stuff is pretty hard," she added.

"You know if it gets too hard, you can always move back down with us!" I suggested eagerly.

Jason nodded. "*And* we have tinsel."

Lupe chuckled. "It's not *too* hard," she insisted. "But I do miss you guys."

I smiled at my best friend and reached for another chicharron. I gazed at it. It used to be that you could get chicharrones at Mr. Abayan's convenience store. He always stocked his shelves with all kinds of snacks from Mexico and the Philippines. But his store got replaced by a 7-Eleven, and now you had to go all the way to Mexico to find chicharrones.

Lupe reached for her textbooks. "I'm going to the library to get started on my homework."

"I'll come with you!" I offered, getting up.

"No, it's okay," Lupe quickly said, backing away and hugging her books tightly. "I'll catch up with you at the front desk!"

I watched as Lupe skipped over to the library, wondering why she didn't want me to come along. Was she afraid I would distract her? I totally wouldn't.

"So did you ask all the teachers for permission yet?" Jason asked, handing me one of his green-tea Pocky sticks.

"Just need English!" I told him as I bit into the Pocky. In a little over a week, my parents and I were finally going on our first Christmas vacation ever . . . to China! I was so eager to see all my cousins and aunts and uncles again, I could hardly sit still at the front desk. Every day I put a big *X* on the calendar, counting down. The excitement—and nerves—jingled inside me. Would my cousin Shen still recognize me when I stepped off the plane? Would I recognize him?

"I can't believe the teachers are letting you take a whole extra month off school," Jason said.

Because the plane tickets were so expensive, and it'd been *forever* since we took a vacation, my parents wanted to go for a full six weeks. So far, all my teachers had said that was okay. "As long as I do my homework, they're cool with it!"

"And the motel?"

"Lupe's parents are covering for us."

Jason's eyes dropped to his Pocky. "Well, *I'm* going to miss you."

I smiled. I knew Jason liked sitting next to me, especially in math, where he didn't always get what the teacher was talking about. "I'll be back soon, and I'll bring you lots of numbing peppers and special spices!"

His face brightened. "And we're still on for the movies next Saturday, before you go?"

"Of course!" As a Christmas treat, Jason, Lupe, and I were going to a movie and then dinner. Now that the economy was doing better, Jason's dad's businesses were flourishing, and Jason got his allowance back. And Lupe and I had our front desk money. Jason had the restaurant all picked out—a new place called Jade Zen. It was right next to the congee place my parents and I liked to go to on Sundays. And we were going to go see *Toy Story*!

I was so excited, I nearly blurted out that it'd be my first time watching a movie in an American theater. But I stopped myself just in time. There were some things I still didn't want to tell Jason, even if I would've told Lupe in a heartbeat.

"It's going to be amazing!" Jason beamed.

The bell rang for third period, and we got up. As we brushed the grass off our pants, Jason leaned over and awkwardly hugged me.

"Oh!" I said, surprised.

"Sorry," he said, blushing. "I just . . . I can't wait for Saturday!"

. . .

Later in English class, Bethany Brett sat next to me, loudly chewing on her gum while Ms. Swann, our teacher, handed back our essays. I looked over at Jason, who was similarly annoyed by our own Miss Violet Beauregarde.

"Da-Shawn, this is *so* good," Ms. Swann gushed. Da-Shawn Wallace had moved to Anaheim from Connecticut a couple weeks before. An African American boy with braces and a Batman pencil case, he was the only person I knew who read more than me and Lupe. He even read sometimes under his desk when Ms. Swann wasn't looking.

"The way you describe being lost at sea, I can *feel* every wave crashing, every drop of rain!"

"Psst," Jason whispered. "I bet yours is better!"

I gazed over at Da-Shawn's paper, curious to see what an A+ paper looked like, but he quickly put it away.

Ms. Swann had given me two As so far this year. She had a bulletin board up by the front of the classroom where each month she recognized the Most Creative Writer, Most Funny Writer, and Most Moving Writer. I hadn't made the Most list yet, but I was hopeful that I was close. As she handed back my essay, I saw another A.

"All right, class, please put your stories away. It's time for our whole-grade photo. Everyone head to the gym," Ms. Swann said.

I looked at Jason. *That's today?* I'd completely forgotten. I put my papers in my backpack and got in the single-file line to go to the gym. Jason took out a comb from his back pocket to straighten his hair.

"How do I look?" he asked.

"Great," I said, studying him. He'd missed a spot, and I reached up and patted a stray hair with my hand. For some reason, that made Jason blush.

As we walked inside the gym, I looked around for Lupe. We *had* to stand together. I found her in the front row.

"Hey!" I said, getting in the front row next to her.

"Did you know this was today?" Lupe asked.

"No, I forgot," I said. I looked down at my jeans and T-shirt of a pickle that said *I'm Kind of a Big Dill.* Had I known our group picture was today, I would have picked another shirt. I gazed over at Bethany Brett, rearranging her five necklaces in front of her sweater. So *that's* why she was wearing them.

Jason squeezed in the front row next to us. "Well, you totally look awesome," he assured me.

"Thanks." I smiled. "*We* look awesome."

The photographer, a white guy named Kyle who had a big button on his shirt that said *Smile with Teeth,* walked over to us.

"You guys need to move to the back row," he told me, Jason, and Lupe.

We looked at him, confused. The people in the back row were a full head taller than us. Maybe Jason would fit in, but Lupe and I would be completely hidden.

"Can we just stay here?" I asked. "Please?"

I really wanted my parents to buy the picture this year. Every year, when we got the flyer to buy school photos, my mom always said they were too expensive. She'd cut out the small free sample pic and stick that on the refrigerator instead. Maybe if they saw me in the front row this year, they'd actually buy it!

"I'm afraid not," Kyle the photographer said.

I looked around at all the other kids in the front row. The other kids were mostly white. Some were even taller than me and Lupe. But he wasn't telling them to move.

"I'm trying to achieve a certain look here," Kyle explained in frustration.

I furrowed my eyebrows. What was *that* supposed to mean?

Lupe tugged on my arm and said quietly, "It's fine."

Reluctantly, I followed her and Jason to the back row, frowning as Dillon Fischer blocked my whole face with his big neck. It just felt so unfair. After all the stuff we'd achieved — Lupe was practically taking high school math and I was a straight-A student — I felt like we'd earned the right to be front and center. But the photographer was still trying to hide us.

As Kyle the photographer told us to smile, I muttered to Lupe, "This stinks."

"I know," she said.

"Nah, it's okay," Jason said. "I don't want to be front and center anyway."

"But that's not the point." I turned to him. "We're not *allowed* to be. There's a difference."

And why? Just because we weren't blonde and blue-eyed and didn't wear a million necklaces like Bethany?

. . .

After English class was over, I went up to Ms. Swann.

"How was the class picture?" she asked.

Not great.

"I didn't get to stand where I wanted . . ." I muttered.

Ms. Swann looked at me sympathetically. "That happens

sometimes," she said. "I remember when I was a kid I was always the shortest one. But don't worry, I'm sure you'll have a growth spurt soon!"

Yeah. I somehow doubted that would change things.

"So what did you want to talk to me about?"

I started telling her about our Christmas trip to China.

"China!" Ms. Swann cried. "That's amazing! I've *always* wanted to go to China. Oh, I'm so jealous you're going!"

I smiled—it was nice to know that not everyone in my school wanted me to hide my culture. Slowly, I explained how the tickets weren't cheap and my parents rarely got a vacation, so I needed to take an additional four weeks off school.

Ms. Swann put a finger to her chin. "As long as you keep up with your English homework, that's okay with me." She glanced around her desk until her eyes landed on a blank notebook, which she handed me. "Fill this up with stories. I want you to write a journal entry on your experience, twice a week. Take me to China and really blow me away—will you do that?"

I promised her I would as I took the notebook. I couldn't wait to show her around my hometown and make her see, taste, and *feel* everything. By the time I got back, I'd definitely earn my position on her Most board.

• • •

"Mom! Dad! I got permission from all my teachers!"

I burst into the front office after school, but my parents weren't there—only Hank heard me shouting.

"These travel agents, they sure are snooty," he said, sighing as he hung up the phone. "They keep saying we don't have enough of a *brand*, so they won't partner with us."

Hank had been trying to get travel agents to work with the Calivista, as part of his plan to take the motel to new heights.

"Why do we need a travel agency again?" Lupe asked, plopping down on one of the stools and putting her math homework on the front desk.

"Because they bring in lots of customers!" Hank said. "Let's say you're sitting at your house in Texas and you want to go to Disneyland. You call up your travel agent and they help you book your flight and your hotel. That could be us. We could be the hotel!"

I sighed, gazing over at the Disneyland poster on the wall, which was peeling at the edges now. Even though we were just five miles away, Lupe, Jason, and I still hadn't been. We'd made a pact to go for sure this year. Maybe when I got back from China. I smiled at the thought. I couldn't wait.

Gently, I took the tinsel Jason gave me out of my backpack and sprinkled it over our cute little Christmas tree.

"Hey, that looks good," Lupe said.

"Thanks!" I smiled.

"We should get some ornaments too. Maybe a Mickey Mouse one . . . I'll try to find one at the dollar store!" Lupe said.

"That'll be great! But we'll get an official one—when we go to Disneyland."

"For sure!"

A loud *BANG* interrupted us. It was coming from the construction work next door. Both the Topaz and the Lagoon were under renovation, curiously at the same time, making us the only motel on the block.

"What are they *doing* over there?" I asked, watching the tinsel shake on our little tree.

"Whatever it is, I hope they never finish," Hank said. His eyes twinkled as he walked over and opened up the cash register. It was full of cash!

"Holy moly!" Lupe said.

"I know. Isn't it great?" Hank beamed. "It's been a full house since the Topaz and Lagoon closed."

I grinned as I thumbed through the thick stack of registration forms.

Lupe gazed out the window at the Lagoon's green mesh netting concealing their renovation, as Mrs. Davis walked into the front office.

"Well, I'm all done for the day! Just came in to grab my purse," she said. Hank got it from under the front desk, thanking Mrs. Davis for her help. Mrs. Davis was the cleaning professional from the local cleaning agency, Happy Clean. Now that my mom was studying full-time for her math teaching licensing exam, my dad needed help cleaning thirty rooms a day. Mrs. Davis was especially good at changing sheets, having worked in a nursing home before.

My dad walked in right behind her.

"You're a lifesaver," he said to Mrs. Davis. "I don't know how I'd get all these rooms clean by myself."

"Well, luckily you don't have to," Mrs. Davis said with a warm smile. "I'll see you bright and early tomorrow."

After Mrs. Davis left, I turned to my dad.

"Guess what? My teachers said I could go to China for the full six weeks!"

"That's fantastic!" Dad said, patting the sweat off his hairline with a rag from his pocket.

Just then, my mom came walking out of the manager's quarters to the front desk, holding a white envelope. Her hands were shaking.

"What is it?" Dad asked.

She peered up at us with big, watery eyes. "I did it! I passed my substitute teaching exam!"

Lupe and I jumped up and down, shrieking, "Oh my God! Oh my God! Oh my God!" Dad took Mom into his arms and hugged her as Hank grabbed the phone to call the other weeklies. My mom had been studying *so* hard. And now her dream of being a teacher in America was finally coming true!

CHAPTER 2

That night, we all gathered in the kitchen of the manager's quarters for a celebratory dinner. As my mom prepared kung pao chicken and spring rolls, Hank stood over the stove grilling up his signature saltine burgers. I turned to my dad.

"Was there any mail for me?" I asked.

"As a matter of fact, there was," he said. "I put it in your room."

Just then, Lupe's mom and dad arrived with a pot full of tamales. Lupe stayed in the kitchen to help her dad, but I escaped to my room and quietly closed the door behind me. My heart thumped as I walked up to the envelope sitting on top of my dresser. Carefully, I tore it open. *Here goes.*

Dear Mia,
Thank you for submitting your work to the opinion section of the *Los Angeles Gazette*. The editors regret to say it does not suit the needs of our newspaper at this time, and we are unable to publish it. We wish you

well, and we thank you for thinking
of our newspaper.

Kind regards,
The Editors
Los Angeles Gazette

I blinked my eyes hard before a tear could escape. *Stop it*, I told myself. *Getting a rejection is normal, part of being a professional writer.*

Except it wasn't my first. It was my seventy-ninth.

Ever since the piece I wrote on Proposition 187 was in the *Los Angeles Times*, I'd been trying to get published again. At the library, I looked up the addresses of newspapers all over the country so I could mail them my opinion pieces. And all year, the editors from those papers mailed my letters right back. The rejections all said the same thing: My writing "didn't suit their needs at this time," they weren't interested in the daily goings-on at the motel, and my stories weren't serious enough.

I sat down on my chair with a heavy sigh, letting the *Gazette* letter fall from my hand to the floor.

The worst thing was, not a single person knew. Not Hank, not Lupe, not Jason. I hadn't told them because I kept waiting and waiting for my luck to turn around. Now I was starting to think maybe I was just a one-hit wonder.

"Hey, Mia?" Lupe knocked on my door. "It's time to eat!"

"Be right there!" I called.

I took the letter and stuffed it deep in my closet, with all my other hidden rejections.

Walking back into the kitchen, I watched my mom's face melt as she bit into Hank's burger. "This is the best burger I've ever had!" Mom proclaimed.

Hank chuckled. "Well, you deserve it! Congratulations!"

Mom pointed to the dark circles under her eyes. "I look like a panda, I've been studying so hard! I was so worried I wouldn't pass."

"*I* wasn't worried for a second!" my dad said, holding a can of cream soda up for a toast. "To my brilliant wife, who as of today is officially on the main road!" He leaned over and kissed my mom on the cheek. "I'm so proud of you."

"Hear, hear!" we all said, and clinked soda cans.

Lupe reached for a spring roll as I helped myself to a tamale.

"What were you doing in your room for so long?" Lupe asked.

"Just homework," I lied. Turning to my mom, I said brightly, "So, do you know where you're going to be teaching?"

"The letter doesn't say exactly, but it'll be in the Anaheim Unified School District." Her eyes flashed. "Wouldn't it be amazing if I was *your* math teacher, Mia?"

I coughed, glancing over at Lupe. Bethany Brett would *love* to see that.

"Or mine," Lupe said quickly. "I think you should be mine!"

My dad chuckled. "You've already got kids fighting to be in your class!"

"When do you start?" asked Mrs. Q, one of the weeklies.

"Right after we get back!" Mom grinned at me and Dad. "I can't wait to see the look on my sisters' faces when I tell them!"

Ever since my mom's sisters turned her down for money when we were trying to buy the motel two years ago, things had been a little tense. I was glad Mom had something great to tell them.

If only I had the same.

"Just think, maybe one of these days, we'll finally be able to buy one of the houses with a white picket fence we've been looking at!" Mom said.

I nodded eagerly. After our weekly Sunday breakfast at the congee shop, my parents and I drove to open houses. We didn't have enough money to buy a house yet, but my mom said it was important to visualize what we wanted to achieve. Maybe one day soon, we wouldn't just visualize — we'd actually achieve!

The front office doorbell rang. Dad got up to go deal with the customer while Hank updated everyone on the travel agency project.

"We'll find something," José encouraged him. "And even if we don't partner with a travel agency, we're doing fine. We've been killing it!"

"Because the Topaz and the Lagoon are both closed. But when they reopen . . ." Hank shook his head.

Billy Bob swatted the concern away. "When they reopen, you'll still have to drive by us to get to them. Remember, in real estate, it's location, location, location!"

"Yup!" I seconded. I'd heard that expression from several real estate agents at open houses.

Mom craned her neck, looking toward the front office. "What's taking him so long? The food's getting cold."

"I'll go get him!" Hank said.

Billy Bob clicked on the television to check the latest scores from the Dodgers game.

"What'd I miss?" my dad asked, sitting back down at the kitchen table. He looked around for the sweet chili dipping sauce to dip the spring rolls in.

"Oh, sorry, I didn't have time to go to 99 Ranch to buy the chili sauce this week," Mom said.

"Don't worry about it. I can run over to the Asian Mart after dinner and get some," Dad said, referring to a tiny store by the library that sold Asian spices and sauces. Jason also liked going there.

"I tried going there, but it was closed," Mom said.

My dad raised his eyebrows. "Closed, really?" he asked. He put his chopsticks down. "I hope they didn't move."

Mrs. T leaned in. "Have you noticed all the shops changing in our neighborhood?"

Mrs. Q nodded, and I realized I'd noticed too. There was Mr. Abayan's convenience store, which was now a 7-Eleven; the hair salon with the giant scissors in the window by the high school, which was now a Supercuts; and my favorite stationery store, where I got my sparkly green pencil. It closed because it couldn't compete with the Office Depot.

Hank walked back in.

"All good?" Dad asked. "What room did you give her?"

Hank shook his head. "It was so weird. Once I took over, she changed her mind. Didn't want to stay anymore."

"Didn't want to stay?" Dad asked.

In the background, the evening news took over from the baseball game.

"Despite efforts to improve racial tensions," the anchorman was saying, "polls show that since the OJ Simpson verdict, race relations have worsened across the country. Many Americans feel that OJ Simpson, a Black man, should have gone to jail for the alleged murder of two white people."

Fred got up and turned off the TV, while Hank sank in his chair.

"Every time something like that happens," he said, pointing at the TV, "it's like a presumption of guilt that extends to all us Black folks." Hank rubbed his weary eyes. "I'm just so tired of it."

"Me too," I said. Gently, I told everyone what happened with the photographer at school.

"That's horrible!" Mrs. Q said.

"I'm going to call up the school tomorrow and make them retake the picture!" Mrs. Garcia said, fuming.

"No, please don't, Mom," Lupe pleaded. "Some of the other kids already think it's weird that I'm in algebra."

"Why's that weird?" Mrs. Garcia asked.

Hank shook his head. "Man, the systemic racism in this country . . ."

Billy Bob put a hand on Hank's shoulder.

"Maybe I need a vacation," Hank murmured.

Just then, a wild idea came into my head.

"Hey, why don't you come with us to China?" I asked. I looked over at Mom and Dad, who nodded eagerly.

"That's a wonderful idea!" Dad said.

"No, no, I was just kidding. I'll be fine," Hank insisted.

"But why *not*?" I asked him. "You haven't had a vacation in years. And you'll *love* it there! You can meet my family!"

"Think of all the great food you'll eat!" my dad added.

"And the sights you'll see!" Mrs. T hollered. "The Great Wall of China!"

"The Forbidden City!" Mrs. Q added.

"But what about the motel?" Hank asked.

José smiled. "We'll take good care of it. Don't you worry, amigo."

"That's right!" Mrs. Garcia said. "You don't have to worry about a thing!"

Hank looked at me and my parents. "Tickets must cost a fortune," he said. "And I don't have a visa."

"You can get a visa next week at the Chinese consulate!" Dad said. "I'll take you!"

"And I'll bet you can get some cheap last-minute fares too, if you go to the right travel agent," Mom said.

"Don't get me started on travel agents!" Hank replied, and we all laughed. Turning to José, Hank asked, "Are you sure you guys are going to be okay without me?"

"We'll be fine!"

Then Hank turned to Lupe. "Don't forget to hang the special stockings on each guest room's door at Christmas. With a little chocolate and card inside?"

Lupe crossed her arms. "Hey, I work here too, remember?" she asked. "I got this!"

Hank laughed as Dad slapped his hand on the table.

"That settles it!" he announced.

I grabbed Hank's hand. "Hank!!! You're going to China!!!" I shrieked.

CHAPTER 3

Over the next week, my parents helped Hank get his visa and a discounted last-minute plane ticket, and Hank went around town picking up essentials for his big trip to China.

On Friday, I came into his room to find an avalanche of stuff on his bed. "What's all this?" I asked.

He smiled as he held up each item. "Dictionary!" he announced. "Travel insurance, maps, RMB!" RMB was short for renminbi, the Chinese currency, and Hank had gotten lots and lots of it. "Polaroid!" He took the camera, held it up to me, and clicked for real this time. I giggled. "Band-Aids! Batteries! Bottled water!"

"Wait a minute, you're bringing *bottled water* to China?"

"I read they don't have all the stuff we do. I just want to be prepared!"

In addition to water, he also had toothpaste, soap, shampoo, trash bags, and even toilet paper.

I grabbed a roll. "We *have* toilet paper!" I informed Hank. I didn't know why it bothered me that Hank thought we didn't have toilet paper in China, but it did. It wasn't like we were going to the Stone Age!

"I'm sorry, the guidebook said—"

"Well, the guidebook's wrong!" I said. I suddenly felt

overwhelmed with emotion that that's what people thought of my old country. I covered my eyes and ran back to the manager's quarters.

"Mia, wait!" Hank called after me, but I kept running.

. . .

Later that night, I was looking at my rejection letters when I heard a knock.

"May I come in?" Hank asked.

I quickly stuffed the letters back in the closet. When they were hidden again, I let Hank inside and he sat down next to me on my bed.

"I'm sorry. You're right. It was silly of me to just go by the guide-book. I should have talked to you first." Hank looked into my eyes. "Will you forgive me?"

I nodded. "It's okay. I don't know why I got so upset. I'm just . . ." I closed my eyes, the emotions brimming under my lids. "I'm going through a lot."

"What's wrong?" Hank asked.

I shook my head, not really wanting to get into it.

"Is it about the class photo?"

Yeah, that hurt. Kyle the photographer was just another reminder that if I wanted to be in the front row in this country, I'd have to work ten times harder and be more accomplished than Bethany Brett. But how was I supposed to ever get there if I kept getting rejected?

When I didn't say anything, Hank patted my hand. "A brilliant writer once said, 'No matter how bad something is, it's a lot worse if you have nobody to tell it to.'"

That was a line I'd written. I looked into Hank's eyes, then slowly, I got up and opened my closet. The pile of letters fell out onto the floor.

"What's all this?" Hank asked. He knelt down, picked one up, and started reading. "Oh. How long have you been getting these?"

I swallowed hard. "Just . . . about a year."

"A YEAR?! Why didn't you tell me?" Hank put the letter down. "Does Lupe know?"

I shook my head. "I kept hoping I'd get good news. *Then* I'd tell you guys."

"Mia, you can't just bottle up the bad stuff and only tell people the good," Hank said, looking into my eyes.

I nodded, biting my lip. Then I fell into Hank's open arms.

"I wanted to tell Lupe, but then she got into algebra at school. And I just . . ." I sniffled. "I wanted to do something amazing too."

Hank stroked my hair. "Listen, you *are* doing something amazing. Just by keeping at it, continuing to send your work out there. That's incredible, you know that? Most kids your age would have quit by the third letter, but you — you *persevered*."

I smiled a little, grateful for his words. But I couldn't tell him my biggest worry: What if I only had one amazing work in me, and I'd spent it already?

"My advice to you is forget about these letters," he went on. "Part of being a great writer is not just sitting in a room and writing. It's also about getting out there and living! We're about to go on a great trip together — me, you, and your parents!"

Hank was right. We were finally going on vacation. I'd waited *years* for this moment. And we were going to China, where everyone looked like me. No one would ever try to hide me in the back row because

I didn't have the right hair color. I couldn't wait to show Hank around my hometown. We might not have everything—okay, maybe I *would* bring a bottle or two of my favorite Pantene Pro V shampoo—but what we lacked in brand-name toiletries, we made up for in warm hospitality. Hank would see! And who knew, maybe it would be just the thing to replenish my creative well!

CHAPTER 4

On the night of our big movie and Christmas dinner with Jason, Lupe called and said she was sick.

"I think I've got a cold," she said, sniffling.

"Oh, no! Should we postpone?" I asked.

"No, no, you leave in two days!" she said. "I'll just take it easy at home. I want to be well rested for when we take over the motel! You guys go ahead without me!"

"Okay," I sighed. "I hope you feel better soon."

When my dad dropped me off at the theater, Jason was already there, waving at me from the ticket counter. I waved back, clutching his Christmas present in my hand. I'd gotten him a collection of gourmet sea salts and a chef's apron with the words *Jason Yao — World's Greatest Chef* ironed on.

"Pick you up at eight at Jade Zen," Dad said, pointing to the restaurant, which was right across from the movie theater. "Don't forget to get me a to-go bowl from the congee shop!"

I nodded. "You got it!"

As Dad drove away, Jason ran over, holding up two tickets.

"You didn't have to buy mine," I told him. I dug out the twenty-dollar bill my dad had given me. "I've got my money right here."

"No way," Jason said. "Tonight's my treat. Where's Lupe?"

"She's sick," I said, and felt my face fall a little. I was bummed I was seeing my first movie in an American theater without her. We were supposed to do it together!

"Don't worry," Jason said. "As soon as she's better, Lupe and I can go again! Maybe over the break!"

"But you'll have seen the movie already."

"So? I've eaten dan dan noodles a million times too. Do you see me getting sick of *that*?"

I laughed. Jason did love his dan dan noodles. He brought them from home for lunch and mixed them with hoisin sauce and chili oil.

Jason pointed at the package in my hand, which was all wrapped up in glossy red wrapping paper from the dollar store. The paper was so nice that my mom said if Jason opened up his present at the restaurant, I should take it back so we could reuse it.

"What's that?" he asked.

"This is for you," I said, handing it to him. "Merry Christmas."

Jason's eyes lit up. "You got me a present?"

I nodded. "Of course."

"I *love* it!" he declared, hugging the package tight.

"You haven't even opened it," I said, laughing.

"It doesn't matter. Even if there's nothing inside, I'll still love the box."

I giggled as we walked inside. Jason opened his present as the previews played. He loved the apron so much he put it on right there in the theater!

The movie was *incredible*. The whole time as we were watching, Jason kept looking over at me. I was sure he was thinking the same thing — *Toy Story* was a feat of imagination and animation. I'd never seen anything like it, and watching it on the big screen made it even more out of this world. When the movie got to the part where Woody was worried about Buzz Lightyear replacing him as Andy's favorite toy, I accidentally squeezed Jason's arm, thinking it was the arm rest between me and him.

"Sorry!"

"It's okay!" Jason said. I hoped he didn't think I was *trying* to hold his arm in the dark.

Afterward, Jason and I headed across the street to Jade Zen, gushing over how good the movie was.

"I bust a gut when Woody was all, 'YOU. ARE. A. TOY!'" I said.

"And when Rex was all, 'What if Andy gets another dinosaur? A mean one? I just don't think I can take that kind of rejection!'" Jason shrieked.

If Jason only knew how much I could relate to that.

"Oh, and when Woody said, 'The word I'm searching for I can't say because there's preschool toys present!'" Jason cried, laughing so hard, he almost fell off the curb.

At the door to the restaurant, I stopped, confused.

"What happened to the congee shop?" I asked Jason. It used to be right next to Jade Zen, but now the sign was gone.

Jason shrugged and pushed open the door. "Forget the congee shop. You're going to love the food here. It's amazing."

As I walked inside the lavishly decorated gold-and-jade restaurant, I looked up at the giant murals and mirrors on the walls. Jade Zen certainly looked fancier than the congee place. Still, I'd promised my dad I'd bring him home a bowl of congee. Then I noticed a newly added wing of the restaurant and realized what had happened.

"Oh my God, Jade Zen *ate* the congee shop!" I pointed at the wall that used to separate the two establishments — it was gone. Now Jade Zen customers sat eating pricey lettuce wraps on toothpicks where my parents and I used to slurp our congee.

"Please, right this way," the hostess said, leading us to our table.

"I'm not eating here. We have to leave," I told Jason, this time tugging on his arm for real.

"No way," he whispered back, following the hostess. "This place is so much better!"

I let go of Jason's arm. The congee shop was authentic. The owner was from Guangzhou, and every morning, he made sixteen different types of congee, including shredded ginger chicken congee, my mom's favorite.

"The congee shop was a random mom-and-pop restaurant. Jade Zen is a *chain*," Jason said, sitting at the table we'd been led to.

"So?" I asked.

"So that means they're more successful."

I sat down across from him. "So the Calivista is *not* successful?" We were a "mom-and-pop" place. Literally: There's my mom and there's my pop.

"That's not what I meant," he said.

A waitress came by with menus, but Jason barely looked at his.

"We'll have the oven-baked turnip cake with Parma ham, dumplings with porcini mushrooms, and stir-fried pea sprouts with saffron," he told her. "That okay with you, Mia?"

He hadn't given me a chance to even look at the menu, but I nodded. It all sounded delicious. Besides, I wanted to get back to what we were talking about.

"So what *do* you mean?" I asked as the waitress walked away.

"Just that chains are bigger. They've proven themselves." Jason shrugged.

"We've *proven* ourselves," I argued. Hadn't we quadrupled occupancy in the last year?

"You know what, forget it," Jason said. He looked around. "Isn't this place great?" He pointed at the stainless-steel chairs with soft leather backs. "Have you ever seen a Chinese restaurant like this?"

I had to admit, I hadn't. Most Chinese restaurants my parents and I went to had plastic wraps on the tables so they were easier to clean, and a menu wall with pictures so it was easier for white people to order.

"When I grow up, I want to start a chain just like this. But even nicer, with white tablecloths and waiters in suits that stand real straight." Jason held up his hand as straight as a ruler.

I had to laugh at him.

Jason's lips stretched into a dreamy smile. "And I'm going to serve authentic, gourmet Asian fusion . . . not the kind of rich French food we have to make at cooking school, like potatoes dauphinoise." Jason made a face. "Ugh. It's way too creamy."

As he was talking, the waiter brought out our dumplings with porcini mushrooms. I took one and smiled as the mushroom melted against the paper-thin wrapping in my mouth.

"What'd I tell you? This place is better than the congee place, right?" Jason said.

I thought as I chewed. "Not better," I decided. "Just different."

"Well, I like it better," he said.

I reached for another dumpling. "So why do you have to make rich French food?" I asked.

He groaned. "My teacher says I have to master the classics if I want to be a chef of fine dining," he said, dipping his dumpling in some vinegar.

I furrowed my eyebrows. Was Chinese food not a "classic"?

I thought about that as the waiter brought out our other dishes. The pea sprouts glistened, reminding me of the stir-fried snow pea leaves my grandmother used to make. I was so excited to see her in two days. I wondered if she would like the pea sprouts with saffron or if she preferred the traditional way, sautéed with garlic. She used to be very traditional, my grandmother. I wondered if she'd changed.

"Here," Jason said, serving me some pea sprouts with his chopsticks. He was much better at using chopsticks than I was. "Can't you see us one day? Me running five-star restaurants and you with a chain of hotels?"

I didn't know about that. "I want to be a writer, remember?"

Jason nodded, considering this. "How's that going?" he asked.

"Not that well," I confessed to the pea sprouts. I slowly began telling Jason about the stack of rejection letters in my closet, embarrassment settling in my stomach on top of the dumplings.

"I'm sorry," Jason said, putting his hand over mine. "But you can't give up. The first time I tried to make crème brûlée, I overdid it with the blowtorch and nearly set the kitchen on fire!"

"Seriously?"

"People called me Blowtorch for weeks."

"I'm so sorry," I said.

"It's okay. But you know what? I kept cooking," he said. "That's the key." He fumbled for his backpack. "Oh, that reminds me — your gift!"

He pulled out a small package and handed it to me.

I looked down at it, curious. It was the size of a small remote control, and for a second, I wondered if that was what was in it, a universal remote? That'd be pretty cool, actually.

"Open it!"

There was a card taped to it, which I opened first.

Dear Mia,
Merry Christmas. I hope you have a wonderful time in China. I'm so happy we're friends. These last three years have been the best years ever.

Yours,
Jason

Above his name, he'd written half a dozen other closings and scratched them all out before finally going with *Yours*.

"Open it! Open it!" Jason shrieked. He had the patience of a customer without air conditioning. I giggled.

Carefully, I unwrapped the shiny gold paper. Inside the slim box was a gold necklace with a key pendant.

"I saw it and I thought, 'That's so Mia.'" Jason beamed. "A key, get it? Because you work in a motel?"

I smiled. It was *very* sweet.

"I love it."

As I reached up to put the necklace on, Jason leaned over the table — and kissed me. On the lips.

I nearly fell off my chair. He sat back, and my hands flew up to my hot lips.

"Why'd you do that?" I cried.

"I don't know. It just happened. . . ." Jason was bright red.

I didn't know what to do. I couldn't believe he'd kissed me. Without asking first. We were *friends*. Just friends. It said so on his card! And now what were we supposed to do?

I tossed the necklace on the table and grabbed my backpack.

"Mia, wait —"

I didn't look back. I just kept walking, my frustration mixing with the honey saffron inside me.

CHAPTER 5

On Monday, I sat squished between my mom and dad in the car, try-ing not to think about the kiss from Jason. Fred and Billy Bob were driving us to the airport. My mom brought so many presents, lov-ingly picked from Mervyn's, we had to take two cars. When we got to LAX, Fred gave my parents a hand with the luggage, piling the suitcases onto the cart my dad wheeled over.

"Five dollars for a cart! Can you believe it?" he complained, shak-ing his head.

"Relax, we're on vacation!" Mom reminded him.

My dad smiled, and Billy Bob and Fred spun me in the air, wish-ing us safe travels. As we hugged good-bye, Hank reminded Billy Bob to water his cherry tomatoes. Billy Bob said no problemo and reminded Hank to bring him back some tea.

"Don't worry, I'll bring back lots of souvenirs for everyone!" Hank promised. He looked over at my dad. "Shall we do this?"

My dad's eyes twinkled with excitement. "Let's do this!"

Laughing, my parents rolled our luggage cart into the terminal. We were on our way!

. . .

On the airplane, I sat in a row with my parents and Hank enjoyed two empty seats next to him in the row in front of us. As soon as the flight attendants delivered the first meal service, my dad started squirreling away little packets of butter and jam and ketchup, just as he had when we first flew over to America.

"Again?" I asked.

My dad turned to me. "These aren't for us; they're for our relatives. They've probably never had ketchup!"

It was hard now to imagine anyone never having tasted ketchup, but I guess I hadn't either before we moved to the US.

"How are you feeling? You excited to see your cousins again?" Mom asked.

I nodded eagerly. I was *especially* excited to see my cousin Shen. Growing up, we were as thick as thieves. I couldn't wait to see what he was like now! Hopefully, hanging out with my cousins would take my mind off my rejections *and* what had happened on Saturday—I wanted to crawl out of my skin every time I thought about the kiss.

"You never told me about your night out with Jason," Mom said, reading my mind in the worst way. "How was it?"

"It was okay," I muttered. I didn't want to get into it here, on a packed flight.

"Was the restaurant good?" Dad asked.

"It was fine," I said. "I'm sorry again about the congee."

"I just can't believe the shop isn't there anymore," Dad said. "It just got taken over by Jade Zen?"

I nodded, and Dad pressed on the packets of ketchup, hard.

"Hey," Mom said brightly. "We're going to be in China soon. There'll be lots of congee there." She turned to me. "How was the movie?"

"Amazing," I said. "And seeing it in the theater was so awesome."

"I'll bet!" Mom smiled. "Wait till we get back to China. I'll take you to lots of movies."

"Really?" I asked.

Dad perked up. "We'll finally be able to afford things—the US dollar is worth eight times the RMB!" He leaned forward and tapped Hank lightly on the shoulder. "We'll all be rich for a month and a half!"

"I'd like that!" Hank called back. They shared a chuckle.

Dad pulled his airplane blanket over him, closed his eyes, and snuggled in for a nap. I waited a moment, then turned to my mom.

"Mom?" I asked quietly, hugging my pillow. I wasn't sure how to get the words out. "Can a boy and a girl just be friends?"

"Of course," she answered. "Like me and Hank."

I shook my head. That was different. They were colleagues, plus she was already married. "What about when you were younger?"

"When I was younger, I met your dad," my mom answered. She looked over at Dad, who was already snoring gently. "He was my best friend and my first love."

Dad peeked one eye open from his blanket and smiled. "And I hope you'll stick with me," he said. "Even if I don't have a fancy new job."

"Stop," Mom said, slapping his leg.

I smiled at my parents. It must be nice having your best friend as your first and only love. As I watched my mom tuck the corner of my dad's blanket under his leg, I wondered if I would ever feel that way about anyone. And if I didn't feel that way about Jason, could we still be friends?

Four in-flight movies and a little over thirteen hours later, we landed at Beijing Capital International Airport. We pressed our faces up against the tiny plane window, trying to get a view of my hometown. It was nighttime, so I couldn't make out the city too clearly, but I recognized the noodle-like roofs of the traditional Beijing *hutongs* as we touched down. I bounced in my seat in excitement.

"We're here!" Mom declared, the corners of her eyes gleaming in the light. "Can you believe it? We're actually home!"

My dad dabbed his own wet eyes while I repeated the word *home* in my mind. I hadn't thought of it as coming home. If this was home, what was the Calivista?

Hank jumped up from his seat with a Polaroid camera.

"Eggplant!" he exclaimed in perfect Mandarin, to the surprise and delight of all the passengers around us. "Did I get that right?"

My mom gave him two thumbs up while Dad gathered up our carry-on luggage. I patted my backpack. All my presents for my cousins were in there. Hot Wheels, check. Jenga, check. And Twister, check!

We were greeted by a blast of freezing Beijing winter air as we stepped off the plane, followed by the blow of the airport heaters as we hurried into the terminal. Mom walked so fast toward immigration and customs, we had to run to keep up. At immigration, Hank had to go in the foreigner line while I stood behind my parents in the Chinese national line, even though we had US green cards. I didn't *feel* like a Chinese national, but standing in line, I looked around and, for the first time in forever, everybody looked like me. I fit right in.

At the counter, the immigration officer took our passports and examined them. In Chinese, he asked me how old I was.

"Twelve," I said in Mandarin.

He nodded. "Are you guys coming back for good or for vacation?"

"For vacation," I blurted. I glanced over at my parents, just to make sure. They nodded.

My mom chatted with the immigration officer while we waited. "We've been out of the country for years," she said. "In America."

"How is it there?" he asked.

"It's . . ." Mom searched for the right word. "Different than we expected, but we love it."

Dad smiled.

"Well, welcome back," the officer said, handing back our passports.

I grinned and ran ahead to find Hank at the luggage carousels. The airport carts in Beijing were free, so I grabbed one.

"Now that's what I'm talking about!" Dad clapped his hands, grabbing two more.

When the last of our suitcases was loaded up, my dad turned to me and Mom.

"You guys ready?" he asked.

"Readier than we've ever been!" Mom beamed.

The four of us held hands as we walked out into the arrival hall, pushing the luggage. My eyes scanned the crowd for my cousin Shen, and my heart thumped.

"Mia!!!" a voice cried.

I turned and there was Shen, nose pressed up against the security gate glass, exactly where I left him five years ago. He waved wildly and I laughed. He looked exactly the same and totally different. He had grown about a foot taller, and he had glasses now, with a mop of thick black hair, and the biggest, most excited smile on his face.

"SHEN!" I screamed, running over.

As we hugged and hugged, Shen said, "Told you I'd be right here waiting for you."

I kept grinning as Shen shouted to the rest of my relatives, who were waiting over on the other side of the crowded airport. My aunts and uncles came running over, along with my two younger cousins, eight-year-old Bo and six-year-old Lian.

"Jie Jie!" they greeted me, using the Chinese term for sister.

"Hi, Di Di," I said, calling them the term for younger brothers.

Thanks to the one-child policy, none of us had any siblings. So we were each other's brother and sister.

My mom burst into tears at the sight of her sisters, and they held one another for such a long time, we all wondered if they would ever part. Then one of my aunts noticed Hank.

"Who's this?" Aunt Juli asked in Chinese.

"*Ni hao*," Hank greeted her, extending a warm hand. "*Wo shi Hank.*"

My dad quickly explained that he was a good friend of ours.

"*Huan ying*, Hank. Welcome to China!" my uncle Jo greeted him in English, beaming as he shook Hank's hand. "It's a pleasure to meet you!" Uncle Jo added that he'd had to learn English for his job, so he was delighted to have someone to practice with.

"He's the senior vice president at his company now," Aunt Juli bragged.

My other aunts and uncles all took turns shaking Hank's hand. Most of them couldn't really speak English, so I had to translate. I told them Hank co-owned the motel with us, and besides being one of the weeklies, he was also one of our best friends. Unfortunately, I got the term for *co-owned* wrong, saying *co-children* instead. Everyone laughed.

"Mia, your Chinese!" my aunt Lan remarked.

"I guess that's what happens when you live in the US for five years!" Aunt Juli said.

"She just needs practice," my mom said quickly. "I'm sure after a couple of weeks, she'll be native again."

My face reddened. There was that pesky word again. I hadn't heard it for a while, but here it was, this time nagging me in my hometown.

My little cousin Lian reached up to try to touch Hank's hair.

"Whoa, easy now," Hank said, laughing as he wiggled out of the way.

"What are you doing?" I asked Lian.

"Trying to touch his head!" Lian giggled. "His hair is so curly!"

"I want to touch it too!" Bo chimed in, reaching up.

"You guys, stop!" I said, but they just kept jumping all over Hank. I blew at my bangs in frustration. When we were little, one holler from me and they'd behave. But now neither of them would listen. I looked to Shen for help, and he finally told them to knock it off with a few sharp words in Chinese.

Lian and Bo promptly dropped their hands. I looked at Hank apologetically.

"It's all right," Hank said. "I'm sure they're just excited. Probably never seen an American before."

"Or a Black person!" Bo added in Chinese, which thankfully Hank didn't understand.

I felt terrible. What had I done, dragging Hank here? "Stop," I warned. "Cut it out. And you should apologize."

Lian looked at me, hurt.

"C'mon, you guys must be hungry," my aunt Qin said, directing us toward the exit. "The car's this way."

CHAPTER 6

It was snowing when we left the Beijing airport. I shivered, glancing up at the sky. I hadn't seen snow for years. As my parents rushed to get out sweaters and jackets from the suitcases, I spun around with open arms, trying to catch snowflakes with my tongue.

"Here," Shen said, taking off his thick parka and putting it around my frozen shoulders. He jumped around in the parking lot, running his hands up and down his arms to stay warm, while Bo and Lian copied me, sticking their tongues out. I laughed.

The air smelled kind of funny, like the leftover hickory smoke after a long BBQ at the pool. Hank drew a sharp breath and coughed. Pointing to the chunky blanket of gray hanging over us in the air, he asked, "What *is* that?"

"Oh, that's just fog," my uncle Jo replied.

As we waited for them to pull the cars around, Hank leaned over and whispered to me, "That is not just fog."

Mom gasped when a brand-new Pontiac and a Jeep pull up. "You guys are driving *American* cars??"

"A lot has changed in the city—you'll see." Aunt Juli grinned.

Mom climbed into the Pontiac, nervously clutching her tote bag. It was cloth and covered with ink splotches from her leaky pens, unlike my aunt's leather one. Mom reached into her tote and started to give some Wrigley's bubble gum to Lian and Bo, but my cousins opened their mouth and revealed that they were already chewing some.

"Oh! You have that here too, huh?" Mom asked.

My dad patted her hand reassuringly.

"Mia, want to ride in the Jeep with me?" Hank asked.

"Sure." I waved good-bye to my parents as I squeezed in next to Shen. Hank adjusted the front passenger seat to accommodate his long legs while Uncle Jo drove.

"Wait till you see our house," Shen said. "It's in one of the big skyscrapers! Do you guys have skyscrapers in America?" He slapped his head like *duh*. "Of course you do."

I giggled. "Yup!" I said, thinking about the high-rises in downtown LA. They'd been popping up around Anaheim too. "Are we going there first?"

"No, we're going to Lao Lao's," he said, referring to my grandmother's.

All right! I grinned.

"She's cooking roasted duck and *zha jiang mien*, your favorite!" Uncle Jo said in English.

My stomach rumbled when I heard that. I hadn't had my grandmother's famous noodles in years, and I knew Hank would *love* her roasted Peking duck.

"Is *zha jiang mien* still your favorite?" Shen asked me.

I nodded.

Shen looked relieved. "I thought by now you'd be a burger-and-fries girl." Hank looked over when Shen said *burger* and *fries* in English.

"I like those too," I informed him.

"We have hamburgers here!" Uncle Jo said. "A new American chain opened recently — McDonald's!"

"You guys have McDonald's?" Hank asked. "But those aren't *real* burgers."

I told them Hank made the best burgers.

"Then you'll have to cook us some!" Uncle Jo said, honking his horn at the car in front of us as he got off the highway onto the narrow residential streets. All around him, drivers were not shy about honking. It was like they were having a honk-a-thon! "Tomorrow night!"

"Love to!" Hank said as we turned into my grandmother's *hutong*.

I spotted my grandmother before we even stopped the car. She came running out of her *siheyuan*, a traditional Beijing courtyard home, in her apron and slippers to greet us, not even bothering to wear a coat. Uncle Jo stopped the car, and I jumped out.

"Lao Lao!" I yelled, running into her arms. Her hair was whiter than I remembered and she had more lines on her face, but she smelled the same . . . of sweet pear and spices. I closed my eyes and breathed in deep. How I'd missed that smell.

"Oh, Mia, let me take a good look at you!" she said. I spun around so she could see the full me. Lao Lao laughed as she reached up and felt my bowl-cut bangs.

My grandfather walked up from behind her with his cane. "Welcome home, Mia!" Lao Ye said in English. My grandfather used to be an English teacher at the local high school, so he always tried to use it whenever he could. He shook hands with Hank. "Welcome, I'm Mia's grandfather."

"Hank Caleb, a pleasure to meet you," Hank said with a big smile.

The Pontiac honked behind us. Mom and Dad were here!

"Ying!" Lao Lao cried. She raced over to the Pontiac, nearly slipping on the icy snow.

"Mama!" my mom yelled, leaping out of the car.

"Oh my heavens. Ying, you're back!" Lao Lao held her shaking hands up to her mouth as my mother ran up and hugged her after five long years. As they embraced each other in the snow, I wrapped my arms around them both.

My mother helped my grandmother back into her *siheyuan*, and I followed, memories flooding back. There were the steps where Bo and I twirled each other until I fell and had to get stitches on my chin. There was the little kids' courtyard table where Shen would try to snatch up all the chicken with his chopsticks. The charcoal on the ground we'd used to write with on the sidewalk when it wasn't snowing. The line where we used to hang lanterns at the Mid-Autumn Festival. A million pockets of my past, flashing before my eyes.

"Come inside, Mia, before you catch cold," my grandmother said. "Tell your foreigner friend to come in too."

"His name is Hank, Lao Lao," I told her.

"Han-ka," my grandmother repeated, smiling. Hank turned and looked at her. She pointed a thumb to her chest and said, "Lao Lao."

"Lao Lao," Hank repeated.

My grandmother nodded, pleased. She led Hank to the dining room, then placed him at the head of the table, the guest-of-honor spot.

My aunt Mei, who was pregnant and hadn't come to the airport, carried out a succession of delicious dishes from the kitchen. Roast duck, pancakes to wrap the roast duck in, *zha jiang mien*, dumplings, sweet and sour pork, honey walnut shrimp.

My grandmother set the shrimp in front of Shen, but now Shen didn't try to hog it all—he moved the plate over to me. I smiled. The sautéed shrimp looked almost too delicious to eat.

"Ma, you shouldn't have! This is way too much!" my mom said, to which my grandmother's face lit up like a thousand lanterns.

"You should have seen her, up since dawn, cooking!" my grandfather chimed in. He sat down next to Hank and started picking up shrimp with his chopsticks and setting them down in Hank's bowl.

"You're one to talk! How late did you stay up last night studying those silly flash cards?" Lao Lao asked him.

"I was trying to brush up on my English so I could communicate with my granddaughter," Lao Ye said to me with a smile.

"Last month it was trying to start a poetry slam for the kids in the hutong," Lao Lao said.

"So?" Lao Ye asked. "Just because I'm old doesn't mean I should stop doing stuff. I still got it!"

Aunt Juli sat down. "Will you guys stop bickering?" she asked, taking off her coat. She was wearing a beautiful wool turtleneck with a white silk scarf. My eyes did a double take, and so did my mom's. Then Mom's eyes darted down at her own polyester plaid sweater.

"Anyway, I'm so glad we're all here," Lao Lao said. "As one family. As it always should be."

She added a few more pieces of shrimp to Hank's bowl. There were so many, they were on the verge of toppling over. "Thank you, thank you," Hank said, motioning with his hands *please, that's enough*. He reached for the chopsticks.

Hank was not an expert at using chopsticks, but he'd come prepared—with two small rubber bands. He wound one of them around the middle of his chopsticks, which made them a *lot* easier to use. My relatives laughed and complimented him on his ingenuity.

"Very smart!" Aunt Qin said, giving him a thumbs-up.

Grinning, Hank tossed me the other rubber band. That's when all my relatives stopped laughing.

"Mia doesn't know how to use chopsticks?" Aunt Juli asked, her eyes widening.

"Well, I do . . . just not very well," I said. I looked down at the rubber band and up at my shocked relatives. Why was it "smart" when Hank did it and laughable when I did?

Shen jumped up. "It's okay. I'll get you a spoon!" he said, running to the kitchen.

When Shen returned from the kitchen with two spoons, one for me and one for Hank, my mother reached over and grabbed mine.

"Hey!" I protested.

"You *know* how to use chopsticks, Mia." She lifted her own two sticks, as if by doing it in front of me, I'd magically become an expert. We'd been through this a thousand times before. I rolled my eyes. What could I say—I was just not a chopsticks person.

"Let her use the spoon," Aunt Juli said.

"No. She's using chopsticks," Mom insisted.

Slowly, I got up. "Can I go to the bathroom?"

My grandparents exchanged a look. "Do you remember where to go?" Lao Lao asked.

I looked around the house. "It's outside," Shen said.

"Wait, there's no bathroom inside?" I asked. Then I remembered. None of the old *hutong*-style houses had private bathrooms. It was one of the things about growing up in China that was so annoying: having to use the public toilets — and the public showers — next to all the neighbors. I suddenly missed the Calivista. We had *so* many bathrooms.

"I'll take you," Shen volunteered.

"Are you sure?" my mom asked. Shen nodded, already zipping up his jacket and putting on his boots. I started putting mine on too.

As we walked out into the snow, Shen held my hand, leading the way into the *hutong* like when we were kids.

"Bet you don't have to go out in the snow to go to the bathroom in America."

"Nope," I said.

"I heard that in America, some people even have two bathrooms in their house."

"Actually, we have thirty-two bathrooms."

Shen's eyebrows shot up. "You guys must drink a *lot* of water!" I giggled. He pushed open the neighborhood bathroom door, and I looked inside.

Instead of a normal toilet, it was one where you had to squat. A squat-let! *And* the person before me forgot to flush. *Great.*

"Shen . . . errr . . . are there any other toilets?"

"Not around here," he said.

With a heavy sigh, I pinched my nose with my fingers and went in. *Here goes.*

Gingerly, I closed the door and stepped up to the porcelain edges of the squat-let. But my feet were unsteady and the edges were slippery. Before I knew it, I'd lost my balance. I fell — and landed smack in the middle of the hole!

"Ahhhh!" I screamed, looking down at my soiled feet.

Shen came running in. When he saw me standing in the squat-let, he grabbed my hands to pull me out. "Are you okay?" he cried.

I looked down and shook my head. I was covered in poop, all the way up to my knees! A wave of nausea reached for my throat.

"Don't worry! We'll clean you off," he said. "C'mon."

I followed him back to the house, staring down at the trail of brown footprints in the snow as I walked.

My relatives' jaws dropped when I came inside. My aunt Juli looked up from opening the presents my mom had brought. She set down the polyester polka-dotted Mervyn's sweater that we'd gotten on sale. "What *happened*?"

Lao Lao came rushing over to me. She helped me remove my soiled boots while my mom knelt down beside me, trying to wipe the poop off my leg. Shen explained, and Bo and Lian burst out laughing.

"She can't use chopsticks *and* she can't use the toilet!" Bo giggled.

"Such a melon!" Lian agreed.

I didn't even know what that phrase meant, but I was pretty sure it was bad. It made me feel like a Martian in my own homeland. Frustration mounted inside me. At school I wasn't white enough. Here I wasn't Chinese enough.

"Our new apartment has a bathroom inside," Aunt Juli said. "She should stay with us tonight. She'll feel more comfortable there."

"That won't be necessary," my mom replied, rubbing so hard at my pants, there was a sopping-wet spot.

"But we have a toilet you can sit on," Shen added. "And a shower and bathtub too!"

A shower? I turned to my mom and begged, "Oh, please, Mom, can I stay with them?"

But my mother's face hardened like the charcoal that had been left out in the snow. She shook her head, a firm no. "You're staying here. And that's final."

As my mom dragged me back outside to the neighborhood bathroom to clean off with a fresh set of clothes from my suitcase, I thought about the looks on my relatives' faces as they stared at my soiled feet. I'd really thought things would be different in China. That I would automatically fit in because I looked like everyone else. But as my mom scrubbed and scrubbed, I realized even though I looked the same, I had become very much an outsider.

CHAPTER 7

That night, I tossed and turned in my metal folding bed, trying to hold in my pee. My grandparents had given Hank his own room on the east side of the courtyard and my parents had taken the room on the west side, so I was bunking with Lao Lao and Lao Ye. They slept in separate beds across the cold cement room from each other. I lay shivering in mine, unable to sleep a wink, listening to my *lao ye*'s loud snoring.

My *lao ye* snored *so* loudly. I looked down at the basket of little paper wads my grandmother had given me at bedtime.

"You want me to *throw* these at him?" I had asked her.

"He's used to it. I do it every night," she said, pointing at her own basket. She took a wad and threw it at his bed to demonstrate.

Thirty some wads later, the floor was littered with paper, but Lao Ye's snoring was not any quieter. I wondered if Lupe and Jason could hear him.

At the thought of Jason, I felt my face turn hot. I still couldn't shake the icky, squirmy feeling I'd had since he kissed me. What was I going to do after I went home? Just pretend nothing happened? Or should I make it perfectly clear to him that it could *not* happen again? I weighed my options as I counted the ceiling cracks until the wee hours.

Finally, at half past six, it was time to get up.

"Good morning!" Dad smiled. "Let's go out for some *jianbingguozi*!"

I squinted, shielding my eyes from the bright morning light with one hand.

"*Jianbingguozi?*" I asked. Then I remembered — the Chinese breakfast my dad was always going on and on about.

"C'mon, we better hurry! There'll be a line soon!"

I got up and threw on a sweatshirt and a jacket. My boots were still drying out in the courtyard. I cringed, hoping my little cousins weren't going to talk about my squat-let incident for our whole vacation. I put on a pair of old boots that my grandmother had in her closet. We wore almost the same size now.

"Morning, Mia!" Lao Lao greeted me in the courtyard. "How did you sleep? Did old grizzly bear keep you awake all night?"

"Hey! I do *not* snore!" Lao Ye protested.

I chuckled. "You do, Lao Ye," I answered. "And yes. A bit."

"You can sleep with your mom and me tonight," my dad offered. "We don't mind."

Hank walked out of his room and into the courtyard, stretching his arms in the sun. "How's everyone doing this fine morning? What's for breakfast?"

"*Jianbingguozi!*" Dad announced. "Come, you'll love it!"

Hank and I followed my dad down the tight alleyway of our *hutong* to where the *jianbingguozi* shop was. It was not really a shop, just a guy with a makeshift stove on top of his tricycle. But boy, was he popular! A crowd gathered, waiting anxiously as the guy cooked. Dad told me to order the *jianbings*.

"Coming right up," the cook said in a Beijing drawl.

I smiled, proud I could still order perfectly in Mandarin.

As we waited, all the neighborhood folks wanted to know who Hank was and whether they could take a picture with him.

"Sure!" Hank chuckled, smiling as he said "Eggplant" in perfect Chinese and did the peace sign with his fingers.

"I've never seen a foreigner before who looked like him!" the neighbors said in Mandarin. "And he can speak Chinese!"

"Just a little," Hank said when I translated their comment — or anyway, the last part. I was deeply embarrassed about the first part. My dad handed him his *jianbingguozi*, which the bike cook insisted we eat right there, before it got cold.

I bit into my breakfast and closed my eyes. The softness of the egg melted on my tongue. The crunch of the fried dough mixed perfectly with the kick of the chili pepper and the sweetness of the bean sauce. Wow, Jason would *love* this. My mind tripped on itself. Why was I still thinking about him?

"This is *incredible*," Hank said in between bites. "Worth the trip all by itself!"

He gave the bike cook a big thumbs-up and handed him a five-yuan bill.

"You don't have to tip here," Dad told Hank, but Hank insisted, stuffing the money in the bike cook's metal tin.

We ordered three more *jianbings* for my grandparents and my mom, then headed back.

Shen was waiting in the courtyard, and I ran over to him excitedly.

"You ready to go to my house?" he asked. "It's a teacher exam preparation day! I don't have school!"

I looked over to my mom, who was sitting and chatting with my aunt. "Can I?" I asked.

To my surprise, she nodded yes. I dashed inside to get Shen's present.

"You should come too, Ying," my aunt Juli was saying when I came back out to the courtyard with my backpack. "I'd love for you to see my house."

"All right," my mom agreed, slipping her hand in mine. She turned to my dad and Hank. "How about you guys?"

Hank shook his head. "I thought I'd go to the supermarket. I'm making burgers for y'all tonight!"

"Great! I'll invite your *nai nai* too!" Dad said, referring to my paternal grandmother. "I'll take you to the supermarket, Hank. It's right by my old office!"

My dad handed my mom her *jianbingguozi* as she and I walked over to Aunt Juli's car. While Aunt Juli drove and my mother ate her breakfast, Shen asked me about my life in America.

"What do you do on the weekends?" he asked.

"I work at the motel. Sometimes I go to the lake with my dad."

"I wish I had time to go to the lake with my dad." Shen sighed. "My weekends are usually packed with tutors."

"Tutors?" I asked.

Shen nodded. "I have them for every subject. Math, English, Chinese, science . . ."

"He needs them to keep up, now that he's going to the *best* middle school in all of Beijing!" Aunt Juli told my mom.

I was impressed. But Shen looked down and muttered quietly so the adults couldn't hear, "It's not all that great."

Mom cleared her voice. "Speaking of teachers, I actually recently—"

But Aunt Juli cut her off. "I had to bend over backward to get him in. Luckily a colleague of Jo's knew somebody who was married to a school official. And since Jo is so high up in his company and all . . ." Aunt Juli fluttered her eyelashes with pride.

"Yeah, I'll bet," my mom said quietly.

When we got to Shen's house, my mom and I stepped out of the car, craning our necks to look at the thirty-two-story apartment building. I'd never seen a building that tall in America. Not even the one in downtown LA we went to with Lupe to look for an immigration lawyer. Shen's apartment building practically shot up to the sky—and he lived on the top floor! In the clouds!

My ears rang as we took the elevator to the penthouse. The view that greeted us when Aunt Juli opened the door to her apartment, though, was truly magnificent. We could see all the way to the Forbidden City!

"Oh my God," I said to Shen, who grinned and took my hand.

"Let me show you around!"

He took me through his kitchen, his living room, the bathroom, and the bedrooms. I noted his parents slept in their own room, not in the living room, like mine. I thought back to what Lupe once said about the definition of success in America—not having a bed in your living room. We weren't there yet, but hopefully one of these days, we'd actually buy one of the open houses. Then we'd all have bedrooms too.

In Shen's kitchen, I saw a woman cleaning the cupboards.

"Oh, Auntie Lin, this is my cousin Mia, from America!" Shen said.

Auntie Lin, an older lady with gray hair, put her cleaning rag down. I noticed that under her apron, she was wearing a Mervyn's sweater just like the one my mom had given Aunt Juli.

"So good to meet you," Auntie Lin said. "Can I get you anything? Some fresh soy milk?"

I shook my head as my mom walked over. She noticed the sweater too, and her face turned bright red.

Aunt Juli quietly pulled my mom into her bedroom. "I want to show you something."

I gazed back at Auntie Lin as Shen led me toward his room. How could Aunt Juli just give my mom's present away like that? Did she know how hard my mom worked for it, how many rooms she had to clean while studying at night? How proud my mom was when she returned from Mervyn's with it carefully wrapped in a shopping bag? A *real* shopping bag, not the fake ones we used to carry stuffed with toilet paper. She'd even packed the bag in our luggage.

Shen pointed to my backpack when we got into his room, asking me what I had inside.

"Oh, this is for you!" I said, pulling out his present.

He took the box and shook it.

"It's a game! Twister!" I told him, pulling off the wrapping paper and turning it around so he could see the image of all the people with their legs and hands twisted.

I thought we might open it up and play it, but he simply took the box to his closet and set it on top of a huge mountain of other toys and games. All of them unopened. I scratched my head.

"You're not going to give my present to Auntie Lin too, are you?"

I asked, half joking. I pictured Auntie Lin playing Twister in the kitchen by herself in my mom's polka-dotted sweater.

"Of course not! I'll play it later, when I have time."

I walked over to his closet and examined the stack of boxes. "I don't understand. There's Chinese checkers here. Chess. And look at all these LEGOs!" I never had any LEGOs when I was younger, because they were always too expensive. Instead I'd played cards with the waitresses at the restaurant where my mom worked.

"You don't understand how busy I am," Shen said. "My mom's got me packed to the gills with tutors."

I followed Shen's eyes to the thick tower of workbooks and dictation journals sitting on his desk.

"Not that any of them has made a difference," he said, plunging his face into his hands. "They still call me 'Wrong Pile' at school."

"Wrong *what*?" I asked, sitting down next to him on the bed.

"Pile," Shen mumbled. "Like I should've gotten rejected. That it's only because of my parents' influence that my letter ended up in the acceptance pile."

Whoa. My fingernails dug into my palms. How dare they say such a horrible thing to my cousin? I wanted to find those bullies and fling them halfway across the world into the Calivista dumpster!

"How long has this been going on?" I asked.

"Pretty much since we moved here," he said. "I tried to tell you. . . ."

I thought back to Shen's last letter, which was over a year ago. He had mentioned something about the kids at his new school teasing him about not being from the same neighborhood as them. At the time, I wrote him back something like *Hang in there* and added an article from the newspaper of us buying the Calivista. Now, looking back, I wished I had written him something more thoughtful.

"I'm so sorry I haven't written more," I said in a small voice.

"It's okay," he said. "I just . . . I really missed you."

I put my arms around my big brother. "I missed you too. You have no idea how hard it's been."

I closed my eyes, thinking of all the times I stayed up late at night, especially those first few years when I first got to America. All the things I wanted to say to him, but it was too expensive to call and we didn't have a stable enough address to send letters back and forth.

"But things are better now, right?" Shen asked. "You have those two friends, Lupe and—what's his name?"

"Jason," I muttered, wriggling uncomfortably.

"What's wrong?" Shen asked. I shook my head, too embarrassed to say. "You can tell me."

After a long pause, when I still didn't say anything, Shen added, "Can't be worse than what happened to me the other day. These three big kids in my PE class, they gave me a door-gie."

"What's a door-gie?"

"It's a wedgie where they take your underwear and hang it on a doorknob."

My jaw dropped. "That's horrible!" I jumped up from the bed. "And what did you do?"

"I got my friend Kang to help me get unhung," Shen said. "He's a wrong pile too."

"Did you tell the teacher?" I asked.

Shen shook his head. "The teachers here aren't like in America.

They only care about your marks, that's it." Shen's face fell. "And mine aren't very good. . . ."

With bullies like that, I wasn't surprised. I'd find it impossible to concentrate too if I was getting door-gies! "I'm so sorry you're going through this," I said.

"It's okay. Having Kang there helps. We have a system. You want to know what it is?"

I nodded.

"We pretend we can't understand the bullies. If they ask us a question, we just start talking in a random made-up language. And if they really push us, we say sorry, we can't speak bully."

"That's great," I said. I thought back to my own experience getting bullied in fifth grade. Jason and I were still enemies then and he was constantly making fun of my clothes. With a laugh, I told Shen about the time I smeared Tiger Balm on Jason's pencils and made him burst into tears in class.

"Genius! I'll have to remember that!" Shen said. "So is he still bothering you—Jason?"

"No . . . but . . ."

"But what?"

It was too hard to say out loud, so I leaned over and whispered it into Shen's ear.

Shen jumped up from the bed when he heard. "He *kissed* you?"

I covered my face with my hands. It sounded so much worse when he said it.

"That's it, I'm getting on a plane right now!" Shen said.

As Shen marched around his room, pretending to pack, I had to laugh again.

"Believe me, I made it perfectly clear that I was NOT cool with it," I assured him.

"Good."

"I just don't understand why he did it." I frowned, throwing Shen's Monkey King pillow up in the air. "I mean, he knows we're just friends. And now it'll be so awkward."

"It doesn't have to be," Shen said. "You just have to be firm with him. Just tell him, 'Jason, I don't like you. It's never going to happen.'"

I hugged Shen's pillow and sighed. The thing was, I'd already told him that at the beginning of fifth grade. And he'd responded by making my life miserable for an entire year.

"He'll understand," Shen went on. "Just in case, though, I'm buying you a bulk supply of Tiger Balm to bring back."

I smiled, grabbing a bunch of Shen's pencils from his desk and pretending to slather them. He threw his head back and cackled. As the morning sun filtered in through the penthouse windows, I realized how much I missed hanging out with my cousin. How nice it was to be on the other side of the world, not having to deal with Jason right now. It made me want to stay here, despite all the squat-lets.

CHAPTER 8

In the car on the way home, Aunt Juli and Mom talked about my grandparents' home while Shen and I played Go Fish in the back. Shen didn't know the game, but he was excited to learn. I smiled as we played, thinking of Lupe. She and I played Go Fish all the time at the front desk.

"You see where the toilet is," Aunt Juli said. "And there's no gas heat. Mom and Dad are getting old. They can't keep living like this."

"What do you suggest we do?" my mom asked. I pulled a two of hearts and handed it to Shen.

"I think we should buy them an apartment. A nice, new, modern apartment. Like mine. We gotta get them out of there. The *hutongs*, they're a thing of the past."

I looked up from my cards. Was that really true? I loved the beautiful *hutongs* with their interlocking courtyard homes. They reminded me of old China and our thousands of years of history.

"Is that what they want, a modern apartment?" Mom asked. "Have you talked to them about it?"

Aunt Juli dismissed the question with a wave of her hand. "They always say the same thing—'We're fine where we are.' But what happens when they have a fall in the middle of the night while they're trying to use the bathroom? I say we get them out of there while they've still got their health. Let them enjoy their golden years in comfort."

Shen handed me a six of spades.

"Fine," Mom said.

Aunt Juli did a cheer at the wheel. "So how much can you contribute?" she asked.

I dropped my cards.

"You're asking me for money?" Mom asked.

"I just figured you'd want to chip in. We're all contributing, even Biming and Mei, and they have a baby on the way."

My mom didn't say anything.

"Look, I know things were hard for you before. But now that you own a hotel and all . . ."

I wiggled in my seat in the back, fighting the urge to say, *Yeah, but things haven't changed* that *much*!

At the same time, I wanted to help out my grandparents. I felt so torn, the tension ripping through me like turbulence on a plane. "Aunt Juli—" I started to say.

My mother cut me off with a look. "No, no, of course. I'd be happy to contribute," she told her sister.

"Good." Aunt Juli smiled. "We want to buy soon, before the prices go up again in the summer."

. . .

I tried to do the math in the car the rest of the way home—what did a luxury apartment in China cost? Split five ways? My calculations were temporarily put on hold when we got out of the car and were immediately surrounded by the smell of Hank's delicious burgers. Grinning, I turned to my cousin Shen.

"You're going to *love* this dinner."

As we walked toward my grandparents' courtyard, I noticed a crowd gathered by the entrance to our house. When they saw Shen, one of them asked what that amazing smell was.

"We're cooking *han bao bao* tonight!" Shen explained, using the Chinese word for hamburgers.

Inside the courtyard, my paternal grandmother, my *nai nai*, was waiting for us with my dad's sister, Aunt Pearl, and his brother, Uncle Lin.

"Nai Nai!" I cried, running up to her to give her a hug.

She held me close to get a good look at me, eyes smiling from behind her thick glasses. "Mia, you've gotten so tall!" She chuckled, then turned to my mom and added, "And dark!"

My smile disappeared.

"What's the matter? You haven't been keeping her out of the sun?" Nai Nai asked.

I looked down at my tanned hands.

"We have very strong sun in California," my mom explained.

Nai Nai shook her head. "Sun is the same everywhere. You know what you do? You avoid it."

My mom frowned at Nai Nai and pulled me into her arms. "Well, *I* think she looks great."

Just then, Hank came outside from the kitchen holding a box of saltines. "Guess what I found!"

My *nai nai* looked at Hank. "That guy's *definitely* not been avoiding the sun."

I shook my head. "What's wrong with the sun?" I asked her in Chinese. I was sick of all the remarks about skin color, but people in China seemed fixated on it. "Maybe if you got some *more* sun, you wouldn't be so narrow-minded!"

I said *narrow-minded* in English because I didn't know how to say it in Chinese. Still, my aunt exclaimed, "Mia!"

I didn't answer her, though. Instead I followed Hank and Shen into the kitchen. Patiently, Hank instructed Shen on how to help him grind up the saltines so he could combine them with the ground beef. The crackers gave the burgers an extra crunch. I joined in, explaining that this was Hank's signature recipe, beloved by all of us at the Calivista. Soon, we had a whole assembly line going — grind, mix, grill.

"This is fun! My mom never lets me help in the kitchen!" Shen said. "She says it's the maid's job to cook."

"Cleaning professional," I corrected him, wiping my eyebrow with the back of my hand.

"What?" he asked.

I stopped grinding for a second to explain, "That's the term that people like my dad and Mrs. Davis prefer. Saying 'maid' is very old-fashioned."

"Uncle Li cleans rooms?" Shen asked. "I thought you guys owned the motel."

"We do, but we also work there."

My cousin's mouth formed an O.

"Anyway, your mom's wrong," I continued. "My friend Jason is an excellent cook."

"Tiger Balm's a good cook?" Shen laughed.

I looked down at the saltine crumbs. I knew I'd just told Shen all about how rotten Jason was to me two years ago and how he'd kissed me without my permission. Still, I didn't like Shen making fun of him. "*Jason* is in cooking school, and he might even be promoted to an elite program."

Shen stopped laughing. "You sound like you're really proud of him."

"I . . . I am . . ." I said, confused.

"All right, these are ready," Hank said, putting the cooked burgers on some plates. "Let's serve!"

We each took a plate and carried them out. In the dining room, my *lao lao* and *nai nai* were seated next to each other, chatting away. Their heads turned when we brought in the burgers and my *nai nai* immediately proclaimed it was too much meat for her.

"Just a bite, Ma. You'll like it," Dad said.

"What I'd like," Nai Nai said, helping herself to a bun, "is for you to move back home. You think that's ever going to happen?"

"I'd like that too," Lao Lao added.

Dad and Mom exchanged a glance.

"Oh, leave them alone," Lao Ye said. "Let them go and explore the world!"

Mom sat up straighter. "Actually, we're quite happy in America. Mia's doing well in school."

"She was even published in the newspaper last year," Dad said. "She's quite a good writer!"

I felt my cheeks get warm. I kept my eyes glued to the bits of saltine crackers in my beef patty, trying not to think about my rejection letters.

"Is that so?" Lao Ye smiled, turning to me. "That's terrific!"

"In English," Mom added proudly.

Hank gave me a pat on the shoulder as he squeezed by and handed my cousins their burgers.

"Writing, though, is that really a suitable profession for a girl?" Aunt Juli asked.

"What do you mean?" Mom asked.

"I'm just saying, how much money do reporters make?"

Mom struggled to answer the question. Finally, she muttered, "It's not all about money, you know."

"Said the girl who left to go live in a capitalist country!" my uncle Biming chimed in. Everyone laughed.

"Well, I think writing is a noble profession," my grandfather said. "I'd love to read your work sometime, Mia."

I looked over and gave him a grateful smile.

Uncle Jo held up his burger from the other end of the table. "You guys, I just gotta say, this is the best burger I've ever had!" All around the table, my relatives agreed, giving Hank a thumbs-up.

Hank blushed as he sat down next to Lian. "Awww, thanks," he said, and dug into his own dinner.

Lian turned and asked, "Can you make this for us every day?"

Hank laughed.

Bo reached over and hugged Hank's arm. But as Hank hugged him back, Bo once again reached up and tried to touch Hank's hair.

"Bo!" I scolded.

"It's all right," Hank said.

"No, it's not — it's disrespectful and inappropriate!" I said. I didn't remember my cousins ever acting this way before! What happened to them?

"Cut it out!" Shen told Bo. Our cousin finally let go of Hank and went back to his food.

On the other side of the table, Aunt Pearl was asking my parents how much money we made in America.

"We're . . . comfortable," my mom said. But she took so long coming up with the adjective that my relatives looked curiously at her.

My dad quickly explained, "What she means is we have enough to live on. But not enough to make all of you jealous."

My aunts and uncles laughed.

"But come on, you immigrated to America, the richest country in the world!" my dad's sister said.

"You'd be surprised," he said. "Things were pretty hard for us the first few years. . . ." He turned and smiled proudly at my mom. "But all that's going to change. Tell them about your new job!"

Shyly, my mom told everyone, "I just passed my teaching certification. I'm now an official American math teacher!"

"That's *wonderful!*" her father exclaimed, jumping up. "You'll love teaching! Oh, honey, I'm so proud of you!"

"She always was very good at math," my *lao lao* remarked to me, talking animatedly with her hands. "Even as a little girl, I'd give her five dollars to go to the market. And she'd say, no, Mama, I only need four dollars and seventy-two cents. She did the math all in her head." She leaned close, as if to share a secret. "Her math was even better than my son Biming's, isn't that crazy?"

"Why's that crazy?" I asked.

Lao Lao blinked a few times, not knowing how to answer. "Because he's a boy!"

I stared at her.

"But why teaching?" Aunt Juli asked my mom. "Why not get back into engineering?"

"Well, that's a much harder license to pass," Mom said. She turned to me. "And besides, I want to be around my daughter as much as I can."

"Then you should just stay home. Let your husband bring home the bacon," Aunt Juli said, smiling at her husband.

Uncle Jo winked at her.

"Not everyone can afford to do that," Mom said to Aunt Juli. "Or wants to."

My dad stood up. "I'd like to propose a toast. To family."

"To family!" my grandfather agreed, standing with his teacup. "That includes you, Hank! Thanks for coming to our humble home and cooking us the best burgers in all of China!"

Hank beamed. "It's my pleasure."

• • •

That night, I lay awake jet-lagged again, listening to my parents talk in the dark.

"She had some nerve! 'Why writing? Why teaching? You should just let your husband bring home the bacon, like me.'" My mom mocked my aunt's voice. "Ugh!"

My dad sighed in quiet agreement.

"And can you believe she gave my sweater to her *maid*?" Mom continued. "I can't believe she even *has* a maid."

"Cleaning professional," my dad corrected her gently. "And why do you care so much about her? Are you jealous?"

"No," Mom said.

I turned to my side, trying to read my mom's face in the darkness, but she was too far away.

"I bumped into a colleague today, right outside my old office," Dad said. "He dragged me and Hank to his house to have tea. You should have seen *his* apartment. . . ." Dad's voice trailed off. "What happened to these people?"

"The economy just took off, I guess."

There was a long pause.

"What are we going to do about my parents' apartment?" Mom whispered. "Juli says we have to contribute."

"We'll figure it out," Dad said.

"We're supposed to be saving up for our *own* house."

"But we have to help family," Dad reminded her. "It's what we do — we're Chinese."

"Where were they when *we* needed help?" Mom yawned.

As my parents drifted off to sleep, I thought about all the things big and small that had changed about China. My aunt's new car and clothes. My little cousins not listening to me. Shen and his school. And why'd my *nai nai* have to make that comment about me getting tan? Who *cared* what color my skin was? And my *lao lao*, thinking boys were better at math?

They'd said similar things to me when I was little, many, many times. But now, the colorism and sexism made me feel itchy and scratchy under the thick blanket. China wasn't the only thing that'd changed. I'd changed too.

CHAPTER 9

On Sunday, Hank woke up bright and early and got everyone steaming-hot *jianbingguozi*.

"Let's go sightseeing today!" he said to me.

"Sure!" I nodded eagerly. I couldn't wait to see the Forbidden City, where the emperor used to live, and the Temple of Heaven. Perhaps we'd even have time to go back to my old neighborhood and find Popsicle Grandpa. Popsicle Grandpa used to give me free Popsicles if I told him what I'd learned at school that day.

I jumped up and grabbed my jacket, then called Shen to ask if he wanted to come. But he said he had back-to-back tutors all day. My parents had to take my *nai nai* to the doctor to get her diabetes medication, so Hank and I were on our own.

"Don't worry, I'll be your tour guide!" I told him. I roughly knew my way around the city, but Lao Ye gave me a map just in case. Hank grinned and put on his LA Dodgers beanie.

Before we left, my *lao lao* scribbled our address in permanent marker on two old pieces of cloth. Then she *sewed* the cloths onto the backs of our jackets.

"Is this really necessary?" I complained.

"Better safe than sorry!" Lao Lao insisted. I looked at the signs on our jackets that said, *If I get lost, please return me to 356 Zhangwang Hutong, Beijing.*

Lao Ye told us which buses to take to get to the city center while Hank grabbed his map, wallet, and sunglasses. We were on our way!

Once out of the *hutong*, we found ourselves standing at a huge intersection. A million cars zipped this way and that. And the bikes! There were so many, I felt dizzy. One man cycled by with his toddler daughter strapped to his back with shoelaces! They swerved every which way, blatantly ignoring a red traffic light.

I looked up at Hank. "How are we going to cross the street?" I asked. The bus stop was on the other side.

Hank shrugged. A group of people stood near us, and we all waited patiently for the traffic to stop. The bikes and cars just kept coming. A couple of brave pedestrians made a run for it, tearing into the traffic. But we were too scared.

After about ten minutes, I noticed the swarm of people next to us starting to make a move.

"We have to join them," Hank decided. "Hold my hand."

"But the light's red!"

"But even when it's green, the cars don't stop!"

Hand in hand, we tiptoed onto the road and followed the other pedestrians. We all huddled together like penguins, braving the traffic together. Cars slammed on their brakes as if we were our own moving traffic light. And when we finally got to the other side, everyone cheered and the cars went right back to zooming around as they pleased.

I laughed, my breath like vapor in the freezing cold. It was twenty degrees outside, and Hank and I blew into our hands to warm them.

We followed the crowd to the bus stop, where we caught bus 10, bound for Tiananmen Square.

Tiananmen Square was full of tourists when we arrived. It had started snowing lightly, and parents were snuggling their children in their arms as they posed for photos. Hank pulled out his Polaroid from under his jacket, and we ran over to the entrance to the plaza, where the emperors of China would pass through.

"Let's ask someone to take our picture!" Hank said.

When I went up to a man and asked, he took one look at Hank and exclaimed in Chinese, "It's Samuel Jackson!"

A bunch of people turned and looked. Hank didn't know what was going on. While I translated for him, a crowd gathered around us.

Hank laughed. "They think I'm the King of Cool? I can dig it!"

The movie *Die Hard with a Vengeance* had just come out, with Bruce Willis and Samuel L. Jackson. Nothing I said could convince Hank's fans that he was not a movie star.

"Please, Samuel Jackson, you have to let us take you out to lunch!" three especially rabid fans insisted.

"I am not Samuel Jackson!" Hank said again. "I understand it can be confusing, us both being so devastatingly handsome and all . . . but I am not a famous actor."

"Not yet," I teased.

"We know you want to maintain your anonymity, so fine, we'll call you Hank," one of his new admirers said. "But please let us take you out to lunch, Sam — I mean Hank."

The men wouldn't take no for an answer. So finally, Hank and

I got into a taxi with them and went to Main Street Grill, a restaurant that served the "best American food in all of Beijing."

Main Street Grill was on the twentieth floor of a fancy new mall. As Hank and I rode up in the big glass elevator, I thought of Shen's apartment. I wished he could have come with us.

The owner of the restaurant, a Chinese man named Mr. Fang, welcomed us at the door. He was thrilled to see Samuel Jackson. He insisted on taking a photo with him to put on his restaurant wall.

Hank hesitated. "What happens when the real Samuel Jackson comes and asks, 'Who's this dude?'"

Mr. Fang laughed and pointed at all the other celebrities on his wall—Tom Cruise, Bruce Willis, Demi Moore, Madonna, Eddie Murphy. Something about each of them looked a little funny. We looked at Mr. Fang, and he leaned closer to us, whispering, "That isn't the real Eddie Murphy either."

Then he held up his Polaroid, and before Hank could protest, Mr. Fang shouted, "Eggplant!" and snapped a picture.

We were seated in a big booth way in the back. As we ordered burgers and shakes, everyone asked Hank about his life in California.

"Oh, it's great. I own a little motel in Anaheim with my pal Mia here," he told them. "How about you guys? What do you do?"

A few of them looked down and shifted uncomfortably.

"Well . . . a bunch of us actually just lost our jobs," An-son said, looking down at the packet of tissue paper for napkins. He told me he and his pals were recently let go from their government jobs due to the rapidly changing economy.

When I translated to Hank what they said, Hank reached out a hand.

"Hey, listen, fellas, I've been there. You just gotta get back on your horse and keep trying. You'll find something."

The guys nodded, grateful for the advice and encouragement from their favorite Hollywood actor.

"What did you use to do?" Hank asked them.

"We were steelworkers," An-son explained. "The pay wasn't great, but the benefits were good. We got free meals and housing. We could live comfortably."

The others nodded with pride.

"And now?" Hank asked.

"Now everything's changed. It's so hard finding a job! Housing is not free anymore. Now we gotta live seven people squished into a small apartment." An-son shook his head while I translated for Hank.

Hank grimaced. "We know a thing or two about that, don't we, Mia?"

I nodded.

The men sighed.

"China's changing," An-son went on as the waiter brought our food. "We used to have an iron rice bowl. Now we don't know where our rice is coming from or how much we're going to get."

The men dug into their burgers, and I thought about their words. The new China may be nice and comfortable for some, like my aunt Juli, but it wasn't rosy for everyone. Just like America, on the outside it might look like a big happy Gap Kids commercial—but for most folks, the reality was far from perfect.

"How's the burger?" the guys asked Hank.

Hank smiled politely and nodded. "Not bad," he said. He put his burger down and wiped his hands on a napkin. "But if you guys want a *real* burger sometime, y'all come down to Mia's grandparents' house. I'll show you a real burger."

"It's a deal!"

When it came time to pay the bill, Hank snapped it up. "I've got this," he insisted.

"No, no, no, no, no, you're our guest! It's on us," they insisted.

"Please, I'm a big Hollywood actor — let me pay."

The fight over the bill brought me straight back to when I was a little kid. Every time I went out to eat with my parents and their friends, the adults would grab and pull and even try to trick each other, just so they could be the one to pay.

Today, instead of grabbing and pulling, Hank looked straight into the other men's eyes and repeated a line from *Die Hard*.

"Listen, I ain't your partner. I ain't your neighbor, your brother, or your friend. I'm your total stranger. And today I am *paying* for this lunch."

The steelworkers erupted in laughter and let go of the check. "But we're doing this again soon," An-son insisted, scribbling his number down for Hank. "And next time *we* pay!"

"Deal," Hank said, beaming as he shook their hands.

Walking out of the restaurant, I couldn't get over the fact that Hank and I had shared the most amazing meal with total strangers we'd met in Tiananmen Square. It was pretty unbelievable.

Then again, I thought as I smiled at Hank, *here I am halfway across the world, with a customer I met in a motel.*

CHAPTER 10

After lunch, we stopped by my old neighborhood. I wanted to find Popsicle Grandpa so I could take a picture with him. He must have been getting up there in age — he was already in his seventies when I last saw him.

"And you said he sold Popsicles outside your school?" Hank asked. "And he'd give kids Popsicles for free if you told him what you learned that day?"

I nodded. "He sure did!"

Hank shook his head in amazement. "How'd the guy make any money?"

I shrugged as I turned the last corner — but Popsicle Grandpa wasn't there.

He usually parked his tricycle, with his ice box strapped to the back, right next to my old school. But now there was only a man sitting on the ground selling knockoff American VCDs.

"Excuse me," I asked the new guy. "Do you happen to know where the old grandpa selling Popsicles went?"

"You won't find him selling Popsicles no more." He shook his head. "He had a bad fall last summer, broke his hip."

"Oh, no! Is he okay? Can we go visit him?"

The vendor pointed toward the *hutongs* next to the school. "He lives over in the *siheyuan* around the corner. Number 512." He looked at Hank. "Say, aren't you Samuel Jackson? I got your movie right here. Twenty-five RMB!"

"Just twenty-five RMB? No kidding! That's like three bucks!" Hank peered into the box of VCDs, excited. The guy pulled out a disc of *Pulp Fiction*.

I started to tug on Hank's jacket. "C'mon, let's go," I urged, looking toward where Popsicle Grandpa lived. But Hank looked longingly at the VCD.

"I'll give you fifteen RMB," he offered.

"Twenty," the guy protested. "That's a good price. This is a quality American movie here. Tarantino!"

Hank chuckled and took a twenty out of his wallet. The VCD seller gave Hank his movie and waved as we walked off.

"You know you just bought a pirated movie," I told Hank.

"So?"

"So, as an artist I don't think that's a very good idea," I said, pointing at the cheap plastic cover. "First of all, the quality's probably bad."

Hank turned the VCD over. "You're right. This description is full of mistakes."

"Yeah, and it's probably going to stop working right in the middle."

"I hate it when that happens."

"And most importantly, what about all the people who worked on the movie, like the writer?" I added quietly, "That could be me one day." *If* I ever got over my writer's block.

"Wait a minute, *I'm* Samuel Jackson here," Hank said, pointing at his chest. "If anyone should be offended, it should be me."

I had to laugh at that.

"But I see your point," Hank said, putting the VCD in his jacket pocket. "I'll give it back on the way home."

I smiled.

"So have you written anything since we got here?" Hank asked.

I shook my head. I wanted to! But there was so much to describe about China, an overload of senses, I didn't even know where to start.

One of the other families from the 512 courtyard house stepped out, and I rushed over to them, asking if they knew an elderly man who sold Popsicles.

"Oh, yes!" an older woman said. "Mr. Pang! He lives right in here. I'll let him know you're here. He'll be thrilled to have a visitor!"

Hank and I waited in the courtyard for Mr. Pang while his neighbor went and got him. When he came out, Popsicle Grandpa was in a wheelchair. He had dove-white hair and wrinkles lining his face. But he still had the same warm and inviting eyes, and they flashed with recognition when he saw me.

"Yeye, do you still remember me?" I asked, calling him the affectionate term for grandpa in Chinese. "You used to give me Popsicles when I was a kid, outside my school. This is my friend Hank!"

"Sure, I remember you." Popsicle Grandpa beamed. "You were the kid who always wanted a second Popsicle!" He chuckled. "Oh, what a wonderful surprise! Come in, come in."

Hank and I squeezed by his rusty old tricycle in his cramped living room and followed him into his tiny kitchen, where he put on a pot of tea. As Popsicle Grandpa waited for the tea to boil, he asked what I'd been up to.

"We live in Anaheim, California, now!" I told him.

"America! Wow! What's that like?"

"It's great! Very different from here. Lots of wide-open spaces," I said. "We have beautiful lakes and parks. And the *best* ice cream."

He laughed. "Are you still going to school?"

"Oh, yes, of course, Yeye."

"Good," Popsicle Grandpa said. He handed us cups of tea and sat back in his wheelchair, blowing gently on his. "School is very important. Never take it for granted. I remember when my daughter was just your age, she was such a good student in school. And then, one day, she couldn't go anymore."

I lifted my lips from the teacup. "Why?"

"Because of the Cultural Revolution," Popsicle Grandpa told us. "The Red Guards came and all the schools had to close." He closed his eyes for a moment, shaking his head. "It was a very difficult time."

I had heard my parents talking about the Cultural Revolution before. I knew it was one of the reasons they left for America.

"Who were the Red Guards?" I asked.

Popsicle Grandpa slowly explained that they were a group of students who went around the country trying to purge the Four Olds.

"Old ideas, old culture, old customs, and old habits," he said, setting down his cup. "Unfortunately, I was an 'old.' So our daughter, Tingting, got sent to the countryside."

I put my tea down and reached for his bony hands. "That's horrible!" I said. "Where in the countryside? Was it far from here?"

He nodded. "*Very* far," he said, reaching up and wiping his eyes with the corners of his sleeve. "Millions of young people had to go to the countryside. By the time it was over, it was too hard for her to come back." He shook his head. "She never got to go to school again."

"Oh, Yeye," I said, wrapping my arms around him. I finally understood why he was always asking us kids what we learned in school.

"Education is a gift. Always treasure it."

"I will," I promised. I sat back down and told Popsicle Grandpa about the proposition that had passed last year in California, threatening to take away my friend Lupe's education. And how, luckily, it had been overturned in the courts.

"Good," he said. "I'm glad it got overturned. Tell me more about America."

As I started telling him about Lupe, Jason, and the weeklies, Hank smiled. Popsicle Grandpa listened, enraptured. He was especially pleased to hear that I loved writing.

"Will you write me sometime and tell me everything you've learned?" He looked down at his ailing lower body. "I don't get to see many kids these days."

"Of course," I said. I turned to Hank and said in English, "And we'll bring you around for dinner before we leave, won't we, Hank?"

Hank nodded. "I'll cook him up some ribs!"

"I'd like that," Popsicle Grandpa said, pouring the last of the tea in his cup. "I'm sad to say that my daughter doesn't visit me much." He sighed. "Times are changing in China. Families aren't as close as they used to be."

"She'll come soon," I told him. "I thought I'd never get to come back to see my cousins, and look, here I am!"

Mr. Pang smiled and touched my cheek with his wrinkled hand.

"I'm glad you came. Stay close with your family, little one. In the end, the only thing that matters . . . is family."

Hank and I thanked him for the tea and bid him good-bye.

"That was very nice," Hank said as we left. We linked arms and went to return the VCD. Luckily, the VCD guy gave Hank back his money. After that, we waved down a taxi.

Soon one pulled over and the driver asked, "Going to the Third Ring?"

"How'd you know?"

He laughed. "I read it on the backs of your jackets! Hop in!"

CHAPTER II

My Trip to China

Hi! I am starting this journal so I can remember every detail of my trip to China. So far, it has been an amazing trip. I've only been here three days and I've:

—Eaten three jianbingguozi. They are DELICIOUS. I don't know what I'm going to do when I get back.

—Fallen into the toilet once. It was not pretty.

—Had to jaywalk. I'm not proud of it, but it was seriously the only way to get across the street.

So far, the highlight of my trip has been visiting Popsicle Grandpa. He told me many things about the Cultural Revolution. I think I under—stand more now why my parents came to America. They wanted to escape the anxiety and chaos they'd gone through as kids, suddenly not being able to go to school. And so they took the great leap of courage to come to America, not knowing that what awaited them on the other side was an ocean of uncertainty.

I sat in my grandparents' room, writing my journal for Ms. Swann while my *lao ye* cooked dinner. I was happy to be writing again. This time, the words flowed out.

Next to me, my cousins Bo and Lian were watching the television. My parents were out on a "date night," their first in many years.

Bo and Lian had the volume up all the way.

"Hey, do you guys mind turning that down?" I asked.

As usual, they ignored me.

I put my pencil down and frowned. I was tired of this.

Lao Lao came into the room and asked, "Has anyone seen my exercise fan?"

"What fan?" I asked.

"My traditional decorative fan! I need it for my dance exercise at the park tomorrow morning!"

At the mention of dance exercise, my cousins immediately got up and started prancing around. "This is what Lao Lao does," they giggled, pretending to fan themselves while lifting their arms and legs high up in the air.

"Go ahead, make fun," she said, rolling her eyes. To me she explained, "Chinese seniors live long, healthy lives because we do our exercise in the park every day! I keep telling your *lao ye* to come with me, but he always stays home reading books. What about you? You wanna come with me tomorrow?"

I grinned. "Sure." I helped her find her exercise fan — underneath her bed, beside her basket of paper wads.

When I got back, Bo and Lian were freaking out.

"What's wrong?" I asked them.

"It just stopped working," they said, pointing to the TV. They pounded on it and shook it, but nothing they did changed the snowy static on the screen.

"Let me see," I said, checking the antenna connection. It was small, more basic than the one we had at the motel. The signal was probably weak from the heavy snow falling outside.

"Got any paper clips?" I asked Bo.

He and Lian finally found one in Lao Ye's desk, and I bent it so it looked like an S. Then, carefully, I attached one side to the TV and the other to the antenna. It was a trick I'd watched Lupe's dad, José, do during the occasional thunderstorm back home. To my cousins' delight, it worked! The screen flickered back to life!

"How'd you do that?" they asked, looking at me like I was some TV goddess.

I chuckled. "Just something I learned living at the motel."

Suddenly, I wondered what Fred was doing. And were Mrs. T and Mrs. Q still holding their How to Navigate America classes this week, even though it was Christmas? And Lupe! Did she go with Jason to see *Toy Story*? Oh God, I hoped he didn't tell her about the kiss.

I wished I could pick up the phone and call my best friend. But Mom had said long-distance calls to America were much too expensive for my grandparents. So I went back to scribbling in my journal while Bo and Lian watched TV.

This time, when I asked them to turn it down, they listened. And when I was done writing and asked, "Can I watch too?" Bo and Lian scooted over.

We watched *Monkey King* and the *Adventures of Shuke and Beita Mice* together. It felt just like old times. I laughed with my cousins, feeling proud for fixing something so much more important than an antenna. I'd fixed the doubt that I wasn't "native" enough in their minds.

. . .

Bright and early the next morning, my grandmother woke me up.

"Come! Come! We're going to the park!" she said, pulling me up from my bed. She was dressed in her jogging suit, holding her huge pink exercise fan in one hand and a portable boom box in the other.

"I don't know, Lao Lao . . . I'm not exactly the morning exercise type," I said, yawning. Hank overheard me say *morning exercise* in English and poked his head in.

"Exercise?" he asked.

"Han-ka!" Lao Lao turned to me and told me to interpret. "He can come too if he wants, but he'd better hurry up! They're starting already!"

"Give me five minutes," Hank said. He pointed to the boom box. "What's that for?"

"Exercise music!" Lao Lao grinned, showing Hank the tape in her hands.

"Oh, can I bring one too?" Hank asked before disappearing into his room. Soon he reappeared in his own jogging suit, carrying a mixtape. "Made this for the trip! Gotta have my tunes!"

I chuckled. He really did pack *everything*.

The park was full of people when we got there, most of them seniors. My grandmother quickly found her fan group and joined in. I watched as the group of seventy or so seniors danced in sync with their decorative fans, singing old Chinese songs as they exercised. It was truly a sight unlike any other.

Hank, meanwhile, squeezed past the ladies doing tai chi and the couples tango dancing and a group of gentlemen doing kung fu. He set up my grandmother's boom box on a patch of grass, put in his tape, and pressed play.

Suddenly, a woman's voice sang, *"Everybody dance now!"* and a thumping beat blasted through the speakers.

Seniors in all directions started nodding their heads to the beat. A few dropped their fans and moved toward Hank.

"Hank, look!" I called, laughing.

His jaw dropped as scores of Chinese seniors gathered around him, ready to rock and roll. Hank danced, and they copied his moves. When he turned left, they turned left. When he turned right, they turned right. Within an hour, Hank was leading a hundred Chinese seniors, all of them dancing to C+C Music Factory. It was so awesome!

When it was over, Hank came running to me, breathless from his workout.

"That. Was. Amazing." I grinned, giving him a high five as he sat down next to me to catch his breath.

"Those seniors sure can move!" Hank said, taking a drink from the water jug my *lao lao* brought.

Lao Lao beamed when I translated what Hank said. "I told you we still got it," she said proudly. "Now c'mon, let's go get some *dofunao!*"

As we walked toward Lao Lao's favorite silk tofu breakfast place, she linked arms with Hank and thanked him for giving her and her friends a morning exercise they'd never forget.

"Do you do that every day?" Hank asked as I translated.

Lao Lao nodded. "Yup! We may be old, but we're not slowing down!"

"I feel the same, Lao Lao. That's why I'm here halfway across the world," Hank replied. He reached over and patted my hair. "Mia here keeps me young."

Lao Lao pushed aside the plastic flaps to the restaurant and said, "Now you're about to have the BEST silk tofu in town. Nothing keeps your complexion looking young like tofu!"

It was a small place, with one long communal table surrounded by wooden stools. The steam coming from the kitchen warmed us even more than the heaters did. Lao Lao told us they served only *dofunao*, which is a Northern Chinese dish of tofu, peanut butter, coriander, and soy sauce.

"Peanut butter?" Hank asked. "Didn't think that was a Chinese seasoning!"

"You'd be surprised. The creamy peanut butter goes well with the silk tofu. You're going to *love* it," Lao Lao raved. She waved hi to the other regulars around the communal table, many of them seniors. "I could eat it all day long."

The chef sighed as he walked over with our food. "Not for long, I'm afraid," he said. He pointed to a sign on the wall. "We're closing at the end of the month."

"What??" Lao Lao asked. "But I've been coming here for fifteen years!"

The chef shook his head. "The landlord says rents are going up all over Beijing. He's nearly doubling ours. I wish we could afford it, but we're just a breakfast shop."

"It's a shame," another customer chimed in. "This place is a neighborhood treasure."

"Now where are we going to go for our breakfast after exercise?" another senior said. "McDonald's?"

I gazed down at the silky *dofunao*, which clearly meant so much more than a breakfast to this community. I wished there was something I could do. I put the spoon to my mouth and slurped up the delicate tofu. Jason would lose his *mind* over it.

"Lao Lao, this is *so* good," I said. But my grandmother just sat there staring at the Closed sign.

Hank was deep in thought too. He poked his head into the kitchen, checking it out as the owner gave us a couple of fried dough sticks, on the house.

As we walked home, Lao Lao, Hank, and I took turns munching on the crispy *youtiao*. Lao Ye came running out into the courtyard when we got home. I noticed he was clutching my journal.

"Mia!" he cried, opening to the entry I'd written for Ms. Swann. "This story you wrote — it's wonderful!"

I blushed. "It's just for English class," I explained.

"That part you wrote about visiting Popsicle Grandpa was so moving." Lao Ye beamed as he handed it to me.

I looked up in surprise that he could understand all my English — then remembered he was an English teacher before he retired. "Thanks," I told him. "It was pretty cool talking to Yeye."

"Can I show everyone?" Lao Ye asked. "Tonight at dinner. I'll call your aunts and uncles and tell them to come over. And maybe tomorrow morning, I'll go down to the paper —"

"To the paper?" Lao Lao interrupted. "There you go again, getting carried away with your big ideas!"

"Yeah, I don't think that's such a good idea," I agreed. I didn't need another rejection letter to add to my stack. No thanks. That was *not* the kind of souvenir I wanted.

Lao Ye looked disappointed. "But it's so good!" he protested.

"I'd like to read it," Hank said.

"We'll all read it at dinner," Lao Ye decided.

I was a little nervous, but I also felt a tiny flicker of excitement. It'd been a long time since I'd shared my work with a group of people. If it couldn't be published in a newspaper, maybe my writing could still be published at the table.

. . .

For dinner that night, Lao Lao made homemade *mantou*, a light, fluffy steamed bun. Hank took one bite and said it would make an *amazing* hamburger bun. Lao Lao served hers with ham and eggs and sliced cucumber. As everyone helped themselves, my grandfather read out my story.

"'They wanted to escape the anxiety and the chaos they'd gone through as kids, suddenly not being able to go to school,'" he read. "'And so they took the great leap of courage to come to America, not knowing that what awaited them on the other side was an ocean of uncertainty.'"

My mom reached for my dad's hand under the table.

"Wow. That's a great story, Mia," Shen said, clapping.

"Thanks," I said, smiling. I had to admit, it felt nice to hear my words out loud.

"I wish I'd gone with you to see Popsicle Grandpa."

"You can! Maybe after school tomorrow?" I suggested.

Shen sighed. "I have *so* much homework." Christmas wasn't officially celebrated in China, so none of my cousins had two weeks off from school like me.

"Well, I think this Popsicle Grandpa is being a little

melodramatic, don't you think? Dredging up old history," Aunt Juli muttered, wiping her hands on a napkin.

"You mean about the Cultural Revolution?" Lao Lao asked. "But that's what happened. Don't you remember they went after your father because he was a foreign language teacher?"

Lao Ye shook his head. "It was awful, Mia. I had to wear these humiliating signs during my struggle sessions—"

"Dad! You don't need to scare her," my mom interjected.

"I'm not scared," I said.

"And anyway, Dad, that's *never* going to happen again," my aunt Juli insisted. "Look at all the foreign investment in China now, all the new buildings and businesses that have sprouted. Why, our building has a gym! With a treadmill!"

"It's true." Uncle Jo nodded.

"Our country has turned the page," Aunt Juli said, "and what a glorious new page it is!"

My grandmother sighed. "Not for everyone, I'm afraid. Just today I found out that our favorite *dofunao* place is closing down. They're increasing the rent."

"Actually," Hank said, holding up a finger when he heard the word *dofunao*. "I've been thinking."

Everyone turned to look at him while I translated.

"What if it doesn't have to close?" Hank asked. "What if they rented out their space during lunch and dinner to somebody who wanted to . . . say . . . open up a pop-up restaurant in China?"

"Like who?" Lao Ye asked.

"Like I don't know, someone who made really delicious, authentic hamburgers . . . ?" Hank shrugged.

I put my *mantou* down. *No way.* Was Hank saying what I thought he was saying?

We were all quiet for a minute. Then Uncle Jo cried, "I think it's genius! Absolute genius! You have no competitors other than McDonald's, and their burgers don't hold a candle to yours!"

"Wait a minute, what about that place, Main Street Grill?" Aunt Juli asked.

"Nah, I've been there," Hank said. "The burgers are overcooked and overpriced. Isn't that right, Mia?"

"Hank's are a gazillion times better!" I agreed.

"And I'm not just thinking of dining in. I'm thinking takeout. Delivery. The whole nine yards."

"Delivery?" my aunts and uncles asked. They had never heard of such a thing.

As Hank explained, it was like a lightning bolt went off in my relatives' heads.

"What an idea! You're going to make a killing, buddy!" Uncle Jo said. "I'd like to be the first to invest."

"But wait, aren't you supposed to be on vacation?" Uncle Biming asked.

Hank chuckled. "I think it'll be fun! Besides, I'd love to make some extra cash so I can bring back something real nice for Fred, Billy Bob, Mrs. Q, and Mrs. T!"

Dad exchanged a look with my mom and said, "We'd love to help!"

"My partners!" Hank chuckled.

"Always!" Dad smiled, shaking his hand.

"But that's just two people," Aunt Juli protested. "Where are you going to get the rest of your delivery guys?"

Hank tilted his face in the light, posing with his best Samuel L. Jackson smile. "I think I know some people looking for work. . . ."

. . .

That night, my parents and I stayed up late talking excitedly about Hank's new burger shop.

"You really think the locals will go for it?" Mom asked.

"Are you kidding?" I said. "They'll love the crunchiness of the saltines!"

"And just think, if the burger shop does well, we could use that money to help pay for Lao Lao's new apartment!" Mom said, clapping her hands together.

"Mom?" I asked, sitting up. "Are you sure Lao Lao even wants to move?"

"Of course she does. She won't have to pay for it. We're all going to chip in!"

I gazed out the window at another snowy night. It *would* be nice for my grandparents not to have to go out in the cold to go to the bathroom. Still, the thought of them selling this house, which I'd always thought of as our family gathering place, was kind of sad.

As I curled up in my rollaway bed, I smiled, thinking about my grandfather reading my journal at dinner. It made me feel all warm inside that my relatives enjoyed my words so much. I was about to close my eyes when I remembered. "Hey, Mom, what was Lao Ye talking about? About having to wear a sign during the Cultural Revolution?"

Mom came over and sat on my bed, tucking a lock of my hair behind my ear. "It was a long time ago," she said quietly. "The reason we brought you back here is for you to get in touch with your roots and be proud of where you came from. China has some painful memories, like many other countries. But times are different now." She turned to my dad. "Just yesterday, your dad took me out for a nice Italian dinner. On the rooftop of a mall!"

He nodded. "You should have seen the view."

"Your aunt Juli is right. The economic progress is incredible."

I was glad to hear my parents' rare date night had been nice. But I couldn't help but think of the unemployed steelworkers Hank and I had met. I told my parents about them.

"Didn't they get a severance?" Mom asked.

"What's that?"

Dad explained that severance was an amount of money people were sometimes paid when they were let go from their jobs, to help them out until they found another.

"But it's always better to have a fishing rod than a bunch of fish," he added.

I thought about that as my mom climbed into bed with me. "They'll find something. Remember us? We had to go through several jobs before the Calivista."

Dad walked over and snuggled me and Mom. "Sometimes a loss isn't really a loss," he said with a wink. "It's an opportunity. You just can't see it yet."

I smiled. I hoped Hank's new burger shop was just the opportunity they were waiting for!

CHAPTER 12

The *dofunao* owner loved Hank's pop-up burger shop idea. He showed Hank around the kitchen, pointing to where all the cooking utensils were. Hank offered to give him 30 percent of his profits to help with rent.

The owner and Hank shook hands while I snapped a picture with Hank's Polaroid. Later that day, while my mom ran around town helping Hank buy up all the ground beef and saltine crackers they could find, Hank and my dad called up the steelworkers.

While everyone else was busy, my grandfather pulled me aside. "Listen, I just talked to the editor in chief of *China Kids Gazette*. He wants to meet with you!"

"*China Kids Gazette?*" I asked.

"It's a newspaper that middle school kids here read to learn English. I used to assign it when I was a teacher. Anyway, I sent him what you wrote—"

"Wait a minute. I thought I said not to," I reminded Lao Ye.

"I know, I know, but I couldn't help it! It was so good! And the editor in chief obviously agrees, or else why would he want to meet?"

I looked into Lao Ye's confident eyes, trying to decide whether I should be mad or hopeful. I reminded myself I already had seventy-nine rejections. What was one more?

And what if Lao Ye was right?

"What do you say? You want to take a trip downtown with your old grandpa?"

A smile escaped as I reached for my jacket.

. . .

Lao Ye and I waited nervously on two chairs outside the editor in chief's office. The *Gazette* was in a brick office building just east of the city center. While we waited, a secretary offered us tea, which my grandfather eagerly accepted and I politely declined. I was too jumpy to eat or drink anything.

After my grandfather's second cup of jasmine, the door finally swung open, and a tall man with silver hair and reading glasses that reminded me of Mrs. T stepped out.

"Mia Tang! It's a pleasure to meet you. My name is Wang Jingmu. I'm the editor in chief of the *Gazette*," he said, extending a warm hand. He ushered us back into his small, dusty office filled with newspapers.

"Thank you for meeting with me," I said.

Mr. Wang sat down behind his desk and picked up my grand-father's letter. "We don't get many submissions by actual middle schoolers," he said, chuckling. "Your grandfather tells me you're in seventh grade?"

"That's right."

"Your style of writing, it's very . . ." He paused for the right word, during which I squeezed my eyes shut and braced for the worst. "Readable," he finally decided.

My eyelids popped open.

"I like it. It's very simple and accessible," he continued, echoing the very adjectives the American editors had used in the rejection letters. Except this time, he added, "That's great. You want to know why?"

I shook my head.

"Because our readers are all developing English learners!" He pointed to a framed picture on his wall of Chinese kids reading his newspaper in class. They looked about my age.

"That's awesome!" I said.

"Our readers are thirsty for stories they can relate to. Stories that tell them about the world. And your work has the potential to do both." He picked up my piece. "I love this line here. 'And so they took the great leap of courage to come to America, not knowing that what awaited them on the other side was an ocean of uncertainty.'"

"Isn't it something?" my grandfather agreed.

Mr. Wang peered at me. "Was it really an ocean of uncertainty when you guys got to the US?"

"Oh, yes, sir," I said. "Especially at first."

I started telling him about how when we first got to America, we had to live in Old Man Jimmy's garage. Old Man Jimmy was an out-of-work truck driver who rented half his garage to us for $200 a month. I would go to sleep curled up next to his Dodge Charger, Shelby, and wake up every morning to the jingle of his keys. Even when we moved out, my parents' jobs were barely enough to pay for a small one-bedroom apartment. That's when we applied for a job working and living at the Calivista Motel. But of course the owner, Jason's dad, turned out to be a real miser.

Mr. Wang was riveted, as was my grandfather, who remarked, "Wow! Your parents never told us all that!"

"What do you mean?" I said, turning to him. "Aunt Juli didn't say anything?" I remembered my mom calling Aunt Juli when we were trying to buy the Calivista and telling her about how much we were struggling.

"She didn't mention a word! I had no idea things were so hard for you guys! We could have helped!"

Mr. Wang cleared his throat. "Let's get back to the story, Mia. So then what happened?"

I explained how we were able to buy the motel from Mr. Yao with the help of some of my friends. Then I started describing Lupe and Jason. When he heard that Jason and I used to be enemies, he sat up and pointed at me.

"Now *there's* a good story!" Mr. Wang erupted. "Our readers would love to read about that!"

"About Jason?" I asked.

"Sure, why not?" Mr. Wang replied. "They wanna read about your friends, the motel, your school life, all of it. Call it — Diary of a Young American Girl!"

"Great title!" my grandfather said.

I stared at the two of them. "Are you *sure*?" What about my stack of letters from editors who said they weren't interested in the simple goings-on of my life?

"How about five hundred words for your first column?" Mr. Wang asked.

My eyes widened. "You're . . . giving me a *column*?"

Mr. Wang wrote down his mailing address and fax number. "We'll see how the first one does. But assuming it's successful, then yes."

I couldn't believe my ears. I jumped to my feet and shook Mr. Wang's hand. "Thank you so much for this extraordinary opportunity! I won't let you down! I promise!"

Walking back home, Lao Ye was beaming. "See, I told you it can happen!"

"It was all because of you." I smiled. "Thank you for sending in my story."

Lao Ye shook his head and told me a Confucius proverb. "'A good teacher can open the door, but you must enter by yourself.'"

I tilted my head and replied with a proverb of my own. "Or as my best friend, Lupe, says, 'You can't win if you don't play!'"

"Oh, I like that one!" Lao Ye chuckled.

At the thought of Lupe, my heart swelled. I couldn't *wait* to tell her about my column! Finally, I'd gotten the good news I'd been waiting for—in China of all places!

Lao Ye took me into his proud grandpa arms, and we huddled together like penguins to cross the busy snowy street. He couldn't wait to tell Lao Lao that one of his big ideas paid off. I couldn't wait to start writing my column!

CHAPTER 13

Later that day, I sat at my desk, trying to write.

~~Dear reader . . .~~

Too boring. I didn't want to sound like a junk mail advertisement.

~~Hey, guys! I'm Mia Tang!~~

Too informal?

Finally, I closed my eyes and pictured Lupe. What would I say to her if she were here?

I can't believe Jason Yao kissed me. Talk about gross. There we were, sitting in the congee shop portion of Jade Zen, having just watched <u>Toy Story</u> — which, by the way, is a really great movie — when out of nowhere, he leaned across the table. I was so shocked I jumped up and nearly spilled all the soy sauce on my pants!

Now, I know you're probably thinking: Is this what life in America is like?! And it's not, I promise. This has <u>never</u> happened to me before. I'm Mia Tang. I'm twelve years old, and I go to middle school at Anaheim Junior High in Anaheim,

California. I was born in China and moved to the US when I was eight years old. And for the most part, I really like it. I don't have endless home-work like my cousin Shen. The other day, he brought so much homework to dinner at my lao lao's house, I thought <u>he</u> was the teacher.

Instead, I have time to read and write and hang out with my friends Lupe and Jason. Oh, and I have a job! I manage the front desk of a motel with my best friend, Lupe. My parents, Lupe's parents, my friend Hank, and a whole bunch of other people own the motel together. Right now, I'm on Christmas holiday in Beijing at my grandparents' house. It's been a ton of fun. I get to hang out with my cousins, whom I haven't seen in years. Hank's about to open up a pop-up burger restaurant! But the thing I can't stop thinking about this whole trip, is <u>why would Jason kiss me?</u> After everything we'd been through...

I thought I made it crystal clear to him that we were just friends a couple of years ago, when he told me he liked me and I told him I'd rather like a rock. How could I like him, when his father, who used to own the motel, would squeeze my poor parents for every dime they had?

It is not easy making a living in America, dear readers. People think America is this super-rich country where everyone drives around in a Cadillac. In reality, two people drive around in a Cadillac, and the rest of us run around trying to wash their Cadillac for two dollars, eating Cup Noodles.

I'm happy to report that I no longer have to eat Cup Noodles. I now wear jeans just like all the other kids in my school. Things in general are good. I just have to deal with a friend ... who got a little too friendly.

I stared at my first column, rereading it. As I handed it to my grandpa, I worried a tiny bit about what he would say. Would he be mad that a boy kissed me? And my mom, what would *she* say?

"Maybe it's too much," I said as Lao Ye's eyes moved across the page. I fought the urge to snatch it back.

"No, it's good! Very honest. And different," he added. He put the paper down and looked at me. "I'm sorry your friend kissed you without permission. That was not gentlemanly of him."

I gazed into my grandfather's kind eyes.

"It was brave of you to write about it."

"Really?" I asked.

He nodded. "The kids in China, they'll get so much out of your words."

"You don't think it's too personal?"

Lao Ye shook his head and recited another famous Confucius proverb. "'Wheresoever you go, go with all your heart,'" he encouraged.

I smiled.

I thought back to my story that I wrote in fifth grade, the one that won Best Story in my class. It had also felt too personal at that time, but it turned out great. I guess I had to go with my full heart, like my *lao ye* said.

As my grandfather went over to his desk and got out an envelope, Hank walked in. "How are the preparations going?" I asked him.

"Excellent!" Hank said. "The steelworkers are in! And look what I made!" He pulled out a thick stack of flyers and showed me and my *lao ye*. They read in Chinese:

Hungry after exercise? Order from Hank's Burgers! Delivered straight to your door! Call today!

"Nice translation!" Lao Ye said, looking up from the envelope.

"I got it done at the printer shop around the corner," Hank said. "I'm going to pass them out at the park to all the seniors!"

"Great idea!" I said. Leave it to Hank to find the best marketing strategy wherever he went! No wonder he was our marketing director back at the Calivista!

My parents walked in carrying bags and bags of ground beef and saltine crackers.

"Well, we just about bought out all the saltine crackers in Beijing!" Dad announced, sliding into a chair.

"Mom! Dad! Guess what? I got offered a column by the *China Kids Gazette*!"

Dad jumped back up. "What? That's amazing! When did this happen?"

"Just today! It's going to be called Diary of a Young American Girl!"

Hank grinned. "I like that!"

"Have you written your first column?" Mom asked. "Can I read it?"

I glanced nervously over at Lao Ye, then shook my head. Even though I was ready to show the world my column, I wasn't ready to show my mom yet.

"You can read it along with everyone else when it comes out next week," Lao Ye said, licking the envelope and pressing it shut.

CHAPTER 14

As it turned out, Mr. Wang loved my first column. He decided to publish it even earlier, so it would come out on the same Friday as the opening of Hank's restaurant.

That morning, my mom stood in the busy kitchen of the *dofunao* restaurant, reading my column. Hank and Dad were rushing to get ready—only ten minutes to go until the doors opened!

"So?" I asked Mom impatiently. "What'd you think?"

She put down the newspaper. "It's great. Love the voice. But when were you going to tell me Jason kissed you?"

I lowered my eyes, staring at her black-and-white waitress uniform. *Never?*

"It's kind of embarrassing."

"And yet you have no problem telling a billion strangers?" she asked, putting a hand to her hip.

"Technically, it's only four hundred thousand," I corrected. Even China didn't have a billion middle school kids.

"Ying, you ready?" Hank called out. I poked my head out of the kitchen. *Whoa.* The line of seniors stretched all the way down the *hutong.* The flyers *worked*!

My mom quickly put the newspaper away, wiped the news ink on her black slacks, and picked up a stack of menus. She nodded back at Hank, ready.

"We'll talk about this later," she said to me.

As the seniors crowded inside, excited to try Hank's famous saltine burgers made with my grandmother's homemade *mantous* for buns, my mom swung into action. She handed each customer a menu and helped them to a table.

I took my place behind the cash register, but before I could even get settled, I heard Shen's voice.

"Mia!" my cousin shouted, pushing through the restaurant. He was clutching my column in his hand. "Everyone in my class was talking about your column!"

"And?" I asked. "What'd they say?"

"They *loved* it! They think you're so funny and witty," Shen gushed. Pride and excitement made his cheeks pink. "And when they found out you were my cousin, you should have seen the looks on their faces!"

He grabbed my hands, and the two of us started jumping up and down.

"My wrong pile days are over!" Shen shouted. I laughed, thrilled for my cousin.

"Coming through!" my dad called, squeezing by us with a platter of Hank's crunchy burgers, fresh from the kitchen. As he served them to the customers, my aunt Juli strolled in.

She took one look at my parents and shook her head. "Can't believe you're flipping burgers on vacation," she said, chuckling at my dad's apron and the plaid bandanna tied around his hair.

But Dad's attention was on a man who'd just walked in. The man was dressed in a suit and tie, and when he saw my dad, his eyes flashed with surprise.

"Mr. Chen!" my dad called out. He set the burgers down, wiped his hands on his apron, and gestured to me to join him. "Mia, this is my old boss, Mr. Chen!" I smiled as I walked over and handed Mr. Chen a menu.

Mr. Chen nodded at me, then turned to Dad. "Wow, it's been a long time. How are you, Tang?"

"Good, good!" Dad said.

Mr. Chen turned back to me and declared, "Your dad used to be one of our very best scientists." Eying Dad's apron and bandanna curiously, he asked, "What are you doing here? I thought you were in America!"

Dad yanked off his bandanna. "We are! We're home on vacation, and I'm helping a friend," he said, pointing at Hank. "What about you? I thought you lived out by the airport."

"I do, but my mother lives around the block. She told me to get her a burger."

"One order to go, coming right up!" Dad exclaimed. "Please have a seat!" He showed Mr. Chen to an open table, then went to the kitchen to get the order.

Mr. Chen looked at me again. "How old are you now?" he asked.

"Twelve," I said. Then, just for kicks, I went and grabbed a copy of the *China Kids Gazette* and handed him my new column.

"'Diary of a Young American Girl,'" he read, impressed. "Will you look at that? Published at such a young age. You're going to be a star, like your dad!"

"Mr. Chen!" my mom said, coming over. "What a surprise!"

"Ying, you're helping out here too?" Mr. Chen asked.

My mom blushed. "We . . . uh . . . kinda got bit by the restaurant bug. . . ."

As they were chatting, the door opened, and some customers helped an old man in a wheelchair get inside. It was Popsicle Grandpa!

"Popsicle Grandpa! You came!" I said, running over and hugging him. "You got the invitation I sent!"

"I wouldn't miss it for the world!" he said, beaming. "How are you, my dear? Did you learn anything this week?"

With great pride, I handed him my column. He started reading right away, and I looked up to see that An-son and the rest of the delivery guys were back from their first trip.

"How'd it go?" Hank asked from the back as I translated.

"Wonderful!" They held up the cash so Hank could see it.

"Did they give you a tip?"

The guys looked puzzled. Hank pulled out a few chairs and told them to have a seat.

"Let me tell you how tips work," he said. "This is going to blow your mind."

I turned back to Popsicle Grandpa just as he looked up from my column.

"This is wonderful," he said. "Are these going to be published once a week?"

"It depends on how well the first one does."

"Oh, it'll do well!" Shen called from his table, giving me an enthusiastic thumbs up. "Don't you worry!"

"I'm proud of you," Popsicle Grandpa said.

I smiled at him, then watched Dad carry Mr. Chen's bag with his mom's order out from the kitchen. I noticed he'd taken off his apron.

Mr. Chen thanked Dad and handed him the money, but Dad shook his head. "No way! It's on the house."

"No, c'mon, let me pay you," Mr. Chen insisted. But Dad firmly shook his head. "Are you sure?"

"Absolutely," Dad said.

"Well, thank you. It was great to see you." He shook Dad's hand, then smiled at me. "And congratulations on your column. You guys are obviously doing great things."

"Just my wife and daughter," Dad said, patting my head. "I'm only trying to keep up."

I gazed up at him, waving and smiling at Mr. Chen as he left. Dad waited until Mr. Chen had safely turned the corner out of the *hutong* before putting his apron back on.

CHAPTER 15

The next few nights were a delicious blur of cooking and serving. By the end of the first week, we made ¥3,000 in profits. The steelworkers were tickled pink when they got their paychecks! Even though they didn't get any tips from the customers, Hank gave them tips out of his own cut. The *dofunao* owner was thrilled too at the ¥900 he got to help with rent.

As word got out about Hank's crunchy burgers, it was a full house practically every night. By the middle of our second week, we even got a call from a man asking if we'd cater a dinner party at his house!

"They're paying us a thousand yuan for the night, plus expenses. Can you believe it?" An-son said.

Hank laughed. "At this rate, we might never go back to America again!" I shot Hank a worried look, and he quickly added, "Kidding!"

"Where is it?" Dad asked.

"Out by the Sixth Ring," An-son said. "The man said he's having a dinner party with his colleagues."

As thrilling as everything was at the restaurant, I was secretly worried. My editor still hadn't called, and it had been almost a week since my first column.

Shen came over that weekend to try to cheer me up.

"I'm sure the editor's just busy," he said. "Or he's just taking his time!"

I shook my head. If the response was good, he would have called. "Maybe I shouldn't have written about something so personal," I said. "And now everybody in China knows about my gross kiss!"

"Not everybody," Shen reminded me. "Only four hundred thousand people."

I groaned.

"Hey, they're not calling me a wrong pile anymore at school," Shen said. "That's something."

"It is something."

"Hang in there," he said. "He'll call soon."

. . .

Finally, on Sunday morning, the phone rang. I stared at it and stared at it, almost afraid to answer.

"Hello?" I asked timidly.

"Hi, Mia? It's your editor, Mr. Wang," he said. "Sorry it's taken me so long to get back to you. It's been a crazy week. Anyway, the readers *loved* your piece!"

Relief enveloped me, setting off fireworks inside, like the ones at Disneyland we could hear all the way in the motel parking lot at night.

"They've been writing in letters," Mr. Wang went on. "They want to read more. We would like to make it a weekly column — and we're prepared to pay you! How's fifty yuan per column? Does that sound good to you?"

I closed my eyes and breathed the moment in. It sounded . . . like sweet candied hawthorns on a stick, dipped in a dream come true.

"I'll take it!" I said.

"Fantastic!" Mr. Wang said. He commissioned five columns from me on the spot, with the specific request that I keep them personal, just like in my first column. "Readers *love* that you're opening up to them. It makes them feel like you're their friend."

I smiled. Was it true that suddenly I had four hundred thousand new friends?

"They want to know everything about you. They especially want to know how you and Jason became friends!"

"No problem," I said. "I'll get you the next column by morning!"

That night, while my mom and dad helped Hank and An-son in the kitchen, I stayed at home, sitting at my grandfather's big oak desk. I tore off another piece of paper from my journal for Ms. Swann and began a new column. This time, instead of picturing Lupe, I pictured Jason as I wrote.

For those of you wondering how Jason and I became friends in the first place, well, it wasn't easy. For a long time, Jason and I were at "active war." We hated each other. I mean HATED each other. It wasn't an under-the-radar kind of hate like I have with this girl in my class, Bethany Brett. It was an in-your-face kind of hate, which started when I told him I didn't like him back and he led the entire school in making fun of my pajama-like pants.

I responded, naturally, by smearing all his pencils in Tiger Balm. You see, Jason liked to twirl pencils. Well, that day when Jason twirled his pencils, he got the Tiger Balm all over his hands, and when he reached up to scratch his eye, the powerful menthol made him burst into tears in front of the whole class.

For the record, I do not recommend anyone trying that at home. But he really was a turd back then. Have any of you ever been bullied? It feels horrible, like when you stub your toe and your toenail falls off. And you're walking around for a month without a toenail, worried that someone might step on you again and then it'll <u>REALLY</u> hurt.

That's how I felt for a long time with Jason Yao. But then something happened that made me reevaluate how rotten he was. He did something kind to help me and my parents. And then he did another thing that was kind. And another thing.

I'm not sure if a bunch of kind things cancel out rotten things, like with fractions in math. But they helped. Last year, when I found out he was really good at cooking, that's when our friendship took off. We've come a long way, me and Jason, which is why I don't want to give up on him or our friendship. Even after what he did.

As I read back my essay, I wondered for a brief second what Jason would say if he knew I was writing about him. He'd probably be mortified. On the one hand, he never should have bullied or kissed me in the first place! On the other, maybe I shouldn't send this to Mr. Wang.

But then I thought, *Nahhhh*. Jason would never read it. It was being published in China! And more importantly, this was my first paid writing job!

I took the paper and, with a deep breath, sealed it in an envelope for Mr. Wang.

Here it comes, column number two!

CHAPTER 16

Later that week, Hank and the steelworkers carefully wrapped up *mantou* buns and ground beef, wiped down the trunk of Uncle Jo's car with a rag, and loaded everything up to take to the catering gig. My mom and dad climbed into the car dressed in their waiter uniforms.

"You guys are working so hard on your vacation," Uncle Jo remarked as he pulled onto the street.

"It's not work if it's fun, right, honey?" Mom said, and Dad nodded.

I didn't understand why they didn't just tell Uncle Jo that they were trying to save up to help Lao Lao with her apartment. My parents were always trying to decorate the truth like it was a Christmas tree. I decided right then and there, I was never going to do that in my column. I was always going to be honest with my readers, even if it was embarrassing or uncomfortable.

The dinner party house was all the way over on the other side of Beijing, near the airport. As Uncle Jo turned off the highway, I was expecting another *siheyuan* nestled in a *hutong*, like my grandmother's house. But this was a beautiful modern villa!

"I didn't think they had houses like this in China," Dad said, his jaw dropping as he got out of the car.

For a second, I felt like I was back in California. I looked around, trying to orient myself. If it weren't for the falling snow, I would have sworn I was in Anaheim Hills, standing in front of Jason's old mansion. This house was nearly a replica of Jason's, with the same tall pillars by the entrance and floor-to-ceiling windows. It was like someone had gone to America, taken Jason's house, and flown it to China.

The door swung open, and my dad's jaw dropped. His old boss, Mr. Chen, stood in the entry.

"You made it!" he greeted us, holding open the thick oak-and-glass door. "Come in, come in!"

It took Dad a second to realize what was happening. *Mr. Chen* was throwing a dinner party for his colleagues — all the people Dad used to work with. And Dad would now have to *serve* them!

Dad's face crumbled like a thousand crushed saltines as we followed Mr. Chen up the marble steps. I felt queasy too, looking around the fake Jason house, thinking about what I'd just written about the real Jason.

The place was packed. Quickly, Dad asked to borrow Uncle Jo's blazer. As he slipped it on over his uniform, I knew he was trying to blend in. Soon, old colleagues were slapping him on the shoulder and greeting him warmly.

"Li Tang!" they exclaimed. "Are you back?"

"We're just visiting . . ." Dad said. Mom slipped her hand through Dad's arm as Hank gave him a *we've got this* wave and led the steelworkers to the kitchen.

"How do you like my house?" Mr. Chen asked. "It's modeled after the homes in California. Wait, let me guess. You guys probably live in something far nicer than this, am I right?"

Mom hesitated for a second. Then she told him we did live in something bigger.

"I'm not surprised!" Mr. Chen said. "Li Tang here was one of the smartest guys I ever worked with. You're probably, what, a managing director at a big biotech company over there by now . . . ?"

"I'm . . . uh . . . managing something," Dad said, laughing nervously.

I shook my head and went to the kitchen to find Hank. He was firing up the stoves when I walked in.

"Hot diggity dog, will you look at this place?" Hank grinned, mushing up the saltines on the granite countertops. "This kitchen is bigger than my entire room back at the motel!"

I looked around. It was bigger than mine too. With two ovens and an island you could sit around, it looked like one of the open houses we'd seen. It even had a breakfast booth. Someone obviously watched a *lot* of American TV when they were designing this place.

When the first batch of mini burgers were done, Hank put little toothpicks on them and placed them on big silver platters for me and the steelworkers to carry out. I was especially excited to give waitressing another try. Ever since the humiliating episode when I accidentally spilled about a pound of shrimp on a customer when I was working with my mom in a restaurant, I'd been waiting for a second chance.

"Think you can handle it, Mia?" Hank asked.

I nodded and lifted the platter with my hands. This time, the platter was steady on my shoulders. Carefully, I walked into the living room.

I spotted my mom over by a jade vase, talking to a woman. I walked over to them with my platter.

"Are you surprised by how much China's changed?" the woman was asking my mom. I offered them each a hamburger, hoping Mom would notice my excellent tray-carrying skills, but she was too busy staring at the woman's diamond tennis bracelet.

"It certainly has changed a lot, Mrs. Chen," Mom said.

"Many people took a bet that China would never modernize, and they were wrong," Mrs. Chen went on, sipping a glass of wine. "Do you ever wonder what would have happened if you hadn't left?"

Mr. Chen walked over with my dad. "They're doing quite well in America, actually. Tang here is the managing director of this biotech firm, what is it called? The Calivista?"

I nearly dropped my tray. *A biotech firm?*

"I'd love to hear more about it. How about Thursday? Do you play golf?" he asked Dad.

Dad quickly nodded. "Yeah, sure!"

"No, you don't!" I blurted out.

My dad shot me a look, like *he* wanted to drop my tray.

"Is this your daughter?" Mrs. Chen asked, smiling at me.

"Mia, say hello to Auntie," Mom prompted.

"Hi," I said, putting the tray down on a table nearby. "Thanks for letting us cater your party."

Mrs. Chen looked around to the steelworkers coming out of the kitchen and at my parents. "I'm sorry, I didn't realize you guys were . . ." she said, pointing to my mom and dad as she put two and two together. "The caterers."

"They're just investors in this restaurant thing," her husband said. "I thought it'd be fun to hire them for tonight." He turned to my dad and said, "I *must* repay you for the complimentary burgers."

"Oh." Mrs. Chen relaxed. "How nice."

Mr. Chen pointed at me. "And their daughter was just published in the newspaper."

"Is that right?" his wife asked, impressed.

I nodded. "I write a weekly column called Diary of a Young American Girl," I told her.

Mrs. Chen's eyes flashed with recognition. "I know that column! My daughter just read it to me! The one about kissing a boy?"

"She didn't kiss a boy," my mom corrected. "A boy kissed her."

"Yes, I remember. And you wrote about how you manage a motel with your parents and life was really hard and you had to eat Cup Noodles," Mrs. Chen went on, nodding. She turned to my mom, puzzled. "But wait a minute, I thought you guys flew here first class."

My mom's face turned beet red. "I . . . I . . ."

Mr. Chen looked at my dad. "Are things not going so well over there?"

"No, she was just exaggerating. . . . You know how kids are," Dad said quickly. "Active imagination!"

"And no discretion," my mom muttered in my ear.

Mr. Chen put a hand on Dad's arm. "You can always come back," he said gently. "We'll always have a job here for you."

"We're fine," Dad insisted.

"It pays a lot better now," Mr. Chen said, then added jokingly, "You wouldn't have to sell burgers or anything!" As everybody laughed, my dad gazed down at his hands.

Mr. and Mrs. Chen excused themselves to go entertain the rest of the guests, and Dad sank into a chair. "We shouldn't have come," he whispered to my mom.

Gently I picked up my tray. "Burger?" I offered, hoping that might cheer him up.

"No thanks," he said curtly, turning away.

"What did I do?" I asked.

Mom crossed her arms, ready to dig into me like a pointy toothpick. "You shouldn't have written about our family. A good Chinese girl does not make her family lose face!"

I looked at her angry face, still perfectly attached to her head! I was sick of all these unwritten rules of what a real Chinese person should and shouldn't do. "What are you talking about? I didn't make you lose face!"

"Keep your voice down," Mom hissed. "And yes, you did. Just don't do it again. Don't write about—"

"No! You can't tell me what to write," I cried.

Then I shoved the tray into her hands and ran out of the room. I didn't stop until I was outside, climbing into Uncle Jo's car. If Mom wanted to pretend to be rich and successful, go right ahead. I would rather spend the rest of the night sitting out here in the freezing cold.

Teeth chattering, I waited for the party to end. Several times, my uncle Jo came out and urged me to come back inside, but I refused. He finally got me a big blanket. It did little to warm my legs, though. They felt like icicles by the time the party wrapped up and everyone came out.

I pretended to have fallen asleep, resting my cheek against the frigid window until it went numb. Anything to avoid talking to my parents.

Back at the house, I lay fuming in my rollaway bed pretending to sleep and listening to my mom and dad talk in low voices.

"Don't think about those people," Mom urged Dad. "Who cares about them?"

He sighed. "I know. When I look at my old colleagues, I see what it could have been like if we hadn't left . . . what *I* could have been." His voice shook slightly.

Mom pulled Dad in for a tight hug. "I know. But we took the right road."

As she reminded him of all the wonderful things that had happened to us in America, including her getting her teaching license, I lay very still, feeling the rise and fall of my chest. How could these random people affect Dad so much? Did he really regret leaving?

"You'll see," Mom promised him. "You bet right on America, and on me."

A small smile escaped from the fog of my anger.

CHAPTER 17

I woke up the next morning to my grandfather dropping a stack of letters on my bed. "Get up, Mia!" he said.

"What's all this?"

"Your fan mail!"

Fan mail??

I sat up and tore open the envelope on top of the pile. My mom came in with a glass of warm soy milk for me. I was so excited, I completely forgot that I was still mad at her.

"Mom, isn't this amazing?" I asked.

Dear Mia,

I really enjoy reading your columns, especially your last column about being bullied. I too was bullied last year, by a girl in my class. She spread horrible rumors about me and cheated off me on my tests. I told her to stop, but she wouldn't.

I was so upset I purposely wrote all the wrong answers, then changed them at the very last second. You should have seen the look on her face when she got back her exam — a big, huge 0/100. She never cheated off me after that.

Anyway, I think you should stay away from Jason. I don't think that kind things cancel out the mean things,

like in fractions. They do not have a common denominator.
I think mean things are like prime numbers — they can
never be factored out. Avoid Jason, that's my advice!!!

Your #1 fan,

Sulin Yang

There were five more letters after Sulin's, all offering various thoughts on what I should do about Jason. I couldn't read them fast enough — it was like having Lupe here, giving me advice! Gently, my parents pried the letters out of my hands for a second to get my attention.

"Hey, can we talk to you?" Dad asked. "About last night. We overreacted."

I glared at them both, not ready to let them off the hook. "You're always trying to sweep things under the rug, like they never happened!"

"We're sorry," Mom said. "Can you forgive us?"

I flopped back on my bed. "Why do you care so much what Mr. Chen thinks anyway?" I muttered to my pillow.

Dad was quiet for a long time, then finally said, "I don't know." He reached for my hand. "But you're right, I shouldn't."

As Mom kissed the top of my head, Dad handed me back my fan mail and scooted next to me on my bed. That morning, we read through all the letters together as I sipped my warm soy milk. Then I went with Hank to set up the restaurant for lunch.

"Can you believe I'm getting fan mail?" I asked him. I was so moved I had readers who took the time to write me. And open up to me with their own personal stories!

"You should feel very proud. Always take that responsibility seri-ously," Hank reminded me as he walked inside the restaurant.

"I will," I promised.

I carried the new *mantous* my grandmother made to the kitchen. It was our fourth week at the restaurant and business was good! We were making *mantous* around the clock, even at home, to keep up with demand. Lao Lao had started coming too, to help my mom in the kitchen.

"Thanks for making all the *mantous*, Mama," my mother said to Lao Lao.

"*Bu xie*. I'm doing this for myself!" Lao Lao replied.

Mom turned to her, surprised.

"If the restaurant does well, maybe you guys won't want to leave," Lao Lao explained with a smile.

Mom opened her mouth as if to say something, then closed it. Gazing into my grandmother's hopeful eyes, I realized how much she missed us and how hard it had been to have us gone all these years. It made me think of my own friends back home. As nice as all the fan letters were, I still couldn't wait to get back to my very first fans—Mrs. T, Mrs. Q, Billy Bob, Fred, and, of course, my bestie, Lupe.

CHAPTER 18

The last two weeks of our visit flew by. Customers continued packing into Hank's restaurant. Some were disappointed we were leaving soon, but Hank promised to show the *dofunao* owner how to make saltine burgers so everyone could enjoy them even after we'd gone.

Halfway through my last week of vacation, Mr. Wang called.

"Great job with the column on Jason. I finally had a chance to read all the responses," he said. "The readers *loved* it. The bullying theme really hit home. Can you write more about what school is like in America?"

"No problemo," I said, jotting the request in my notebook.

"Great. And when you go back to the US, where shall we transfer the money to? Do you have a bank account in China?"

I lingered on the phone. I didn't, but my *lao ye* probably did.

"That's fine," Mr. Wang said when I suggested it. "I'll transfer the money to him for all your new columns!"

"So I can continue my column even from America?"

"Are you kidding? Especially from America! We want to know *everything* you're up to!"

"You got it!" I said, grinning.

While my parents and Hank were busy getting souvenirs and giving burger-cooking tutorials, I sat down to write.

Going to school in America is sort of like learning to swim...in the ocean. There are waves crashing at you from all sides, and sometimes it can feel like you're drowning. But then, if you kick really hard, you'll get to the top again. And you might just see a dolphin!

For a long time, I felt like I was thrashing around in the waves. My English wasn't very good. I was the only Chinese girl in my class (which meant people automatically assumed I was good at math and that I liked Jason!). On top of that, because my parents and I moved around a lot, I was always the new kid.

What's it like always being the new kid? For a long time, I walked around with this bubbling fear in my belly that I'd never stay in one place long enough to have a best friend. But I was wrong. On my first day of fifth grade at Dale Elementary School, I met a girl named Lupe who changed everything.

Lupe made school fun for me. Suddenly, I was looking forward to skipping down Meadow Lane every morning. Now when the waves came, we swam through them together. We've been through so much together, from mean comments from our classmates to harsh immigration laws in our state. And you know something? I'm not afraid anymore, because I know I can handle <u>anything</u> with my best friend by my side.

Not only is she my best friend, we also work together after school too, which means I get to see her double! This year, I'm afraid, I don't have any classes with Lupe. We're in middle school now. If school's like the ocean, middle school is like the Mariana Trench, filled with stinging jellyfish.

I miss being able to turn to my right and tell her a joke. Or exchange a knowing look if one of our classmates says something ridiculous. When you're friends with someone for a long time, you can communicate things with just a look. Luckily, I still get to see her at snack and lunch and back at the motel. I can't wait to get back and tell her everything that's happened to me. I miss her so much I could pop.

As I was writing the last words, Mom came inside.

"We counted up all the money from the restaurant," she said.

"And?"

"And after subtracting all our expenses, our cut was about ten thousand yuan."

My jaw dropped—it sounded like *a lot* of money!—but Mom shook her head. "With the conversion rate, it's not enough for Lao Lao and Lao Ye's apartment," she said. "Apparently real estate has *really* gone up in price in Beijing!"

Dad walked into the *siheyuan*, having overheard the conversation. "That's okay," he said. "We'll figure out another way. Ten thousand yuan is a great start!"

Still, Mom looked sad.

"You want to read my latest column?" I asked, trying to cheer her up.

Mom looked at me, hesitating.

"It's not about our family, I promise," I told her. I didn't add that I *still* thought I had the right to write about whatever I wanted.

Mom read my piece and smiled. "It's wonderful," she said. "I miss Lupe, José, and Dolores. I wonder how they're doing back at the motel."

I glanced at the clock on Lao Ye's wall. It was noon in China, which meant it was about 8:00 p.m. in California. Lupe should be getting ready to hang all the keys from the rooms that had been cleaned for the day behind the front desk.

"You think she's going to like my column?" I asked Mom.

"I think she's going to be very, very proud of you. As am I," Mom said, looking into my eyes. "I hope you know that."

It meant a lot hearing her say that, because I wasn't sure, given what she said at the Chens' house. It was scary thinking that I lost my mother's face. I was glad she'd managed to find it again.

CHAPTER 19

On the day that we were supposed to leave, Lao Lao was a puddle of tears.

"I can't believe you're leaving *again*," she said, following my mom around the *siheyuan* as Mom packed up all our things. "When am I going to see you next?"

"Hopefully soon," Mom said, turning to Lao Lao and wiping a tear from her own eye.

"Soon," Lao Lao sniffled. "I'll mark that in my calendar."

Mom reached over and got a package from her purse. Though we didn't have enough money to buy Lao Lao's apartment yet, Mom had gone out and gotten her a present. It was a beautiful new silk exercise fan.

As Lao Lao unwrapped it, her kind eyes smiled. "You shouldn't have," she said, obviously delighted we had.

Next it was Hank's turn. He presented her with a C+C Music Factory cassette.

"Now you and your friends can dance to it anytime you want!" Hank said.

"Thank you, Han-ka," Lao Lao said in English. She'd been practicing. She turned and asked Lao Ye, "Did I get that right?"

Lao Ye did the *perfecto* sign with his fingers. Then the doorbell rang and my *nai nai* walked in. As Dad greeted his mom, and Mom and Hank packed up the million and one souvenirs we were bringing home, I turned to my grandfather and handed him a copy of my latest column, the one on Lupe and school.

"This is wonderful," Lao Ye said.

I told him how I was going to keep writing back in California. "I can send my columns to Editor Wang by fax!"

"Good." Lao Ye nodded. "Your fans are waiting, including me and Popsicle Grandpa." Tears pricked his eyes. "Don't forget us."

"Oh, Lao Ye," I said, throwing my arms around him. How could I begin to thank him? For believing in me and pushing me to go for my dreams, even when I was feeling too rejected to try again. "Thanks for everything. I couldn't have done this without you."

"Thanks for making an old man feel useful again," he said, reaching to wipe his eye. "I didn't always get to use my voice when I was younger." I wondered if he was talking about the Cultural Revolution. I reached out and touched his hand. "But now you do," he went on. "Promise me you'll always use it."

"I promise," I said.

The door opened. Shen and my aunt Juli were here to take us to the airport.

"I can't believe you guys are leaving. Seems like just yesterday you got here!" Aunt Juli said.

"Yeah, and if you didn't load me up with so many tutors, I could have spent more time with Mia!" Shen muttered to his mom.

Aunt Juli ignored him and pulled my mom aside. "What about Mom's apartment? Are you going to wire the rest of the money?"

Lao Lao overheard and chimed in, "I need my daughter, not an apartment!"

Aunt Juli lowered her voice, but I heard her tell Mom the down payment was due in April.

"I promise you'll have the money," Mom said.

When all the suitcases were in the car, we stood in the freezing snow of the courtyard for a final good-bye. I turned to my *nai nai* and gave her a hug. She hugged me back and made no further comments on skin tone, thankfully. Next, I turned to Lao Lao and buried my face in her pear-and-spices apron. I was going to miss her so much. Finally, I turned to Shen.

"Do you know when you're coming back?" he asked, blinking snowflakes from his eyes.

"Soon."

Shen looked down at our shoes. I remembered that first night when I fell into the toilet, my dirty footprints in the snow. I'd wondered then how I could possibly make it through this trip without indoor plumbing. And now part of me didn't even want to leave.

"I'll miss you," Shen said in a small voice.

"I'll miss you too," I said.

"At least I won't have to keep waiting for the mailman this time. I'll be able to read your columns in the paper, along with everyone else!"

A lump formed in my throat.

"I'm sorry, Shen. I promise I'll do a better job keeping in touch."

He stood as still as possible, trying to hold in the tears. "It's okay. I know you were busy."

I shook my head. "Busy or not, I'm still your cousin," I said.

Shen put his arms around me, and we hugged. Tears fell out of my eyes and onto the snow.

The Pontiac pulled up, and Bo and Lian jumped out, running over to join our hug. The scene brought me straight back to the first time I left China. It was as painful to say good-bye now as it was then.

We hugged and hugged until Uncle Jo beeped the horn of his car and told us we had to leave to make our flight.

Taking a deep breath, I wiped my tears and picked up my carry-on. As I put my luggage in the trunk and got into the car, I promised Shen I'd save up to call him, and that I'd be back before he knew it.

Shen smiled. I put my hand on the freezing car window, and Shen put his hand on the other side of the glass. Then he knocked on the glass, and I rolled down the window. He repeated a line he said to me the first time I left for America.

"The time will flash by like *vroom*."

CHAPTER 20

On the flight back, my mom and I were a mess of tears. Dad and Hank tried to console us—Dad offered me his extra packet of butter and Hank handed me all his Polaroids—but as I looked through the pictures, I felt an ache in my heart so sharp, it hurt to sigh.

There was so much I'd learned while we were in China, so many sights and sounds and smells and emotions that were now a part of me, forever. Heart overflowing with emotion, I put the Polaroids away and spilled my feelings out onto a new page in my journal.

My parents told me that China would be this amazing place where I could bike everywhere I wanted, play with my cousins every day, and eat Peking duck till I was red in the face. The only part I really got to do was the duck part, but that's okay.

The most amazing Peking duck I had was at my grandmother's house the first night we arrived. There we were, all gathered around the table, just like the old days. I stared at my little cousins, who had grown so big. When my cousin Shen offered to take me to the bathroom across the courtyard, I went with him, never thinking I was going to fall in. But I did! There I was with my two feet stuck in the poop, wanting to scream because it smelled so gross. Shen could have laughed, but he didn't. Instead, he pulled me out and helped me clean off and told me it was okay.

Everywhere I went, I was struck by the kind-ness, warmth, and generosity of the people, who welcomed me and my friend Hank into their living rooms and their lives. They shared meals with us, or just a laugh. That's the part about China that I will miss the most — the people. I hope the kind-ness in people never changes, no matter how tall or fancy the buildings get.

I learned a lot about my homeland on this trip, and even though it isn't perfect, I'll always be proud of it because it is where I came from. A place filled with a great many people with great big hearts, from the dancing seniors at the park to the Popsicle Grandpa, who I hope is reading this. Thank you for showing me China.

. . .

Thirteen hours later, the pilot's voice came through the intercom and told us, "Ladies and gentlemen, we are approaching our descent into Los Angeles International Airport."

I put my journal away in my bag and looked out the window at the sprawling Los Angeles Basin, feeling a flutter of excitement. I couldn't wait to show Lupe my new column and the mountain of souvenirs! I pictured her on the other side of the arrival hall and smiled, thinking about the last line of my last column. *I miss her so much I could pop.*

CHAPTER 21

The Garcias were not waiting for us at the arrival hall at the airport. We looked around for the weeklies, but Billy Bob and Fred weren't there either.

"That's strange," Hank said.

"Maybe they're extra busy at the motel. Maybe it's a full house!" Dad said.

"That's gotta be it!" Hank said.

Mom and Dad smiled. Eagerly, we loaded up the luggage cart and went out to get a taxi.

Forty-five minutes later, we got back to the Calivista Motel. Never in my wildest imagination did I expect the sight that greeted us. Dirty leaves floated in the middle of the pool. The parking lot was *empty*. Worst of all, the Topaz and the Lagoon were gone — they'd turned into one *giant* motel, called the Magna!

Hank, my parents, and I gazed up at our monstrous new neighbor.

It was a *beast*. At five times the size of the Calivista, the Magna completely overshadowed us, and a sign shooting up into the sky declared it was the "The Cheapest Motel in Town — Guaranteed." Judging from the long line of cars waiting to pull in, the sign was working.

"Oh my God," Dad said, dropping our luggage and putting his hands to his mouth. After a stunned moment, he went to find Lupe's mom and dad.

We hurried after him, across the lot to the laundry room. Mrs. Garcia was inside scrubbing dirty towels by hand. When she saw us, she jumped up.

"You're back!"

"What's going on?" Dad asked. He immediately rolled up his sleeves and took a seat to help with the towels. "Where's Mrs. Davis?"

"She's gone," Lupe's mom said over the roar of the washing machines. "The Magna hired her away. Actually, they hired her agency away. Made them a higher offer, but on one condition — their staff can only clean for the Magna from now on. Can't clean at other motels."

"That's ridiculous!" Hank exclaimed.

"They can't do that!" Dad said, jumping up from the stool. He asked where we could find José, and Mrs. Garcia got up and led us over to room 2. As we walked, I noticed that one of the neon lights on our sign was broken. Now instead of Calivista Motel, it said *Calivista   otel*.

"We didn't have the money to get that fixed," Mrs. Garcia lamented.

"Don't worry, I'll fix it," Hank said.

"Where's Lupe?" I asked.

I pushed open the door to room 2, hoping to find her. José was up on a chair, trying to clean the filter of a leaky air conditioner. My mom quickly grabbed a nearby trash can and put it under him to catch the drips.

"José!" Dad said. "Why didn't you call to tell us things were this bad?"

"We wanted to. But there wasn't much you could have done from China, and we didn't want to interrupt your vacation. How was it, by the way?"

"It was great, but what's going on? The lot's empty," Hank said. "Where are all the regulars? The student travelers? The truck drivers?"

José climbed down from the chair. "They all went next door. That place is just so big, it's hard to compete. Especially since they're offering rooms at seven dollars a night."

"*Seven dollars* a night?" Dad exclaimed.

"They're ripping off our business model of putting bunk beds in the room *and* undercutting us on price." José shook his head.

Fred, Billy Bob, and Lupe came in as he was talking. At the sight of Lupe, I stretched out my arms.

"Lupe!" I cried.

"Mia!" We hugged for a long, long time. "I missed you so much. Have you seen it?"

"The Magna?" Hank asked. "You can't miss it. It looks like a spaceship!"

I made a face. "Yeah, the Death Star!"

"That's what it's felt like," Billy Bob muttered.

"It's been a rough few weeks," Mrs. T agreed. "Thank goodness you guys are back!" She gave me a hug.

I thought of the line in my Lupe essay. *Now when the waves came, we swam through them together.* While the adults talked, I pulled Lupe into the hallway.

"How was your Christmas?" I asked.

"Good," she said. "Actually, I have some good news!"

"Me too," I said, standing on my tippy-toes because I was *bursting* with excitement. "You go first!"

"After the break, my math teacher and my English teacher asked me to take a placement test, and, well, I got into geometry!"

"That's great!" I exclaimed.

"And English literature."

"Really?" I asked, trying to hide the envy in my voice.

She twirled her braid nervously. When did she start braiding her hair? "Isn't that amazing?" she said. "They're both at the high school. So it'll mean in the morning I'll have to go to there. My counselor and I worked out a schedule."

"Wait a minute, you're going to the *high* school?" I asked.

"Only for half the day. I'll come back after lunch," she said.

"*After* lunch? For what? PE?" I'd meant it as a joke, but Lupe didn't laugh.

"Now's probably not the best time to tell you. . . ." She chewed her lip. "But, Mia, I don't think I have time to help out at the front desk after school anymore."

What???

I shook my head and took a step backward. No. This wasn't happening.

She talked faster. "The classes I'm taking—they're really hard. I'm going to need every minute after school to study for them if I want to do well in them."

I could feel her urgency—it was the same drive that led me to write to seventy-nine different editors. Still, I felt like I was losing her, and that felt like a sharp blade in my heart.

In a small voice, Lupe added, "Please don't be mad. I have to do this — for my future. You see how tough it is to prove ourselves here . . . we have to work twice as hard or they move us to the back."

I nodded, but tears pooled in my eyes. I couldn't believe she was leaving me, when the motel needed her most, when *I* needed her most. I turned and walked toward the manager's quarters. Opening the back door, I stood in the colossal shadow cast on me, feeling the full impact of the chill of the Magna — and everything else.

CHAPTER 22

Inside the manager's quarters, I had to shield my eyes from the harsh fluorescent lights shining through the windows from the Magna next door. It was so quiet at the motel compared to Beijing—a deafening, infuriating silence that rang in my ears.

When I finally made it to my room, I banged open my closet door to put my suitcase back inside, and the avalanche of rejection letters fell out. The sight of them, right after Lupe's news, made me sink to the floor, tears pooling in my eyes. The letters had kept me up at night. But Lupe's rejection felt far more crushing.

"Mia?" Lupe's voice called from the other side of the door.

"Go away," I shouted. I quickly got up and sat with my back to the door, locking her out. For a minute, I could hear her breathing.

"Mia, please," she said finally. "Don't be like this."

Like what? I felt like asking. Like someone who actually cared about my friendships and didn't just throw them away? I wanted to succeed and climb to the top too. But did you see me quitting the front desk?

And to think I wrote all those lovely things about her.

"Lupe!" I heard her dad call.

Lupe sighed, and I listened as her footsteps faded away.

I took all my rejection letters and threw them across the room, screaming to her in my head, *You don't just quit! You find a way to make it work!*

I hadn't even told Lupe about my new column. My special news, which I'd been saving and saving, got swallowed up by hers!

At the thought of my new column, I wiped my eyes and picked myself back up. At my desk, I sat down and got out a new piece of paper.

Today, I came home from China to the most devastating news. Our motel, the Calivista, is not doing well. The Lagoon and the Topaz—the hotels next door—have combined into one giant COLOSSAL motel! And that's not even the <u>worst</u> news. The worst news is my best friend, Lupe, said she can't work at the front desk with me anymore!

My heart shattered when I heard this. All last year, when a horrible law in California threatened to take Lupe away, I was terrified about this very possibility. I couldn't imagine being separated from my best friend. And now here it is, and not because of a stupid law—but because of a stupid class!

Lupe is getting the chance to take advanced math and English at the high school. Have you ever felt proud of someone but mad and sad for your-self at the same time? That's how I felt when she told me that she didn't have time to work at the Calivista anymore. Like she'd picked school over me. My brain was crying, "Noooooooo!" even while my heart was cheering "Good job!" <u>What about me?</u> I wanted to say. What about our motel?

I hope, dear reader, that I'll be able to get the motel back on track on my own. But the other question about our friendship is...a lot harder to answer.

When I finished, I let out a long breath, feeling the calm that always followed after I wrote out my feelings. Slowly I walked out to the front office, squinting in the bright light. I stared at the two stools where Lupe and I normally sat. Part of me wanted to knock one of the stools over. The other part of me wanted to run up and hug them, the last remaining evidence of our days together as front desk managers. Instead, I walked by them to the fax machine and punched in the code for Beijing.

Bad things happen, I told myself. Maybe I didn't need Lupe to get through everything. Maybe all I needed was my pen.

• • •

At school the next day, Jason came running up to me.

"Mia! You're back! Oh, thank goodness. Did you hear about Lupe going to the high school?" Jason hoisted his backpack full of text-books and cookbooks higher on his shoulders.

I rolled my eyes and nodded, wishing I could *unhear* it.

"I mean, I'm happy for her, but for the last FOUR weeks, I've had no one to talk to!" Jason said, playing with the French whisk he'd tied to his backpack with a shoelace. "But I have you now!" He smiled and moved so uncomfortably close, I took a step back.

We still hadn't talked about our kiss.

"What's wrong?" Jason asked.

The thought of rehashing what had happened was so embarrassing, I turned bright red. "I just — I gotta go," I said.

When I hurried into English class, Ms. Swann looked up from decorating the Most board. She put down the ribbons and glittery letters in her hand and gave me an enthusiastic smile.

"Mia! You're back! How was your vacation?"

"Great," I said, looking around the classroom. Bethany Brett rolled her eyes at me. I saw she was wearing a new gold necklace, which she probably got for Christmas. It made me think of the photo shoot and I frowned.

"I can't wait to hear all about it!" Ms. Swann said, holding out a hand. "Where's your journal for me?"

I froze. Oh, *nooooooo*! I was so busy helping out at Hank's restaurant and writing all my columns that I completely forgot to do all my homework! "I'm so sorry. I didn't have time. . . ."

Ms. Swann's eyes bulged.

Quickly I added, "I did get published in a Chinese newspaper, though! I have my own column!"

"Well, that's interesting," Ms. Swann said, her face relaxing a little. "You'll have to bring them in and show them to the whole class."

From his desk, Jason called, "I want to read them!"

I cringed as I thought about those columns. My classmates could *never* read them. Especially not Jason. He wasn't even supposed to know about them!

"Err . . . actually . . . I left them all in China," I lied.

Ms. Swann frowned. "Mia, I can't give you credit for work I can't read."

With that, she went to her desk, got out about a million grammar worksheets, and dropped them on my desk. They landed with a cloud of dust. Then she returned to the bulletin board to pull out the name of this month's Most Creative Writer.

No surprise—it was not me. Da-Shawn Wallace let out a yelp as our teacher pinned his name to the board. I slouched in my seat. I probably wasn't gonna make the board anytime soon.

Even if I was being read by four hundred thousand people every week.

· · ·

At lunch, I stared at Lupe's empty seat next to mine, while Jason chatted away about his break.

"Hello? Did you hear me? I said we stayed at one of my dad's new chain motels in San Diego. The Gold Standard."

"The Gold Standard?" I asked, raising an eyebrow. It made me think of the necklace he gave me at Jade Zen. The one I dropped on the table. I wondered if he still had it. "I don't know why you think being a chain is so much better."

"It just *is*!" Jason declared.

I opened my mouth to tell him about the Magna, then thought, *Nah*. He'd probably think it was better just because it was bigger than the Calivista.

"Oh, and I completely forgot to tell you! I officially got promoted!" He smiled. "You're looking at one of the finest junior chefs in the Newport Beach Culinary Academy!"

"That's great!" I said, genuinely proud of him. He was going to learn so much too—the teachers there were all top retired chefs from around the greater Los Angeles area.

"I'm like the only Chinese kid in the whole academy!" He leaned over closer and added, "Sometimes when I pour the sesame oil, they look at me a little funny. Not that that's going to stop me. I *love* sesame oil." He laughed. "Oh, that reminds me, did you get me spices from China?"

"I did indeed!" I reached into my backpack for the plastic bag of Sichuan peppercorns, star anise, cloves, fennel, and five-spice powder.

Jason's face lit up like a firecracker. "You're amazing!" he said, wrapping his arms around me. "These are going to come in handy at the first cooking competition! You've got to come watch!"

I wriggled away from the hug, and Jason looked confused. "What's wrong?"

I didn't want to get into it. But then again, were we really just never going to talk about the kiss? Finally, I muttered, "I don't really want to be hugged. . . ."

Jason put his hands up as if to say, *Whatever!*

I started getting up with my tray. As I walked over to the trash, he called, "The competition is next weekend!"

• • •

That afternoon, I had to lug four weeks of homework back to the motel. My math teacher, Mrs. Beadle, had been especially disappointed at how little work I'd done in China.

"It's so unlike you, Mia, to just let things go," she said.

"I'll make it all up, I promise. Then will you consider letting me take the placement exam for geometry?"

Mrs. Beadle looked at me like I was asking her if I could get a free soda after having just kicked the vending machine. "We'll see," she said, turning back to the Spring Dance poster she was hanging on the wall.

I glanced at the poster. Fat chance I was going. And certainly not with Jason.

The motel was still and quiet when I got there. Aside from the weeklies' cars, the parking lot was pretty empty—but the row of cars waiting to get into the Magna was down the block.

I half expected to see Lupe in the front office, and for her to be like, *Just kidding! Fooled ya!* but only Hank was at the desk.

Billy Bob came out from the kitchen in the manager's quarters as I put my gigantic backpack down. He was making the green tea Hank had brought him from China.

"How was school?" Hank asked, taking a mug from Billy Bob.

I made a face. "I have a truckload of homework. How about here? Things getting better?"

He exchanged a glance with Billy Bob. "You want the good news or the bad news?"

"Good news, always," I said.

Hank cleared his throat. "The good news is, I fixed the sign."

"Oh, yay!" I said, looking out the window at our neon sign, glad it read *Calivista Motel* again. "And the bad news?"

"I went over to the Magna, and I found out what's going on," Hank said. "The Topaz and the Lagoon didn't just merge. They got bought."

"Bought?"

"By a company called Mega Magna Hotels," Hank said. "They have a huge chain of hotels all up and down the state."

"Oh, I've seen their commercials on TV," I said. Their slogan was *A good night's sleep you can count on, everywhere you go!*

"And they're pushing us out of business," Hank went on. "To drive the prices up afterward."

My dad walked in then, his T-shirt drenched with sweat. He slumped down on the chair, exhausted. I couldn't believe he was back to having to clean the entire place by himself.

"*We* didn't do that!" Dad pointed out. "When we were the only motel on the block, when they were closed for renovation, we kept prices fair!"

"That's because *we* actually have a heart," I fumed. I was so angry, my hands were shaking. If those turtle eggs thought they could kick us out of the water by price-cutting us, they could think again! Not on my watch!

CHAPTER 23

That night, I got a call from my editor.

"Mia, thanks for faxing over your columns," Mr. Wang said.

"What did you think?" I asked, grabbing my notebook.

"The one about China is sweet, but it doesn't have enough drama," he said. "A good column should have tension. I *loved* the one about your best friend, Lupe, quitting on you, for instance."

I pursed my lips. It was weird hearing someone talking about my most tender wound with such enthusiasm, but at least one good thing came out of it. I wrote *More drama!* in my notebook.

"Our readers would love to hear more about it," he said. "What Lupe's doing, how high school is going for her. It can't be easy skipping two grades."

I put my pen down and told Mr. Wang we weren't exactly talking.

"So embellish a little!" And with that, he ordered five more columns from me and hung up.

That weekend, I sat at my desk, trying to write while my mom sat at the kitchen table, preparing lesson plans. Her first substitute-teaching job was starting that Monday.

Mom stayed at the table all Saturday, and on Sunday, when I put on my best house-hunting outfit, she was still there, working in her pajamas!

"Aren't we going to the open houses?" I asked.

"Oh, honey . . ." She put her cup of tea down. "I think we're going to take a little break from that. . . ."

"Why?"

"Because we're a long way from buying," she said simply.

"I thought you said, 'We're just looking,'" I reminded her. I didn't understand. It was our *thing*. We'd been doing it every Sunday for almost a year. I'd gotten used to walking around the big bedrooms, trying to imagine what it'd be like to have a walk-in closet.

"There's a difference between 'just looking' and 'just wishing' . . ." Mom sighed, and I shook my head.

I walked outside and headed to my usual spot by the back staircase.

Mrs. T spotted me. "Hey, Mia!" she said, walking over. "Shouldn't you be at the congee shop with your parents?"

"It closed," I said. Mrs. T took in my sad, long face and sat down beside me on the stairs.

"What's wrong?" When I didn't answer, she said, "One of those days, huh?"

I nodded and told her what my mom said about going from *just looking* to *just wishing*. "And now we'll never be able to buy a house. . . ."

"Oh, Mia, nonsense," Mrs. T said. "You will. Though I hope you'll still want to live here with us. I can't imagine this place without you guys."

I leaned my head against her shoulder. "Me neither. But owning a house is kind of the American dream. . . ."

Mrs. T chuckled. "There's a lot more to the American dream than that."

"Like what?"

She was quiet for a minute. "Like doing things you love, helping your community, and being with your friends," she said.

"Yeah, well . . . *that's* not happening," I muttered. I fiddled with the peeling paint on the staircase railing and told her about Lupe.

"I was wondering what she was studying for at the desk," Mrs. T said. "Wow. But good for her, going to high school for math!"

"Yeah, it's great."

Mrs. T gave me a look. "As her friend, you should be proud of her."

I felt a twinge of guilt. "I am," I said. "But I'm also . . . sad for me."

Mrs. T took off her glittery cat-eye glasses and looked into my eyes. "Give it time, little one. Remember that friendship is kind of like a river — there are ebbs and flows. Just because you're in an ebb doesn't mean the whole river's dried up."

I smiled, making a mental note to use that in my column when I wrote about me and Lupe making up.

If we ever made up, that was.

. . .

Bright and early Monday morning, Mom ran around the manager's quarters, trying on five different first-day outfits.

"Will you drive me?" she asked Dad, applying another layer of lipstick.

Dad was sitting on the couch, sorting through our bills. He looked down at his T-shirt, which smelled of Lysol, sweat, and room freshener. Most of Dad's T-shirts smelled of Lysol, sweat, and room freshener.

"Fred can give you a lift."

Mom stopped applying her lipstick. "It's kind of an important day for me," she said.

"Which is why Fred should drive you," Dad insisted. When Mom gave him a *huh* look, he explained shyly, "You don't want all your colleagues knowing your husband's a maid."

"I thought you were a *cleaning professional*."

Dad turned back to his bills. "I just don't want to screw it up for you," he muttered. "If business continues to go down, we'll need your steady paycheck." He pointed at the stack of bills on the coffee table. "And your benefits . . ."

Mom walked over, knelt down, and looked into his eyes. "You're *not* going to screw it up for me."

But Dad stayed put, and Mom finally called Fred for a ride. As she waited for him, I asked if she knew which school she'd be teaching at today. She said she'd find out when she got to the school district office.

"Good luck!" I told her. "Knock 'em dead!"

"You too," she said with a smile. I didn't know about that. I had so much homework left to do, I was starting to feel like my cousin.

"Hey, do you think I can give Shen a call?" I asked.

"An international call?" Mom glanced back at Dad, who looked up worriedly from the bills.

"Just for a few minutes?"

I knew money was tight, but I'd made a promise. Besides, I missed Shen so much, especially now that I didn't get to see Lupe every day.

"Maybe this weekend," Mom finally said.

I smiled and gave her a hug. "Thanks, Mom!"

CHAPTER 24

On the walk to school, I made a list of all the things I wanted to tell my cousin. With only a few minutes I'd have to be fast. Thirty seconds about Lupe quitting. And a few about how I hadn't seen her Friday afternoon, even though she was supposed to be back at our school. I was half convinced that she'd done such a great job in her morning classes, they'd asked her to stay at the high school for the whole day.

After Mrs. T's advice yesterday, I put all my energy into finishing my homework. Maybe I really could take the placement exam for geometry and catch up with Lupe.

But Mrs. Beadle was not at her desk when I walked into math. I slumped into my seat next to Jason just as the door swung open, and I turned around to see our substitute. My jaw dropped.

"Good morning, class. My name is Mrs. Tang, and I'm going to be your substitute teacher today."

Jason and I exchanged a glance, his eyes said, *Don't worry, I won't tell if you don't.*

But the name Tang was not lost on my classmates. Everyone turned to look at me.

"Tang? Are you guys related or something?" a boy asked.

"Of course they are!" Bethany said loudly. "Everyone from China is related! That's why they're all Wangs, Yangs, and Tangs!"

Her loud laugh rang in my ears, and I lowered my head, cheeks turning the same shade as my mom's lipstick. I don't know why I was so embarrassed; I should be proud of her. I should have told everyone she was my mom. But just like that, I'd waited too long, and now it would just seem weird.

As my mom walked over to pass out the math warm-ups she'd been preparing all weekend, I leaned over and quietly whispered, "Mom —"

"Don't," she whispered. "I don't want the other kids thinking I'm giving you special treatment!"

With that, she walked back over to the whiteboard. For the next half hour, my mom tried to teach us the Pythagorean theorem. Except every time she said *Pythagorean*, she kept mispronouncing it as the *pathetic* theorem. All around me, kids giggled. I slid farther and farther down in my seat.

"The pathetic theorem is one of the most important theorems you'll ever learn," Mom went on, oblivious. "You can use it to find the missing leg of a triangle!"

Stuart, the class clown, got up and started jumping around on one leg. "Help! I'm missing a leg! Where'd it go?"

"I'll help you find it!" another boy shouted, pretending to search.

"No! You're not pathetic enough!" Stuart yelled. Everyone howled with laughter.

"Stop that! Sit back down! That's not how you use the pathetic theorem!" Mom cried.

It was excruciating. Several times, I opened my mouth to say, *Stop it, guys. She's my mom!* But the words stubbornly refused to come out.

I wished Lupe was there. With her by my side, I'd have the strength to speak up. Instead, I sat in my desk paralyzed—and ashamed of myself for being paralyzed.

When the bell finally rang, I waited until everyone left and then walked slowly up to my mom. "It's 'Pythagorean,' not 'pathetic,'" I said quietly.

She turned to me, her face red. "Is that why they were laughing?"

I nodded.

Mom sank into her teacher's chair. "Why didn't you say something?"

I shrugged.

"You were embarrassed," she said.

I looked down, more ashamed than ever. Even if it meant weathering Bethany's jokes for an entire year, I should have stood up for my mom. "I'm so sorry. . . ."

"You can't tell your father this, you understand?"

The determination in her eyes knocked the breath out of me. But I nodded, swallowing hard. I wouldn't tell anyone. I wouldn't even write about it.

"They must have thought I was totally unqualified. That I was such a fool." She sorted through her papers for a couple of minutes, then looked up and said, "I'm just trying to make a better life for us." Her voice broke, and I wrapped my arms around her.

"I know, Mom," I said. "You're doing great." I stood back and added, "Forget them. They do that every day. With everybody."

Mom rubbed her eyes. "With you too?"

"When I first got here," I admitted.

"And now?" Mom asked.

I chewed my lip, wishing I could tell her Bethany Brett no longer made fun of me. That Stuart never made wisecracks at my expense. Instead I said, "Now I just don't let them get to me."

My mom sighed. "I guess I'm still figuring that out."

The bell rang again, and her next class started piling in. I wished there was a way to protect my mom from the crashing waves of middle school, the way Lupe had protected me.

But all I *could* control was how *I* responded when my classmates made fun of someone. I hoped next time, I'd find the courage to do better.

CHAPTER 25

In English, Ms. Swann passed out our school photo packets. As usual, there was an order form inside, along with small sample photos. I took a look at my individual sample photo and smiled. It would be so cool to have this next to my name in my column!

"Hey! I'll trade you for one of yours," Jason said. "After you order them."

Maybe, I thought, but didn't reply. I didn't want Jason getting the wrong idea about us.

Instead, I turned to the sample group photo. Lupe's face and my face were practically hidden in the back row. I wondered if she was looking at this too and feeling similarly bummed.

When I got home that afternoon, I called her.

"Hey . . ." I said when she picked up the phone. "It's me."

"Hi!" Lupe said. "What's up?"

"Have you seen it? Our photo?" I stared at the sample group photo on the front desk. Every time I thought about that day and that photographer, it made me furious all over again.

"Yeah, it's pretty bad."

"Are your parents buying it?" I asked.

"Nah . . ."

"Mine either," I said with a sigh. I'd shown the packet to my mom, but she took one look at the prices and shook her head.

"I'm still going to keep the sample and put it up by my desk," Lupe said. "As a reminder."

"Of what?"

"Of how hard we have to work so they can *never* hide us again, even if they want to."

Timidly, I asked her how geometry was going.

"Great," Lupe said. "It's actually less work than I thought."

I sat up. "So you can come back to the front desk?"

"Well, I still have a lot to do for English. Oh, and, Mia! I overheard the college counselor talking, and guess what he said? The only way to get into good colleges is to do extracurricular activities after school! We have to do, like, Math Olympiad and Model United Nations and stuff. But those are so expensive! You have to travel and everything. What are we going to do?"

"There's plenty of time to worry about all that later," I said. "College is in a million years. Besides, we already *have* an extracurricular after school," I reminded her. "And it's suffering right now."

There was a long pause.

"I know," Lupe finally said. "How's it going? What's the latest?"

I shook my head, not feeling like recapping it all, as if she was one of our paper investors, people who had invested money but rarely came around. She was supposed to be my partner, right here next to me, going through the thick of things together.

Instead I end our conversation with an invitation: "Come back and I'll tell you."

. . .

The next day at school, while all the other kids returned their filled-out photo order forms to Ms. Swann, I sat at my desk reading the note I'd found in my locker.

Dear Mia,

I wish I could come back to the front desk right now, but I can't. You know I want to. But you should see how much homework I have for English literature! We're learning all this complicated text, and there's a new paper every week! And I can't get a bad grade because now that I'm in high school it goes on my official record for college!

So far I'm hanging in there, but I have to spend every minute trying to keep up or I'll never make it. I even study at lunch, sneaking my sandwich in the high school library (not like I have a lot of friends to sit with at the picnic tables).

Anyway, I miss you very much. Hope you're not too mad at me still. I miss you.

Hope business at the motel is getting better. My dad says things are still slow, but I just know they'll pick up.

Write back.

Love,
Lupe

I opened my notebook.

Dear Lupe,

I miss you too! And I totally get it about the homework overload! Why don't you come over and we'll do our homework together? I promise I won't distract you. I have a ton of homework myself, since I completely forgot to do any while we were in China (that's a whole <u>other</u> story). But I'm slowly getting through it.

Things at the motel are not great. Mrs. Davis can't help my dad clean anymore because the Magna made her agency promise they'd be exclusive to the Magna. So my poor dad has to clean all the rooms by himself. And though we're saving some money, it's a lot of work and my dad is so tired every day. I don't know why they won't let Mrs. Davis work for us again! Hank says the Magna is trying to price-cut us out of business. We'll see about that!

Seriously though, Lupe, we need you back. Forget about all those INTENSE high school classes and don't even WORRY about pricey extra-curriculars. We can navigate all that stuff TOGETHER when we're both in high school. It'll be more fun that way. You don't need to be like Doogie Howser — I love you just the way you are!

Please come back.

Your friend,
Mia

I signed the letter with the swirl of my pen and, when English was over, stuck it in Lupe's locker. The rest of the school day, I walked around with a smile on my face, certain she'd like the idea of doing our homework together at the motel.

After school, I waited at the front desk for her. But the only people who came in the door were there for Mrs. T and Mrs. Q's How to Succeed in America class. It used to be called the How to Navigate America class, but now that most of the immigrants knew how to open up a bank account, Mrs. T and Mrs. Q moved on to more advanced topics, like how to save your money and start a retirement fund. Since the immigrants' English was getting better, they didn't need me to translate for them anymore. I sighed, thinking of last year when Lupe and I would translate together.

One other person walked in—the mailman.

"Mia Tang?" he asked.

I nodded.

"I've got a bunch of letters for you from China!" He set a thick stack of envelopes on the desk.

My fan mail! I was so glad I'd left my Calivista address with Mr. Wang!

"Thanks!" I said, eagerly tearing open the letter on the top of the pile.

Dear Mia,

I was so sad to read about your best friend, Lupe, not wanting to work with you anymore. How horrible! She's so selfish! Even if she comes back, you should never forgive her. Trust me, you're better off without her!

You deserve a much better friend than Lupe, such as me. I've been reading your columns ever since they first came out, and I feel like we're already the best of friends. I feel like I know you! And I just know we'll hit it off.

Will you please write back?? Below is my address. You can write to me anytime, or better yet, come and visit me. I'll be waiting for you. Till then, stay away from Lupe — I mean it!!!

Your #1 fan,
Lina Li

There were five more letters, exactly like Lina's — so many words of caution to stay away from my best friend. They had gotten it all wrong; Lupe just sent me a very nice letter! We might be going through a tough patch, but we were still best friends. I pulled Lupe's letter out of my backpack and put it face-to-face with my fan letters, as if to show them.

But it was no use, of course. In my hurry to get out my feelings in my last column, I realized I might have exaggerated a few things.

I reached for a new piece of paper and started scribbling, hoping I could correct my mistake.

Lupe sat in her high school math class thinking maybe she'd made a terrible mistake. She missed her best friend, Mia, terribly, especially at lunch.

My mom walked in as I was writing.

"How did your classes go?" I asked her.

She collapsed in the armchair with a sigh. As she kicked off her Payless pumps and rubbed her aching feet, she told me she'd been to the other middle school all day. I walked into the kitchen to grab the sesame oil. Sometimes when Mom was having a hard day, I gave her a sesame oil back rub.

Closing her eyes, she said, "Middle school kids are not easy."

"You're telling *me*." I chuckled.

Hank and my dad walked in from the back. "Long day?" Dad asked.

Mom wriggled free from my sesame hands. "No, it was fine," she said brightly. "The kids were great!"

Dad sat down on the couch. "Well, we've been on the phone all day with our investors. Everyone's really worried."

I wiped the sesame oil off my hands with a tissue.

"Maybe we could cut our prices," I suggested. "Even if we lose money in the short run, at least we'd get some of our customers back!"

But Hank and my dad shook their heads.

"When they go low, we can't go lower," Hank said. "We don't have deep pockets like they do."

I looked down at my own jean pockets. They weren't the ones you could put your hands into. They were sewn shut, pretend pockets, just like me pretending to know exactly how Lupe was feeling in high school.

Hank glanced out the window at the parking lot.

"At least the parking lot looks full today," he said. "Thanks to Mrs. T's class."

Dad reached out a hand and I poured him some sesame oil. As he rubbed the stuff under his sweaty T-shirt, Mom asked him how he was coping.

"I'm pretty pooped, but I'm hanging in there," Dad said as he massaged his shoulders.

"If you need help, maybe I can stay home tomorrow," Mom offered.

"What about your job?"

"I could switch to part-time . . . just for a little while," Mom said.

I glanced at her. She wasn't giving up on her dream, was she? Because of what the kids said?

"No, you focus on your teaching," Dad said. "The future of this family depends on you!"

Mom gazed down at the sesame oil bottle on the coffee table.

"That's a lot of pressure," she muttered.

"Don't worry," Hank jumped in. "We'll find someone else to help Li clean. Until then, I'll help him. It's not like the front desk is packed with customers during the day."

Dad laughed. "Silver lining!"

"Hey," I said, "why don't we meet with all the investors next week over dinner? Then we can put all our heads together and discuss what to do."

"Great idea!" Dad said.

I grinned. Finally, a chance to talk to my best friend—in person!

CHAPTER 26

At school the next day, I got another note in my locker.

Dear Mia,

I've been thinking about Mrs. Davis leaving and what to do about it. So last night, I made a flyer! Do you like it? My dad's going to put it up at the Mexican grocery store. There's a bulletin board where people can post different jobs. I wrote it in English and Spanish and put the Calivista number on it. Hopefully someone will call soon!!!

Miss you!
Love,
Lupe

I smiled at the attached flyer. Along the sides, Lupe had drawn adorable little cleaning products—Lysol, Pledge, Clorox, Windex, Ajax, and 409. Leave it to Lupe to make my dad's sweaty job look so cute.

I put the note and the beautiful flyer in my backpack and hurried to math. Maybe Dad and I could put it up at the Asian grocery store, and the Ralphs and Albertson's, too! At the end of math class, Mrs. Beadle handed out her own flyers — for the Spring Dance.

I saw Jason take one and was worried when he turned to me. But all he asked was "How's your mom doing?"

I sighed, walking with him to the courtyard. "I think being a sub is harder than she thought it would be."

We sat down on a patch of grass and got out our snacks.

"Well, I think she did great," Jason said, munching on a five-spice bagel chip he'd made himself. "Who *cares* how you pronounce Pythagorean? It's just a name."

I gave him a half smile. Sometimes when Jason said stuff like that, it made me want to forget what happened.

He offered me a bagel chip, and I took it. It reminded me a bit of the *jianbingguozi* in China, and my tummy filled with nostalgia.

"I just wish my mom didn't have to deal with any of that. . . ."

"Hey! I know what might cheer you up. How about going to the dance?"

My face reddened. "No thanks," I said flatly.

Jason looked stunned, like he had *no idea* why I might be turning him down.

I shook my head. "You kissed me, remember?"

Jason blushed hard. He looked down at the blades of grass and whispered, "I know, and I haven't been able to stop thinking about it. . . ."

"Me neither! It was disgusting!"

He flinched.

"Jason," I said, staring defiantly into his eyes. "I don't like you like that. I've been trying to tell you. For *years*."

He crossed his arms and turned, sitting with his back to me and his face to the tree.

"I don't want to hurt you, but I just don't—"

"I heard you!" he snapped. "You don't have to be mean about it." Then he scrambled to his feet. A dusting of chip crumbs fell on the grass as he grabbed his backpack and walked away.

CHAPTER 27

I thought about Jason's words all day—*you don't have to be mean about it.* How was I being mean? By turning him down?

That weekend, I decided not to go to Jason's cooking competition. Instead, I called my cousin Shen. We only had two minutes, so I tried to talk as fast as possible.

"Hi, Shen. It's me, Mia. How are you? How's school? You're never going to believe it. The two motels next to ours became one massive motel. It's as big as a spaceship! Oh, and my best friend, Lupe, stopped working at the front desk with me because she's too smart for middle school, so she's going to high school now to take all these fancy classes."

"Whoa, whoa, slow down," Shen said. "I read about Lupe in your column. I'm so sorry. What spaceship are you talking about?"

"It's not an actual spaceship. It's just as big as one."

"Like can it move and stuff?" Shen asked.

"No. You know what, forget about the spaceship," I said, realizing maybe it was a poor analogy.

"So Lupe just stopped coming around?" he asked. "She probably has too much homework. I can't *imagine* going to the high school; I'm already buried in homework as it is! And I'm only in middle school!"

I chuckled. "How are the kids at your school treating you? Tell them if they don't leave you alone, I'll totally write about them in my column!"

"Thanks," Shen said with a laugh. "And yeah, they're leaving me alone. For now."

I smiled. "Good."

"Do you miss China?" Shen asked.

"I miss *everything*! Lao Lao's *mantou* and the *jianbingguozi* at breakfast. I miss the snow, the seniors exercising in the park, and Popsicle Grandpa. I even miss the squat toilets." I chortled. "Okay, maybe I don't miss those."

"Well, *I* miss pulling you out of them." Shen giggled, and then we both sighed at the same time. "Wish you lived closer," he said.

"Me too."

"Mia, time to get off," Mom said, tapping at an imaginary watch on her wrist.

I groaned. "I gotta go," I told Shen.

"Awwww," he said.

I heard my aunt in the background, calling, "Hey, I want to talk to her mom about the apartment!"

I covered the mouthpiece with my hand and asked my mom if she wanted to talk to Aunt Juli. She gestured with her hands no.

"My mom says maybe another time," I told Shen.

"Cool. Thanks for calling. And, Mia?" Shen asked. "Keep writing your columns. Everyone at my school loves them."

I beamed. After I hung up the phone, I thanked my mom for letting me call him, then skipped to my room. Encouraged by Shen's words, I sat down to write another column.

Yesterday, I finally let Jason know that it was not cool for him to kiss me. I was proud of myself for telling him but also very sad to hurt him.

To give him space, I am skipping Jason's cooking competition today. Space. It's something we have a lot of at the motel these days. And it's given me a lot of time to think. Why does it bother me so much that Jason kissed me? Should I not have made such a big deal out of it?

I think it bothers me because he changed our friendship without asking. He just went for it. And I know that every day on TV, people are always kissing other people, and they don't ever stop and ask, they just go for it. But I think they <u>should</u> stop and ask. If Jason had asked before he kissed me, here's what I would have said:

Jason, you are my dear, dear friend. I need you so much right now, especially with Lupe gone. I want to be there for you and cheer you on because I'm so proud of you. Watching you go for your dreams inspires me to go for mine. I'll bet right now, you're whipping up the most amazing five-spice dumpling soup with tortilla chips or something totally awesome like that, which I can't even eat because I'm not at your competition.

I'm sorry I hurt your feelings, but I needed you to know I don't want you to change what we have. You're my friend, someone I am privileged and honored to know. I don't ever want us to do anything to change that.

As I fed my column into the fax machine, I hesitated. But it was fine; Jason would never read it.

. . .

"Are you ready for the big investors' dinner?" Dad asked later that day. "We're going to the all-you-can-eat buffet!"

"I'm ready! Hey, did we get any calls from any people looking for a cleaning job?" I asked him and Hank as I made copies of Lupe's flyer with the fax machine. Mom was in the bathroom drying her hair.

"Not yet," Hank said. He patted his tummy. "Let's go. I'm starved! Been driving around all day, talking to used car dealers."

I raised an eyebrow. "You're getting a new car?"

Hank shook his head and laughed. "I wish! I was trying to convince them to put some of their used cars in our parking lot."

"Why?" I asked.

"So the place seems fuller! Nothing looks worse for business than an empty lot!"

"I totally agree," Dad said, slapping Hank on the shoulder. "Genius idea!"

"That's why they pay me the big bucks," Hank said with a grin. "Or medium bucks."

"I know what you mean," Dad said. "I've been trying to save up to take Ying on a date to celebrate her new job. We had such great dinners out in China."

Mom came out of the bathroom and asked, "What are you guys talking about?"

"Nothing."

"Is it about my sister? I know we need to call her back to talk about Lao Lao's apartment. . . ." Mom sighed.

Dad took her hand. "Have faith. Things are going to turn around, I promise."

I put on my jacket, accidentally knocking the Spring Dance flyer out of my pocket. Dad picked it up.

"I'm not going to that," I blurted out.

"Why not?" he asked.

"You could go with Jason," Hank suggested, then immediately remembered what I wrote about in my very first column.

My dad took in my forlorn face. "Hey . . . it's okay. You don't have to go." He turned to my mom, his eyes sparkling with nostalgia. "You remember the first time I asked you to a dance?"

Mom blushed.

"At the time, I thought no way she'd say yes. But you did. And now look at you." He smiled. "A big-shot teacher in America. I'm so proud of you."

Dad's face beamed with pride. But Mom looked away.

CHAPTER 28

At Buffet Paradise, the investors sat around the long family table. I was only half paying attention—Lupe and her dad were late, so I was eagerly watching the door. But I knew everyone's focus was *not* on the crab legs and rib eye steak, for once. As my dad proceeded to explain how the Magna undercut our prices, tension was at an all-time high.

"We can't just sit on our hands and watch the Magna take all our business!" Uncle Zhang said.

Mr. Lewis, one of the paper investors, agreed. "I say we stand in front of the Magna with some picket signs—"

"That's not going to work," Mr. Bhagawati said. "When the owner of my shop was trying to sell, some of our customers tried that, but he sold anyway."

Mr. Bhagawati used to work at the Laundromat down the street, before his boss sold it to the chain CleanShine Dry Cleaners. Now it cost six dollars to get a shirt dry cleaned, and they didn't even do as good of a job.

Finally, José and Lupe walked in. I waved at Lupe as she took a seat at the other end of the table, and she smiled and waved back. She was carrying her geometry textbook. Lupe brought *math* to an all-you-can-eat buffet?

Mr. Cooper, one of our biggest investors, cleared his throat. "An interesting offer has come in from a company called Vacation Resorts," he said. "They're interested in acquiring us."

"How much are they offering?" Hank asked. I turned to Hank, surprised. He wasn't seriously thinking about selling, was he?

"Almost double what we bought the motel for," Mr. Cooper said.

Mr. Lewis whistled. "Double??"

I jumped in before everyone got too excited. "Why are they so interested in us?" I asked.

"Well, Anaheim's changing," Mr. Cooper explained. "That's why the Topaz and the Lagoon sold. The economy is improving, and real estate is going up. Vacation Resorts wants to expand in Anaheim. They have big plans to turn the Calivista into a boutique hotel for young, sophisticated travelers."

"Wow!" Mr. Lewis said. "A boutique hotel, imagine that!"

Even my parents looked excited. "Would we be able to keep our jobs?" Dad asked.

Mr. Cooper's face fell. "Unfortunately, no," he said.

"Oh, then forget it," Hank said, frowning. Dad and José shook their heads in agreement, a hard no.

"Hang on," Mr. Cooper said. "Before you guys turn it down, we should all think about it. It's a great opportunity for *all* of us to double our investment and get out while we're ahead." He looked around the room. "These are tough business circumstances we're operating in. Everyone knows we're bleeding cash. And the situation with the Magna is only going to get worse."

"But we can't just give up!" I protested.

Lupe must've heard the urgency in my voice, because she put

her math textbook down and jumped in. "Mia's right," she said.

"I agree!" Dad said. "We have to face our problems head-on, not sell out to the first buyer!"

I was encouraged to see many investors nodding at what we were saying. As the adults continued brainstorming ways to compete against the Magna, I walked over to Lupe. I gave her a hug and pointed at her book. "Is that . . . ?"

"Geometry, yeah."

I narrowed my eyes at the textbook—my nemesis. She was dark green with a barf font and thick spine. This was who I'd lost my best friend to.

"Thanks for backing me up," I said. "And for all the flyers you made."

"No problem!" she said. "I feel so bad not being able to be there to help."

"Well, you can come back anytime. . . ."

Lupe's gaze slid toward her textbook. "I know," she said. "But my classes—"

"Why do you have to take them right now?" I asked, trying to keep my voice even. In her note, she hadn't answered my question about why she needed to skip ahead.

"Because the college counselor said I need to be in geometry now, so I can take Algebra II next year, then Precalc, then AP Calc and AP Statistics—" She rattled off courses a mile a minute!

"But do you have to take them right this *second*? You have so much else going on right now . . . the motel . . ." *Me*, I wanted to add.

Lupe frowned. "You know, you're always so supportive of Jason when he wants to do something hard. But when it comes to me moving up in school, you're like, 'Are you sure? Come back, you can't handle it.'" She shook her head. "It's like you don't think I can do it."

"That's not—*you're* the one who said your classes were hard!"

"They *are* hard. But that doesn't mean you give up!" Lupe said. "You just said that yourself!"

"Yeah, well, I didn't say you should give up on *us*," I snapped. I went to the other side of the table as Lupe turned back to her textbook.

For the rest of the night, I sandwiched myself between Auntie Ling and my mom, sneaking glances at Lupe. She made it sound like I didn't support her—of course I supported her. But right now, we really needed her back at the motel. Mr. Cooper was literally talking about selling the Calivista!

I cracked a crab leg in half in frustration as Auntie Ling peppered my mom with questions about our vacation.

"So what was China like?" she asked. The table went silent, and all the other immigrants turned to face Mom, hungry for details. "Is it true what they say, that it's really nice now?"

My mom stared at the wonder and fear and curiosity in their eyes. I knew from listening to enough of my parents' conversations that what they were really asking was *Did we make the wrong decision moving here?*

There was a long pause.

"No," Mom lied. "It hasn't changed a bit."

CHAPTER 29

Over the weekend, as Mr. Cooper insisted on arranging a meeting between us and the Vacation Resorts people to consider their offer before we turned it down, I poured my frustrations onto paper.

It's like Lupe doesn't care about our motel anymore. All she cares about is college, which isn't for like a gazillion years! What about the people who need her right now? That's realer than anything in a textbook!

If our motel gets sold, what's going to happen to all the weeklies? To all the immigrants who rely on our How to Succeed in America classes? There are <u>real</u> people with <u>real</u> problems who need her!

The thing that hurts the most is, it's like all of a sudden, she thinks she's outgrown the motel or something. Like she's outgrown me.

My editor *loved* that one. He called me after school that week to gush about it. "This is *exactly* what I wanted—the drama! The tension!"

I was glad he found my life blowing up so entertaining—that made one of us.

I put the phone back as the front doorbell rang. I pressed the buzzer, expecting to greet a customer. Now that Hank had arranged for more cars to be in our lot, some people were starting to trickle in again. But it wasn't a customer—it was Mrs. Davis!

"Mrs. Davis!" I exclaimed, letting her in. I quickly phoned my dad in the laundry room and called out to Hank, who was cleaning the pool. Dad ran over and took off his plastic cleaning gloves, giving Mrs. Davis a big hug.

"You're back!" he exclaimed. He rubbed his eyes with the back of his hand, trying to contain his emotions.

"When you came over this morning and said how much trouble the Calivista was in, I just knew I had to help," Mrs. Davis said.

"But what about the ban?" I asked.

"I quit the agency!" Mrs. Davis announced. "It wasn't working out anyway. You won't believe how hard they worked us over there at the Magna. We had to clean each room in less than seven minutes!"

Hank's eyebrows shot up. It usually took my parents forty-five minutes to clean each room; my dad, a former geneticist, still cleaned like a scientist.

"Management didn't care how dirty anything was," Mrs. Davis explained. She lowered her voice, as if they could hear us. "Sometimes, when things got real busy, they told us to skip the vacuuming. And just rinse the bathtubs, not scrub them."

Dad flinched. "You're kidding! You guys would *skip* the vacuuming?" He spent *so much* of his time vacuuming.

Mrs. Davis nodded. "That's not even the worst of it. They had these motion detectors in the rooms when we were cleaning. If we stopped to rest even for a few minutes, our pay would be docked."

"That's outrageous!" I said. It filled me with such anger that the Magna had such little respect for their staff. Poor Mrs. Davis!

"Unbelievable," Hank said.

"So I told the agency I quit," Mrs. Davis said. "I'd much rather work for a place that treats staff with compassion."

"You always have a job with us," Dad said, putting a hand on her shoulder. "You don't know how hard it's been, trying to clean all the rooms by myself."

"Well, now you have me," Mrs. Davis said. "I won't let you down, partner."

Dad smiled as Mom walked into the front office. "Is that Mrs. Davis I hear?" she asked.

"Yup! She's back!" I said, handing Mom her purse from under the front desk where she kept it. Some cards fell out, and Mom kneeled to pick them up. I glanced at the cards—my mom had scribbled things on each of them, probably math formulas.

"It's so great to have you back," Mom said to Mrs. Davis, coming around the desk to shake her hand.

"I'm excited to get to work!" Mrs. Davis replied.

My mom looked at her watch. "Me too! I'm teaching at the high school today!"

"I've been meaning to ask," Dad said to Mom, "what are you doing Saturday night?"

"Nothing," she said, setting the cards and her purse down on the coffee table.

"Well, I might have a little surprise for you," Dad said, smiling.

"Okay!" She grabbed her purse again, kissed Dad on the cheek, and rushed out the door.

My eyes fell on the notecards on the coffee table.

"Mom, wait!" I called. I ran out the back to try to catch her, but when I got outside, she was already gone. There was nothing but a bunch of old cars sitting in the lot.

I looked down at the cards.

Polynomial	*Poly-no-meal*
Perpendicular	*Per-pen-dic-u-lar*
Congruent	*Con-grew-ant*
Trapezoid	*Traa-pah-zoy-d*

I smiled — then frowned. Were the high school kids going to give my mom a hard time too?

• • •

At school, Mrs. Beadle let out a little squeal when I handed in all my completed homework. "Well done, Mia. I'm impressed!"

"Thanks! Can I take the geometry placement test now?"

Mrs. Beadle reached into her drawer to pull out the test. "I'm fairly certain you're in the right class," she said. "But if you insist . . ."

I took the paper from her and hurried to my desk. At his seat, Jason was poring over his own papers. I took a closer look — French recipes. He quickly covered them up when he saw me.

"Where were you this weekend?" he asked, upset. "You didn't come to my competition!"

"I'm sorry," I said. "I . . . was busy."

He made a face. "Well, you'll be happy to know I lost."

"Why would I be happy to know that?"

Mrs. Beadle shushed us. "Mia, no talking! If you don't know a question, just guess and move on to the next one!"

I turned back to the test. Lupe wasn't kidding—geometry was no picnic. These questions were *hard*.

Jason leaned over to peek at the paper.

"You're trying to ditch me for geometry too?" He threw his hands up. "Perfect!"

I opened my mouth to reply, but a *shhhh* from Mrs. Beadle cut me off. I turned back to the test and tried to ignore Jason for the rest of class. I made myself think of Lupe and how if we were in the same class again, everything would go back to normal. I was sure of it. I could say all the things I didn't get to say that day at the buffet and things would be good again.

When I was all finished, I walked up to Mrs. Beadle's desk, hoping my score was enough to get my best friend back.

CHAPTER 30

Walking out of Mrs. Beadle's class, I tried not to think about the fact that half my answers had been guesses, or that I had no idea what a rhombus was. It sounded like a type of dance that the old folks in the Beijing park did.

Instead, I tried to think of other things. Like what Mrs. Davis said about the Magna. How could they dock her pay and ask her to cut corners on cleaning? Wasn't the whole point of being a bigger motel and having so many customers to spend more on their staff? And I was dreading the upcoming Vacation Resorts meeting, which was in less than a week.

In English, Ms. Swann smiled when I handed in my thick stack of papers.

"Doesn't it feel good to get all your work done?" she said.

I wished I could give her my columns—then she'd see I'd been working *all* month. But I just smiled back, and Ms. Swann turned to the rest of the class and clapped her hands.

"All right, kids, our next unit is a group writing project."

A group writing project? I furrowed my eyebrows. How was that going to work? I imagined me writing half a column and Lupe writing the other half (which was *never* going to work, given what I wrote about in my first half).

"Jason, you're working with Bethany," Ms. Swann said.

"What? No!" Jason protested.

Bethany made a face too. "I don't want to work with him! He smells like paprika half the time!"

Jason held up a finger. "That would be cloves. Get your spices straight."

I suppressed a chuckle.

"And, Mia," Ms. Swann continued. "You will be working with Da-Shawn."

Da-Shawn Wallace? Aka this month's Most Creative Writer?? I spun around, but Da-Shawn's eyes were glued to his journal. He was probably writing a five-thousand-line free-verse poem shaped like a swan.

Ms. Swann finished pairing people off, then directed us to take our stuff and move seats. Reluctantly, I walked over to Da-Shawn.

"Hey," I said.

"Hey," he said back, barely looking up from his writing.

I sat down in the seat next to his. "Whatcha writing?"

"Nothing."

He continued writing, and my eyes peeked over at his journal.

Sheets of glazed ice that turn slightly metallic in the sunlight, like they're winking at you, smiling on cold winter days when you can see your breath before you can feel it, is what I remember the most about my old school.

Wow. The imagery and details and flowery language — it was so beautiful. No *wonder* Ms. Swann made him Most Creative Writer.

"That's really good," I said.

He shrugged as he tore off the page, folded it into a thousand tiny squares, and put it into his Batman pencil case.

"Not like I can do anything with it," he said. "At my old school, we had a student newspaper. But they don't have that here." He sighed.

"You want to get published?" I asked.

He nodded. "You probably think that's stupid."

"No . . . I think it's amazing," I said.

Da-Shawn looked up.

"I . . . I like writing too," I confessed.

"Really?" Da-Shawn asked.

I nodded.

"What kind of stuff do you like to write?"

"Just really simple stuff, about my life," I said, a little embarrassed. My sentences were such potato chips compared to his literary souffles. Still, it felt good to share my love of writing with somebody else at school. That was one of the things I missed the most about not having Lupe here.

"You know, if you want to get published, there are ways," I added.

"Like what?"

Color rose in my cheeks. I didn't want to exactly tell him about my column in China, so I said, "Maybe *you* could start a student newspaper. . . ."

Da-Shawn shook his head. "They'd never go for that. Not from some new kid."

I put my pencil to my mouth, still thinking about Lupe. "You'd be surprised. My best friend always says, 'You can't win if you don't play.'"

"I like that!" Da-Shawn said.

He jotted the words down in his journal, and I smiled, missing Lupe. Her wonderful phrase had helped me so much these last couple of years.

As Da-Shawn and I started working on the project, I spied Jason across the room. He wasn't working with Bethany at all. He was staring at me and Da-Shawn, gripping his pencil so hard, I thought it might crack in half.

CHAPTER 31

That weekend, at a tall, fancy building in downtown Los Angeles, the investors, my dad, the weeklies, Hank, José, and I all went in to meet with Vacation Resorts. I was hoping Lupe would be at the meeting too, but she wasn't there. There were six Vacation Resorts executives present, including Mr. Smith, who welcomed us into a conference room and shook our hands.

"So great to meet you. Thank you guys for coming in," he said. When he saw me, he leaned over to his assistant and asked, "Do we have a book or maybe a coloring pad for this girl so she doesn't get too bored?"

Coloring pad, seriously? "I'm Mia Tang, front desk manager of the Calivista," I informed him.

Mr. Smith put his hands up. "Sorry!" he said. "We don't get a lot of kids working as front desk managers in our hotels, do we?"

The executives next to him all chuckled. As they whispered among themselves how "cute" I was, my face grew hot. I didn't want to be cute. I wanted them to take me seriously.

I leaned forward, folding my hands on the mahogany conference table. "So what exactly is your plan for the Calivista?" I asked.

Mr. Smith cleared his throat. "Our plan is to take the Calivista into the twenty-first century. We want to make it a true destination!"

As he proceeded to explain all the ways in which Vacation Resorts would modernize and innovate our motel, turning it into a high-end boutique hotel, I could see that our investors were impressed. They had many questions, like *How much was the Vacation Resorts offering?* and *Was this going to be an all-cash sale?*

Then Dad asked, "And what are your plans for the staff?"

Mr. Smith looked at his associates. "Normally when we acquire an asset, we bring in our own professional management team to run it. They're very experienced."

"But they don't know our motel like we do," I said. Hank, José, and my dad nodded.

"I assure you, once we acquire the asset, it'll be in great hands," Mr. Smith said. "We have an excellent track record. . . ."

I frowned. Why did he keep referring to the Calivista as an asset? It was a motel. With people who lived in it and loved it.

"Everyone we hire goes through our extensive Vacation Resorts training. Most importantly," Mr. Smith added, looking at me and my dad, "they all have legal working visas for employment and they're all of working age."

"Hey!" Dad protested. "Are you saying we don't have visas?"

"We *all* have papers," José added.

"As for legal working age," I said, "the federal family-business child-labor laws say it is okay for children to help out in a business their parents own or operate." I remembered looking it up in the library last year, when my teacher was unusually curious about what I did after school.

"But if your parents no longer own it," Mr. Smith pointed out, "then I'm afraid that rule no longer applies."

He had me there.

By the time the meeting was over, I felt like I'd been to another school photo shoot. After all the work I'd put into the Calivista, the big guys still saw me as just a kid and wanted to move me to the back row. I looked around the room as Dad and Hank and the other adults shook one another's hands. I wondered if the meeting would have gone better if I hadn't been the only kid there.

. . .

When we got home, Hank and Dad and I sat at the front desk, talking over the offer, while I tried Lupe on the phone.

"I think it's baloney that they can't hire us," Hank said. "We busted our butts building this place."

"Tell me about it," Dad said.

"Not only that, we'd do a much better job than those corporate suits," Hank went on.

Dad nodded, pointing toward the Magna. "You know over at the Magna, they charge people for another day if they're fifteen minutes late checking out?"

"What?" I asked in disbelief, putting the phone down. Lupe wasn't picking up. "They charge people a whole extra *day*?"

That would never happen at the Calivista. One time, we let a customer stay for an extra two hours because his baby was taking a nap.

"That is crazy harsh!" Hank shook his head.

It suddenly occurred to me what we could do to compete. I reached for another blank piece of paper from the fax machine. Hank and Dad both stared as I quickly made a flyer:

Come to the Calivista, where you'll always be
greeted with a friendly smile!
— The Calivista Motel, an independent business
since 1984

"I love it!" Hank cheered, reaching for paper to make more.

"Let's put these up all over town!" Dad said. I nodded, decorating the sides with keys and little packets of soap, just like Lupe's flyer. Then I jumped down from the stool and went into my room to find the Scotch tape.

Mom was sitting at my desk, making more notecards. She hadn't been at the meeting with Vacation Resorts either, because she volunteered to help out at a weekend professional development conference for teachers in Long Beach. She didn't have enough money for a badge, but by volunteering to set up the chairs, she could still sort of attend.

"Hey, how was the conference?" I asked her.

"Good!" she said. "I learned some classroom management tricks. I'm sure they'll come in handy." She got up and closed the door so my dad couldn't hear. "Yesterday, a kid pulled the fire alarm on me."

"What??"

Mom nodded.

"I think that part of the problem is I'm a substitute," Mom said with a sigh. "They probably wouldn't act like this if I were their real teacher."

"You *are* a real teacher," I encouraged her.

"But to teach the same class full-time, that requires more school, I'm afraid," Mom said. "And we don't have the money for that.

Anyway. How did the meeting with Vacation Resorts go?"

"Not very well," I muttered. "They don't want to keep any of the Calivista staff after the sale."

"That's terrible," she said. "No wonder your dad was so quiet when I came home."

I sat down on the bed, listening to the traffic outside the window.

"I saw Lupe at the high school today," Mom said.

"How was she?" I asked.

"I only saw her for a second. I was walking by her class. She looked . . . stressed. And lonely. She was sitting all by herself."

I scrunched my eyebrows. "Really? She didn't say anything at the buffet." Though, come to think of it . . . in her note, she had mentioned not having a lot of friends to sit with at lunch.

"People keep things bottled up inside for all sorts of reasons," Mom said, reaching for my hand.

I knew she was right. I'd been keeping all my rejections bottled up for the whole year, and Mom herself still hadn't told Dad about her own challenges as a substitute teacher.

That night, after all the flyers were made, I tried calling Lupe again. I hoped she knew she could always talk to me if she was going through something. We might have our ebbs and flows, as Mrs. T says, but I was here for her always. My fingers curled around the phone cord, hoping she'd pick up.

When she didn't, I put the phone back and reached for another sheet of fax paper. I needed to submit another column. So I started writing down what I wished I'd said to Lupe in person.

At the top I wrote *Should you go for your dreams?* as the title.

I believe you should absolutely go for your dreams, even if they are hard. I'm going for mine — that's why I'm writing this column. And I know that sometimes it can feel lonely, going after your dreams. Like you're the only one in the whole school, the whole universe, going through something. But chances are, you're not.

I discovered this yesterday when I had to work with Da-Shawn Wallace in English. I'd never talked to Da-Shawn before, though I'd spent a lot of time staring at him from across the room, secretly wishing he'd get hand arthritis. That's because my teacher Ms. Swann wouldn't stop gushing about how great his writing was.

Well, I finally read it for myself. And guess what? It really was that great. His words made me want to jump into the story and pitch a tent right underneath the paragraph so I could read it over and over again.

I couldn't help but compare my own simple words to his elaborate prose. As I was reading, I felt like one of the used beater cars we have in our parking lot, masquerading as a real customer's car.

But the more I talked to Da-Shawn, the more I realized he's actually a lot like me. He's new to the school, and while I'm not exactly new, I still feel new sometimes. He misses his old friends in

Connecticut just like I miss Lupe and Jason. He wants his writing published too. I would have never guessed that we have so much in common, which just goes to show, you never know with people. Sometimes we're a lot less alone than we think. All we have to do is look around.

As I sat back and read over my column, a crazy thought crossed my mind. I should send this to Lupe! Then I quickly reminded myself why that was bucketloads *not* a good idea, because then she'd want to read all my columns, including the ones I could *never* show her. I sighed. Lately, some of what I'd written in those earlier columns made me feel a little bad.

I could rewrite my words as a letter, I thought as I punched in my editor's fax number. But some things were easier to say to four hundred thousand people than to just one.

CHAPTER 32

Mom and Dad were getting ready to go out on their big date when the phone started ringing.

"Hi, I'm in room five, and there's a blazing light coming in my window," Mr. Mason complained. "I've tried closing the curtains, but it's no use. I feel like I'm onstage at the Beach Boys concert in Vegas! How am I supposed to get any sleep tonight?"

"Sorry, sir, we'll look into it!" Dad promised.

No sooner had he hung up the phone than it rang again.

"What in the world is that light?" asked Ms. Templin in room 2. "It's like I'm in a Xerox machine!"

"Apologies, ma'am, I'll find out and call you right back!" Dad said. He hung up and grabbed his jacket.

"Where are you going?" I asked.

"To go talk to the Magna!"

The Magna was lit up like a second sun as Hank and I followed my dad over there. We found three tired men sitting behind the check-in counter. They wore T-shirts that said *Magna Motels: A Good Night's Sleep You Can Count On, Everywhere You Go*. But judging by the looks on their faces, I wondered when was the last time *they'd* gotten a good night's sleep.

"Hi," Dad said to them. "We're from the Calivista. Your new pool light is shining directly into our guest rooms."

"Yeah, so?" one of the men replied.

"So you think you can turn it off?" Hank asked.

They exchanged a few words among themselves, then turned back to us.

"Sorry, corporate policy. Our pool light needs to be on at all times."

"But it's beaming *directly* into our guest rooms! Our guests need to sleep!" Hank told them.

"Have you tried closing the curtains?" one suggested.

"Of course our guests have tried closing the curtains!" I said.

"Well, maybe your curtains are just too weak!" the first man said, perking up now. "Here at the Magna, we have the latest, state-of-the-art blackout curtains."

Hank rolled his eyes. "Listen, I don't care what kind of curtains—"

A loud beep interrupted us—a machine behind the desk was sending an alert. The curtains guy spoke into a walkie-talkie clipped to his shirt pocket.

"Front Desk to Tidy Nine, Front Desk to Tidy Nine," he said.

A woman's voice came on. "Yes, this is Tidy Nine."

"Tidy Nine, this is Billy at the front desk. The motion detector alerted me of recent inactivity in the room you're cleaning. Can you please explain?"

Oh my God . . . that was what Mrs. Davis told us about!

"I'm sorry, I stubbed my toe when I was cleaning and it was so painful, I had to catch my breath for a second—"

"I'm sure it was," Billy cut her off. "But please get back to work, Tidy Nine. We're on a schedule."

"Yes, sir," Tidy Nine told him.

My mouth hung open when he clicked off the walkie-talkie. Who *talked* to their staff that way? Was that our future if we sold to Vacation Resorts—we were gonna be referred to as numbers instead of having names? (If we even had the opportunity to work there at all.)

Billy looked back at us. "Anyway, there's nothing I can do about our pool light. I suggest you change your curtains to blackout curtains."

Dad shook his head as we walked out.

"Wow," Hank muttered.

"And I thought Mr. Yao was bad . . ." I said.

"Those guys are in a whole other league!" Hank agreed.

"What are we going to do?" Dad asked. "Blackout curtains cost an arm and a leg."

The phone was ringing off the hook when we got back. It was getting darker out, but the pool light kept the rooms illuminated like broad daylight. We could've played night baseball at the Calivista! Guests were threatening to get a refund and move to the Magna unless we did something.

"I could get some thick fabric from the crafts store and try stitching it onto the curtains myself," Mom suggested.

Hank and I nodded—it was better than nothing.

So that night, instead of going on their date, my parents took me to the fabric store, and Dad spent the money he had been saving up for a nice candlelit dinner on fabric by the yard.

"Some evening this turned out to be . . ." Dad apologized as he and I helped Mom hold up the fabric in the guest rooms as she stitched.

"It's all right," Mom said. "These things happen."

Dad shook his head. "They don't just happen." He glared at the light from the Magna. "They're the work of a big bully."

I felt the anger bubbling inside me. It just wasn't fair. I wished there was some way my parents could get back their date night. And for the Magna to *back off*.

CHAPTER 33

In class the next week, Mrs. Beadle delivered the crushing news that unfortunately, I could *not* go to geometry with Lupe. It was not entirely a surprise, given I'd guessed half the questions. Still, I was bummed. Mrs. Beadle encouraged me to try again next year.

"Next year? Lupe'll probably be in grad school by then," I groaned.

Jason raised his hand to ask if *he* could take the test.

"You too?" Mrs. Beadle asked. "You're barely caught up with your homework! Where are my problem sets from last week?"

Jason smacked his forehead. "I'm sorry, I totally forgot. I had to go to these extra cooking classes. We're getting ready for this *big* competition —"

Mrs. Beadle held up her hand to quiet him. "Jason, this is the third time this has happened. I'm afraid I'm going to have to send a note home to your parents."

I turned to Jason, worried. "Really?"

"What do you care?" he snapped at me. Then he went back to studying his recipes. I leaned over and saw that it was for potatoes dauphinoise. I thought he *hated* potatoes dauphinoise.

"What happened to the Asian fusion dishes you were making?" I asked.

"Not doing them anymore," Jason muttered.

"Why not?"

Jason put the recipes down and crossed his arms. "So now you're suddenly interested in my life? You didn't even show up to my cooking competition. And what's going on with you and Da-Shawn?"

Before I could tell him that Da-Shawn was just a friend, Jason grabbed his math textbook and got up from his chair.

"You know what, forget it." Turning to Mrs. Beadle, he asked, "I'm sorry, Mrs. Beadle, but can I sit at the carpet? I'm having a hard time focusing at my desk."

I threw my hands up. Now *I* was distracting Jason?

"Of course," Mrs. Beadle said, handing him a cushion to sit on. As Jason dumped his stuff on the carpet, I slumped back at my desk.

Great. Now I had *no* friends in math class.

· · ·

In English, Da-Shawn showed me a new piece he'd written over the weekend, about drinking Slurpees in Connecticut in the winter and getting brain freeze *and* finger freeze. It made me laugh so hard, I got the hiccups. I put my hand over my mouth and passed Da-Shawn one of my own stories. Not one of my super-personal and embarrassing columns, but the piece I wrote on visiting China. The one my editor said wasn't "dramatic" enough. I still liked it, though. I hoped Da-Shawn would too.

As Da-Shawn's eyes moved across the paper, I waited anxiously for his reaction.

"This is *amazing*!" he finally said.

"Really?"

"It's so moving and honest! I want to read more."

I smiled, feeling all warm and fuzzy inside. "But it's so simple," I said, pointing to some of my sentences, which were short little pebbles compared to his long caterpillars that stretched lovingly across the page. Before I could stop myself, I blurted, "All my readers in China are still learning English. So short sentences are better for them." I quickly put my hand to my lips.

"Your *readers*?" Da-Shawn asked, his brown eyes growing bigger.

Oops.

"I kinda write for a newspaper in China," I said.

"Oh my God! Like a column?" he asked.

I nodded.

"You're a *columnist*?"

"*Shhh,*" I whispered, putting a finger to my lips. But the way he said *columnist*—I liked the sound of it. *A lot.*

"That's *so* cool," Da-Shawn said, looking at me in awe.

I smiled back at him.

"You got any more?" he asked, pointing to my column.

It felt so good to finally tell my secret to someone, after weeks of hiding it! And not just anyone—a fellow writer!

"I'll bring you some tomorrow!" I said. "But you have to promise not to tell anyone."

Da-Shawn zipped his mouth with his finger and threw the key away. As he returned my piece to me, our fingers touched and I felt a little jolt of electricity. I blushed from behind my paper.

CHAPTER 34

What was happening? Did I *like* Da-Shawn?

I was thinking about him so much, I couldn't concentrate on grocery shopping with my mom. We were at Ralphs because we didn't have enough time to go to 99 Ranch, the Asian grocery store. Mom had to go to a new-staff mixer at the school district later that night, so we had to hurry. And I had to stop obsessing over Da-Shawn!

"Let's just get something easy so all your dad has to do is microwave," Mom said, peering at the selection of frozen dinners.

"Isn't Dad going to your thing?" I asked.

Mom shook her head. "I asked him, but he doesn't want to go." She sighed. "You know how he is."

I didn't know why Dad was being so shy about going with my mom to her new work. I grabbed a box of pepperoni pocket pizzas and was reading the instructions on the back when Jason and his mom pushed their carts into the aisle next to us.

"Mia, it's so good to see you!" Mrs. Yao said with a smile.

"And Jason!" my mom replied.

"How are things at the motel?" Mrs. Yao asked.

"I'm sure you've heard about our neighbors, the Lagoon and the Topaz?" Mom said. "They got bought out by this chain, Magna. It has *not* been easy competing with them."

"My husband's started a chain down in San Diego," Mrs. Yao said. "It's actually been tougher managing it than we thought."

"Really?" Mom asked.

Mrs. Yao nodded. "Oh, yeah. They've got staff turnover issues. Customer complaints." She rolled her eyes. "Lots of problems."

I poked my mom, encouraged by this. *Maybe it's possible to win against a chain!* But my smile wavered when I looked at Jason's sad face. I remembered how proud he'd been that night at Jade Zen, when he told me about his dad's new chain.

Jason pointed at the box at my hand. "What are you getting?"

"Just some frozen pizza," I said, showing him the box.

My mom quickly explained, "I have a work thing tonight." She stood tall and proud as she informed Mrs. Yao, "I'm a substitute math teacher now at the school district."

"So I've heard." Mrs. Yao beamed, sharing a knowing look with Jason.

Mom glanced at Jason in alarm. He didn't tell his mom about my mom's humiliating first day substituting, did he? He better not have!

"We could take Mia," Mrs. Yao offered. "She could have dinner at our house!"

"NO!" Jason and I blurted out at the same time.

Our moms frowned, not sure what to make of our joint outburst.

I pointed to Jason's cart. "That's a lot of butter," I said, trying to distract everyone. It was true too: There were about thirty sticks, enough to make a croissant the size of a car.

"Jason's making *chaussons aux pommes*," Mrs. Yao said, pronouncing the words with a French accent.

"They're just apple turnovers," Jason muttered.

Mrs. Yao turned to him. "Jason, I thought we agreed. If you're going to be a French pastry chef when you grow up, you have to learn to pronounce everything perfectly." In a low voice, she added, "It's bad enough you don't *look* French."

What? Okay . . . there were so many things wrong with that statement.

I turned to Jason. "Since when do you want to be a French pastry chef?"

"Since his teacher at the academy said he showed real promise," Mrs. Yao said proudly. "Frankly, I'm relieved. The margins on French pastries are a lot higher than noodles."

"It's not just noodles, Mom. It's Asian fusion." Jason put his hands up. "Never mind."

As Jason dragged his mother away, I stared at their cart full of butter.

"I hope Jason doesn't let his mom tell him what to do," I said to my mom after they left.

Mom put a hand on my shoulder. "She can try, but it's not going to work." She winked. "Take it from me."

I had to laugh at that.

As Mom went to find frozen stir-fry sesame chicken for Dad, I grabbed a box of lasagna and put it discreetly in the cart. I was working on a secret idea for getting my parents their date night back.

. . .

Back at the motel, a couple was waiting in the front office, holding the flyers Hank and I had made.

"Do you have a room?" the wife asked. "We love to support independent businesses whenever we can."

"We sure do!" I said, glancing at the row of keys. "And thanks! We're one of the few left on our street."

As I led the couple to their room, we passed Hank, and I hollered, "Hey! The flyers are working!"

Hank gave me a thumbs-up, dropped his tools, and went to move one of the beaters to the street so our real customers could park.

. . .

Later that night, we called the investors to report that our new advertising plan was working.

"We've been putting the flyers up all over town!" I told them.

"Good! I'll translate it into Chinese and put them up in my neighborhood too," Auntie Ling offered.

"I'll do the same in Spanish!" Lupe chimed in. I smiled, glad she was on the call this time. It was good to hear her voice.

I promised I'd fax them a copy straightaway, and everyone agreed to pass on the Vacation Resorts offer — for now.

"But! If things get worse with the Magna, we have to think seriously about what we're going to do," Mr. Cooper cautioned. "A little flyer isn't going to save us in the long term."

"You'd be surprised," I said. "A good flyer with a killer design? Who can resist little soap and keys along the edges?"

Lupe laughed.

"I'm sure it's very cute," Mr. Cooper said. "But is it *enough* to get the numbers back up?"

I didn't have a reply to that one — not yet. But I hoped I would soon. After everyone got off the conference call, I stayed on the line.

"Lupe?" No one replied. Still, I added softly, "Thanks for being on the call. I miss you."

I waited for a long while, holding my breath and listening to the silence, before finally hanging up.

CHAPTER 35

On Friday, while my dad cleaned with Mrs. Davis and my mom locked herself in one of the guest rooms to grade quizzes, I went to work on my secret plan — Operation Date Night!

The first step: decorations. I fished out the Christmas lights from the supply closet. Carefully, I hung them up around our pool, which thankfully was *not* already lit by the Magna flashlight.

Next I draped a spare white sheet from the laundry room over one of our pool-side tables. As I laid out plates and silverware, I remembered what Jason said at Jade Zen — how he wanted to start a Chinese restaurant with white tablecloths and waiters that stood straight as a board. I smiled, standing up tall.

When the table was all set, I walked back into the manager's quarters. Now for the main course!

Hank walked in as I was pulling the lasagna from the freezer.

"Whatcha doin'?" he asked.

I told him about my secret plan to get my parents their date night back. Hank frowned, though, when he saw what I was planning on serving.

"Allow me," he said, putting the box away and pulling out a skillet.

As Hank made his signature burgers, I went to find my parents. Mom's smile was a mile wide when she heard what we were doing.

She set her papers down and went to change into a dress, while my dad hopped into the shower and shaved.

That night, under the flashing Christmas lights by the gleaming pool, Mom and Dad went on a "date." I was their waitress, pouring them drinks under the full moon, as Hank passed me dishes through the small front office window.

"Honey, this was so, so sweet," my mom said. "We can't thank you and Hank enough!"

I smiled.

"Sir, could I interest you in some sparkling water?" I asked my dad.

Dad nodded.

As I poured the soda water, he said to Mom, "I've been meaning to take you out to dinner ever since you started your new job."

"That's sweet, but you don't have to take me out. I'm happy just spending time with you at home," Mom said. "Now that you don't have to clean all the time." She smiled and reached for Dad's hand. "I'm proud of you."

"For what?"

"For getting Mrs. Davis back," Mom said. "For trying so hard these last few weeks, trying to turn the motel around. And holding down the fort while I teach."

Dad tried to wave off the compliment, but I could tell Mom's words meant a lot. He raised his glass. "To us."

Mom said, "To us!" and they clinked glasses.

Dad asked how Mom's job was going and I held my breath—but Mom just said, "It's going well."

"The kids treating you okay?" Dad asked.

"Yes," Mom said.

Dad smiled. "I wouldn't be surprised if they made you principal one day!"

As Dad reached across the table to hold Mom's hand, I looked at her face. Maybe she was waiting for the right moment to tell him what was really going on, like I had been waiting to tell Lupe about my columns. I hoped she didn't wait too long, because sometimes things got harder to tell the longer you waited.

• • •

When I walked into English class on Monday, Da-Shawn was talking to Ms. Swann about the possibility of starting a student newspaper.

"I'll speak to the other faculty members and see if we can start something up," Ms. Swann said.

"Good for you!!!" I said when we sat down together.

Da-Shawn grinned. "I just thought, if Mia can put herself out there in front of everyone in China, I can at least try with my new school. Thanks for giving me the courage."

I crossed my fingers and my toes, hoping Ms. Swann would make it happen. "Can I write for it too?"

"Of course! Actually, I was thinking I could run a profile of our school's most successful columnist in the first issue!"

It took me a second to realize he was talking about me. "I don't know about that," I quickly said. I didn't want people knowing about my columns, especially the ones I wrote about Lupe and Jason.

Da-Shawn patted my hand and told me he'd only write it if I was comfortable. I looked down, once again feeling the tingling of electricity.

That night, I pulled out a fresh page of fax paper.

How do you know when you like a boy? It's really easy to tell when you <u>don't</u> like them. You have no problem burping in front of them. Or telling them their hair looks like a billy goat's. Or rolling out of bed in your pajamas and going to school. That's what I used to do with Jason (and I kind of miss telling him everything).

But when you like a boy, does that change how you're supposed to act? I recently discovered that I may have a tiny, eensy-weensy crush on Da-Shawn Wallace, my classmate in English. You may recall that Da-Shawn is the new boy whom I once wished hand arthritis upon.

Well, I no longer wish him hand arthritis, in part thanks to a group project we've been work-ing on, which has been going really great, by the way. We're writing a collection of stories on what it feels like to move schools. Every time I'm around him, the time goes by so fast. We both love writing, and we can just talk on and on and on about stories. And sometimes, when our fingers touch, I get this tingly feeling. Like a jolt of elec-tricity. And I'm NOT talking about the kind you get when you touch the doorknob of room 5. I'm talking about the good kind.

It used to be that when I wrote a story, the

first person I wanted to show it to was my editor or Ms. Swann, in the hopes that I'd get my name on the Most board. Now when I write a story, the first person I want to show it to is Da-Shawn. I haven't even <u>thought</u> about the Most board in like a month. That's how I know I like Da-Shawn.

The question is, what to do about it. Obviously, I'm not going to make the mistake Jason made and kiss him. Should I say something? But what if he doesn't like me back? I don't want to lose what we have — I need all the friends I have at school right now. On the other hand, if I never tell him, then he'll never know. And what if ... what if he feels the same about me?

When I was done writing, I held the column to my chest. *This* was my most personal one yet. Did I really want to share my secret crush with four hundred thousand strangers? But then I looked at the reminders on my desk — *More drama! Always be honest!* — and thought about my editor's eager face and, if I was being honest, about my own need to feel like a successful columnist.

I walked over to the fax machine.

CHAPTER 36

That weekend, Hank and I made a bunch more flyers to hand out at the bowling alley. He'd taken Lupe, Jason, and me to Lucky Lanes once over the summer, and even though it wasn't exactly Disneyland, we'd had a total blast.

Now I wondered if we were ever going to go to Disneyland together. We'd planned on going when I got back from China, but so much had happened since then.

"Why the long face?" Hank asked.

I shook my head.

"Is it Jason?" Hank asked. "He still bothering you at school?"

I took my time thinking about how to describe it. "Things are just weird."

I wished we could go back to that day at Jade Zen and undo the kiss. Was there a time-machine ride at Disneyland?

"Have you tried talking to him?" Hank asked, turning onto the street of the bowling alley.

I nodded.

"And?" Hank asked.

"And he just stormed off," I said. Turning to Hank, I added, "But I did make a new friend at school! His name is Da-Shawn!"

"That's great!" Hank smiled. "What's he like?"

"He's sweet and funny and he loves to write, just like me!" I said.

I could hardly contain the excitement on my face, and Hank gave me a knowing smile. "I see what's happening," he teased.

"What?" I tried to make my face stop blushing.

"Mia has her first crush!"

"I do not!" I lied, turning *bright* red now.

But I didn't have a chance to convince him, because when Hank pulled up in front of the bowling alley, the low building with its warm neon sign was gone — and a luxury apartment complex stood there instead.

"Oh my God, Lucky Lanes is gone!" I cried.

"When did this happen??" Hank asked as we got out of the car. "That's such a shame. I'd been hoping to take you again, once business got better!"

I stared up at the building, flanked by palm trees too perfect-looking to be real.

"Look at these trees. They must have taken them from somewhere else and plopped them in here," Hank said, reading my thoughts.

All this change suddenly reminded me of China and I sat down on the curb, wondering how the *dofunao* owner and the steelworkers were doing.

"Hey, Hank, do you ever miss your pop-up restaurant?" I asked him, blocking the sun with one hand.

"Course I do."

He sat down on the curb next to me, and a cool spring breeze blew between us.

"Sometimes I wonder if I'd stayed and opened a proper restaurant, could the business have taken off?" Hank added.

"You could still go back . . ." I said, joking. But the look on Hank's face told me he'd considered it too. I shivered.

"Nah," he said quickly. "I have a responsibility to the motel. And to you guys. This is my home." He stood and pulled me up, looking at the high-rise apartments one last time. "But sometimes I do wonder. . . ."

"I'm glad you're here with us instead of taking China by storm with your burgers," I said, bumping my shoulder into his arm.

"Me too," Hank smiled.

Luckily the local ice rink was still there, so we managed to hang some flyers that afternoon. Later, at home, I sat at the front desk writing.

All around me, my city is changing. The taqueria down the street where I used to eat chimichangas after school with my friend Lupe is now a Jack in the Box. The local bowling alley where Jason got his first strike got turned into an upscale apartment building. And the thrift store where my mom used to go to buy all my clothes is now a Pottery Barn.

I used to hate the thrift store. Hated wearing flower pants that looked so different from everyone else's blue jeans. Back then, I would have done anything to fit in. To be seen but not stared at. Like the taupe walls of the Pottery Barn that look exactly the same no matter which city you go to.

But now, as I stroll through my city, I want to shout at the overpriced throw blankets and the soggy tacos: <u>Where'd my city go?</u> I miss Mr. Abayan's convenience store, which carried not only Cheetos and Doritos but snacks from the Philippines too. I miss Mr. Bhagawati's old dry cleaner shop, where you didn't even need a ticket because he knew everyone by name.

I even miss the Topaz and the Lagoon, our former competitors. Sure, they'd annoy us from time to time, but there was enough business for all of us. Our new neighbor, the Magna, doesn't believe in "enough." Mega Magna Hotels believes in total annihilation and won't rest until it takes every last customer and towel.

As a small business owner, I refuse to give up or to be intimidated. I think the only way to com—pete with big business is with big heart. And so I will carry on, doing the same thing I've been doing since the first day I arrived at the Calivista Motel: treating each customer like they're family.

As I was finishing up my column, I heard the voice of a commercial from the TV in the living room.

"Ever find a bug in your bed? Clogged toilets? Don't risk a good night's sleep on a small, unknown place. Come to the Magna, a member of Mega Magna Hotels! Our rooms are held to *national* standards of cleanliness!"

Those rotten melons! Dad and Hank raced in from the back. They'd both seen the commercial in one of the guest rooms.

"*National* standards of cleanliness!" Hank said. "They don't even vacuum their rooms!"

"What are we going to do?" Dad asked. "This is all over the TV!"

Hank fumed as he paced the living room.

"I say we hit 'em back with our own ads," Hank said. "How much does it cost to run a thirty-second spot? We can get a loan from the bank."

Dad shook his head. "You said it yourself—when they go low, we can't go lower."

"What about putting out more flyers?" I suggested.

Hank shook his head. "A piece of paper can't compete with TV."

"Well, we've got to do *something*!" I wailed. "We can't let them attack us like that! We'll lose all the customers we worked so hard to get!"

As Dad and Hank debated what to do, I headed over to the desk to call Lupe. Her homework would have to wait—this was an emergency!

CHAPTER 37

"What are we going to do?" I asked Lupe on the phone.

"Okay, don't panic. Did they specifically say the Calivista?" Lupe asked. I heard her turn on her TV and surf through the channels, looking for the commercial.

"No. But we're the only other motel on the block! It's clearly directed at us!"

Suddenly, Lupe turned the volume on her TV way up. I listened to the commercial again through the phone.

"Those plague sores!" Lupe shouted.

I let out a surprised laugh. "Those whats?"

"Sorry, I learned that in English class. Shakespeare."

"Oh." I tried to hide the envy in my voice. My class was still on *Where the Red Fern Grows*.

"Anyway," Lupe went on, "I know it's bad, but I agree with your dad. I think we should sit tight."

"What about our customers? We're finally starting to get people coming in again. . . ."

"It'll blow over," Lupe said. "They're not going to be able to run the ad all the time — it'll be way too expensive."

I didn't know about that. I got the feeling that when it came to trying to put us out of business, no expense was too big for the Magna.

No sooner had I hung up the phone with Lupe than Mr. Cooper called.

"It's not too late to accept the Vacation Resorts offer!" he said.

"We're not going to throw in the towel because of one commercial, Mr. Cooper."

"It's not just one ad, Mia," he argued. "Who knows what they're going to do next? We have to face facts . . . they're a behemoth with way deeper pockets than us! We're an ant just waiting to be squished!"

I frowned into the phone.

"Arrange a call with the investors, and we'll put it to a vote," Mr. Cooper demanded, then hung up on me.

. . .

The next day I was so distracted, Da-Shawn had to ask twice whether I had reviewed our project that weekend.

"Yeah, sorry," I said, taking my edits out of my backpack and handing them to him.

"What's wrong?" he asked.

I debated whether to tell him about the Magna. I hadn't exactly told him I lived in a motel, though it was possible he'd heard about it from someone who went to elementary school with me. Then again, Da-Shawn usually kept to himself at break and lunch, preferring the company of a good book.

Before I could say anything, though, he went on. "You know, I was thinking. You should try to get your columns published here too, not just in China. It could run in the *Anaheim Times*!"

"I don't think they want it," I said, shaking my head.

"Why do you say that?" Da-Shawn asked.

I had about seventy-nine reasons why.

"It can't hurt to send it," Da-Shawn said. "And even if they turn you down, so what? You're already a published columnist!"

I peeked at him, a chuckle escaping. Every time Da-Shawn used that word, *columnist*, my face lit up even brighter than the Magna's pool light. I glanced over at the poster of the Spring Dance and gathered my courage.

"Hey, Da-Shawn, do you want to go to the dance together?"

I held my breath and told myself it was cool if he said no. That would be just fine. Then at least I'd know the answer to my question and we could carry on being good friends.

But he smiled and said, "Sure."

"Really?" I asked, fireworks exploding inside me.

"Yup! It'll be fun!"

Walking out of class, I hugged my notebook tight in my arms, temporarily forgetting all about my Magna woes. I was going to my very first school dance with my very first crush!!!

CHAPTER 38

That night, all the investors gathered at the Calivista for an emergency meeting. Most of them had seen the Magna commercial and agreed with Mr. Cooper.

"We should take the offer from Vacation Resorts," he said at the beginning of the meeting. "We can't compete with a massive television campaign!"

"But," I quickly pointed out, "if we sell, we'll be losing a lot more than the motel! What about our How to Succeed in America classes for the immigrants? What about all the things the Calivista represents besides a place to stay?"

"People *need* those classes," Mrs. T agreed. "We've been running them for two years!" Mrs. Q nodded. "We've bonded with people!"

"This is a motel," Mr. Cooper snapped. "It's a business. You're not supposed to *bond*. That's what you all haven't gotten since day one. None of this is personal!"

"Maybe not to you," Mrs. T said. "But we *live* here."

The weeklies, my parents, and I all suddenly fell quiet. If we sold—where exactly *were* we going to live?

"Maybe we don't need to make our decision tonight," Dad said.

"Fine. But if we don't make the call soon, it's going to be too late," Mr. Cooper warned.

After everyone left, Lupe stayed behind, following me out to the pool. I sat near the shallow end, unable to do anything but stare at the lapping blue water. Lupe took off her shoes and dangled her feet over the edge.

"Are you okay?" she asked.

I nodded.

"Don't let that notable coward get to you," she said.

I looked up at her and smiled. "That another Shakespearean insult?"

"Yeah."

I sighed. "I wish we never sold all those shares to Mr. Cooper," I said.

Lupe bumped her feet with mine lightly, trying to make me feel better. "But . . . I don't know, do you think he has a point?"

Not her too.

"I'm just thinking out loud," Lupe said, noticing the look on my face. "If we sold, we could all make some money and—"

"And what? Where would the weeklies and my parents live? What would they *do*?"

Lupe looked down at the water, quiet.

"You're right," Lupe said. "I'm sorry, I was just thinking about college and all the expenses coming up. But you're right. We shouldn't just give up."

I gave her a small smile.

"But what are we going to do about the ads?" Lupe asked.

In the crystal-blue water, I tapped her big toe with mine.

"We'll figure it out," I promised. I didn't know what exactly, but I knew we had to — soon. Or Mr. Cooper would win.

The two of us sat shoulder to shoulder, smiling into our reflections in the water, the tall palm tree swaying above us. For a second it felt just like old times.

CHAPTER 39

The next week, I sat in the lobby of the office of the *Anaheim Times* newspaper. I'd taken a bus after school. A wild idea had come to me in the middle of the night before. It was a long shot. But fueled by the serious shareholder meeting — and Da-Shawn's suggestion — I thought I'd give it a try.

"And who did you say you are again . . . ?" the receptionist asked.

"Mia Tang, columnist," I told her, with as much confidence as I could muster. "I have some urgent information about the motels in Anaheim that I need to speak to the editor about."

The secretary raised a curious eyebrow as she dialed the phone. A few minutes later, she nodded to me. "The news editor will be out in a sec."

I wiped my sweaty palms on my jeans. Three minutes later, a man came out and introduced himself as Robert Hadden, news editor. "Why don't you come on back?" he said.

So I followed him into the newsroom, which was a mass of reporters sitting at cubicles and desks, writing and talking on the phone and drinking coffee.

This is where all the magic happens!

I looked around for the reporter Annie, who had written a feature on the Calivista last year. I asked Mr. Hadden about her.

"Oh, Annie moved to the Bay Area earlier this year, to chase a big story."

Chase a big story, I repeated in my head. That just sounded like the coolest thing ever.

When we finally got to Mr. Hadden's office, I took a seat across from his messy desk. It was a smaller office than Mr. Wang's and filled with twice as many newspapers. Some were framed and hanging up on the wall. Others were scattered on the floor.

"So, what is this regarding?" Mr. Hadden asked.

Quickly, I explained to him what was going on with the Magna. Mr. Hadden listened intently, scribbling notes in his reporter's notebook.

"How do you know all this?" he asked.

"I manage the front desk of the Calivista, right next door," I explained.

Mr. Hadden's eyes did a double take. He held up a finger, *just a minute*. I waited as he punched a few numbers on his phone, then stepped out to talk to one of his colleagues. I figured it was about some urgent news, but when he returned, he said, "Follow me."

"Where are we going?"

"I'd like you to speak to our editor in chief about this," he said. "Unfortunately, I can't authorize a story based on what you're telling me. It's not that I don't believe you. But we have these journalistic guidelines—" He reached for a pamphlet from the document tray in the hallway and handed one to me. It said *Anaheim Times Journalistic Integrity—Source Credibility and Guidelines on Objectivity.* "But maybe you can convince our editor in chief."

Nervously clutching the pamphlet, I followed Mr. Hadden to the other side of the newsroom. He pushed open the door to the editor in chief's office, and I was happily surprised to find a woman sitting at the desk inside. She had short gray hair and wore reading glasses on a chain, just like Mrs. T.

"I'm Katherine Addison, editor in chief," she said, getting up and shaking my hand.

I smiled. "I'm Mia Tang. Thanks so much for making the time to see me."

"No problem," she said, nodding at Mr. Hadden.

"I'll leave you to it, boss," he said, shutting the door behind him.

Ms. Addison turned back to me. "Rob said that you and your family manage a motel over on Coast?" she asked. "And you're worried about the health and safety of our motels?"

"Yes," I said. I dug in my bag and got out my copy of Annie's article. "You guys ran a feature story on us last year."

"Oh, yes, I remember this piece," she said, smiling. "And how's the Calivista doing?"

I shook my head and started telling her about the Magna and their TV commercials. Katherine peered into my eyes, studying me as I talked.

"And the ads are lying—they say the Magna is a lot cleaner than our local motels. But I've met people who've worked at the Magna next door to our motel, and they say they have to skip cleaning things in order to save time and money."

"That's very interesting," she said. "But we can't just write that. We have to prove it. How do you propose we go about proving such a claim?"

I took a deep breath. "Well, I was thinking the health department could check. To see which motel was actually cleaner."

I knew it sounded crazy, but I'd stayed up all night thinking about this. We needed to accept their cleanliness challenge and prove who was *actually* cleaner. And if the media happened to be there when the inspection was happening . . . well, then that would be even better than advertising.

Katherine Addison took off her glasses, shocked. "You want us to call the health department on *your* motel?" she asked.

"*I'll* call the health department. You guys just need to be there."

"I have to hand it to you — that's bold," she said. She scribbled a few notes down onto her pad of paper and pointed her glasses at me. "Has Rob given you our guide to journalistic integrity and objectivity? You'd have to promise not to do anything different with your motel for the inspection. You can't secretly dust everything to perfection."

I held up the pamphlet and promised to study it. "You have my word, as a columnist. We won't do anything differently."

"How old are you again?"

"Twelve," I said, then quickly added, "But I've been writing a long time."

"Which newspaper do you write for?" she asked.

"*China Kids Gazette.*" I took some of my columns out of my backpack.

She sat back and put on her reading glasses. The whole time she read my articles, my heart pitter-pattered in my chest. It got so quiet that I could hear the ceiling fan spin.

"I really like this one," Ms. Addison said at last, pointing to my latest column on Anaheim changing, which I hadn't even faxed to my editor yet.

I looked up, surprised.

She read aloud, "'I used to hate the thrift store. Hated wearing flower pants that looked so different from everyone else's blue jeans,'" and smiled. "I know exactly what you mean. My mom used to make me wear these long colorful skirts when all I wanted were jeans."

"Me too!" I said.

"So when is this being published in the *Gazette*?"

"I haven't sent it to them yet," I said.

"Well, I'd love the chance to consider it, when it's ready," she said, handing it back to me.

Was she offering . . . *to publish it*?

"Of course! And I can totally make it more dramatic," I told her.

Ms. Addison smiled. "No, no, that's not what I meant. In fact, if you read our pamphlet, you'll see we're strongly committed to reporting just the news. Not embellishing the news."

Oh.

"We don't need more drama. We need more analysis. More research. Our opinion pieces tend to be around seven hundred to eight hundred words. Yours is only three hundred."

I stared at her, wondering how she knew that without counting. It must be a trade thing, like how my dad always knew exactly how many towels were in a pile just by looking at the stack.

"I can make it longer!" I offered. "I could go to the library and research other businesses in Anaheim, and talk to the people who used to work there."

"Great!" she said. "If you can flesh it out, send it to me. And let us know when you call the health department."

She reached over and gave me her card.

"So you'll do it? You'll cover the story?" I asked.

"That's up to the reporter. But I'm happy to send someone over," she said.

YESSSSSS!!!

As she walked me to the door, I looked down and noticed she was wearing a bright yellow skirt. It had little blue pencils on it and it ran all the way down to the floor. Ms. Addison followed my eyes and chuckled. "Like my skirt?"

I nodded. I did *a lot*. But what about all the stuff she said about her mom?

"I guess I eventually stopped caring what everybody else thought," she said, reading my mind.

I grinned all the way home, armed with the knowledge and excitement that now *two* editors in chief were interested in my work! *And* I had a solid plan for getting back at the Magna! I couldn't wait to tell Da-Shawn. Yet again, Lupe was right — you can't win if you don't play!

CHAPTER 40

I called the health department as soon as I got back to the front desk.

"Hi . . . Yes . . . I'd like to report a health issue at the Magna and the Calivista Motels . . ." I said, nervous but excited too. "Magna. C-A-L-I-V-I-S-T-A."

Afterward, I sat on my stool, hands trembling. I couldn't believe I'd just reported my own motel. My dad would murder me if he knew! His face turned green whenever we even *talked* about the health department. But it had to be done and I was confident that we'd win the inspection war.

As soon as the health department came, I'd call the newspaper. The guy said he couldn't tell me exactly when they'd come — it'd be a surprise. I flipped through the pamphlet on journalistic ethics as I waited.

When I got to the section on fairness, I swallowed hard. It said:

In the interest of presenting truthful, fair information to our readers, the journalist must approach stories with an open, skeptical mind; must try to examine contrary information and viewpoints; and must keep their personal biases and opinions from influencing their story.

I stared at the last line — *must keep their personal biases from influencing their story.* Uh-oh. Had I been breaking this rule in my columns? I definitely did *not* keep my personal biases from influencing my stories about Lupe, nor did I get her side of those stories. Worse, I didn't even change her name. If Lupe happened to get on a plane right now and go to Beijing, every middle schooler she met would know exactly who she was and what she did to me.

Stop . . . stop, I told myself. She wasn't going to China.

Still, the knowledge that I'd broken an important journalistic rule nagged at me. I should just come clean and tell her. I knew if the roles were reversed, I'd want her to tell me. But what if she never forgave me? This could push us further into an ebb, right when we're *just* starting to flow again. . . .

Slowly, I reached for another piece of paper. Instead of writing a column, I started working on a letter.

Dear Lupe,

Thanks for coming over the other day. It was great to see you and hang out for a bit by the pool. It felt like old times again.

There's been so much that I've been meaning to tell you, starting with: I'm proud of you. I should have said that a long time ago. The words have been sitting in my mouth since the other day when we were at Buffet Paradise. I was scared to say them then because I was worried you might study even harder and I wouldn't get to see you. Looking back, I realize that was pretty selfish of me. I'm sorry.

The truth is, I miss you. There have been so many things that have happened, some good, some bad, that I don't even know where to begin. Do you ever feel like you've kept something inside for so long that now it's kinda stuck?

That's how I feel. But I want to unstick them. I hope you want to unstick them too. If so, please come by the motel sometime and we'll get unstuck together!

Miss you,
Mia

When I was done, I sealed the letter into an envelope and added stickers to the front. Then I grabbed another piece of paper.

Dear Jason,

I don't know what's going on with us. But I want you to know that I'm sorry for not coming to your cooking competition. I wanted to, but I didn't want you to get the wrong idea about us, or for things to get more weird. You're my friend and always will be. But it's been really hard for me to get over what happened. You have to understand that. I'm hopeful that with time we can go back to the way things were.

Mia

The next day, I took both letters and stuck them in Lupe's and Jason's lockers. I was still at Jason's when he spotted me from down the hall.

"Hey!" he called.

"Hey," I said back.

He pointed to a poster of the Spring Dance across from us. "You going with anyone?"

I bit my lip, wondering whether I should tell him.

"No way! Who?!" Jason asked when he saw my face.

"Da-Shawn," I admitted.

"He asked you?"

"Actually, I asked him."

Jason's jaw dropped. "I can't believe it," he muttered.

"Why?"

Jason grabbed his hair with both hands. "He doesn't even have a real name! His first name is literally Da!"

I stared at him. It was so upsetting he was making fun of Da-Shawn's name, and it almost made me want to yank my nice letter out of his locker.

"Well, *I* like it," I finally said.

Jason turned, and in one furious grasp, he reached up, pulled the dance poster off the wall, and stormed away.

Anger welled inside me as I kneeled down to pick up the torn poster. I got that he was disappointed, but why did he always have to get so angry? Couldn't he listen to me for once?

CHAPTER 41

I sulked all the way back to the motel that afternoon. The health department wasn't there, but there was a stack of letters waiting for me.

I sat down and opened them.

Dear Mia,

I can't believe you like this boy Da-Shawn Wallace. You barely even know him! You've already gotten kissed by one boy. Don't you think that's quite enough?

A girl should know that her heart is precious. She shouldn't give it away to every boy she sees, like it's candy. When you first wrote about getting kissed by Jason, I was on your side. But now I'm afraid you're becoming too Qing fu.

My mom worries that if I read more columns by you, I'll become Qing fu too. But I like reading your columns. My English has improved a lot since I started reading them. I just wish you'd be more proper in the way you behave and think about the consequences of your actions.

Your disappointed fan,
Meixin Fung

My cheeks burned. There were ten more letters, all accusing me of being too *qing fu*. I didn't know what it meant. Finally, I took my mail and went out back to the laundry room.

"Mia, what's wrong?" Dad asked, looking up from the towels he was washing by hand.

Hot tears sprang to my eyes. I didn't know why, but I felt really embarrassed. I handed my dad the letters.

As he read the first one, his face tightened.

"How could they accuse my daughter of being *qing fu*?" he asked, flinging the wet towels down in anger. Soap splattered everywhere. Quietly, I asked him what it meant. He refused to say at first, but I pressed him.

"It means 'boy crazy,'" he finally told me.

"Boy crazy?" I asked, confused.

Dad nodded. "A girl who only thinks about boys."

"That's absurd!" I erupted. "I don't only think about boys! I think about my writing, about the motel—"

"Of course you do, sweetheart," Dad said.

"I don't understand," I said, looking down at the wet towels. "I wrote one thing—one thing!—about *maybe* liking Da-Shawn. And they're labeling me *qing fu*? What about Jason? Nobody called him girl crazy even though *he* kissed *me*!"

"That's because people think boys can behave a certain way that girls can't," Dad said. Then he kneeled down and looked into my eyes. "They're wrong."

I nodded, but I was still fuming. Walking back to the front desk, I tried to put it all out of my mind. But I was so humiliated. And mad at myself for being so humiliated. Why did I care so much what complete strangers thought of me? And yet . . . it nibbled and nibbled at me.

That night, I couldn't sleep a wink. All I could think about was *qing fu qing fu qing fu*. Even burying the letters deep in my closet didn't work. It was like swallowing a bug, one that wriggled inside me.

• • •

At school the next day, I could barely look at Da-Shawn, worried about acting *qing fu*. To be safe, I kept it strictly professional, keeping my eyes glued to my paper and only uttering short replies.

"What's the matter?" Da-Shawn finally asked.

"Nothing."

"You're acting kind of strange."

"No, I'm not."

After a long pause, he guessed, "Is it the dance? Do you not want to go?"

"No! I still want to go!" I blurted, looking up at him.

Da-Shawn's face relaxed. "Good," he said. "I do too. As a reporter for our newly formed school newspaper, I feel it is my duty to attend."

I looked from Da-Shawn to Ms. Swann, who stood up from her desk with a big smile.

"Listen up, guys!" she said. "I have some great news! The faculty officially approved Da-Shawn's idea for a student newspaper. The first issue is coming out after the Spring Dance—you're all going to be able to contribute!"

I hugged Da-Shawn, temporarily forgetting about the *qing fu* label. Da-Shawn laughed as he hugged me back.

"I'm so proud of you!" I said.

"Of *us*," he corrected me. "You're going to write for the paper too!"

"You bet I will!" In fact, I had an idea for my first article. I would love to interview girls in my school who'd turned down a boy and been labeled "mean" or liked a boy and been labeled "boy crazy." Maybe I could interview them at the dance! I couldn't be the only girl dealing with this. But this time, I'd put my personal biases aside.

As the bell rang, Jason walked over and tossed a letter on my desk. Cautiously, I opened it.

Mia—

Hey, I got your letter. Thanks for writing me the note and for putting the poster back up. (I'll admit I have "impulse control issues," as my culinary teacher says, which I know I have to work on if I want to be a good chef—but it's hard.) Tell me what I have to do:

☐ Don't talk to you until you get over it.

☐ Like someone else.

☐ Wait fifty years until someone invents a time machine, then go back in time, and undo what happened.*

*Please don't make me wait fifty years. We'll both be old and leathery by then.

The leathery part made me laugh. I looked over at Jason and gave him a slight smile. I was glad he took the time to write me and acknowledged he'd been wrong.

But I didn't know why he didn't include *Say sorry to you* as an option.

CHAPTER 42

Later that day, I was walking through the motel parking lot when I heard someone call "Mia!" Hank was leaning over the upstairs balcony.

Before he could say anything more, I knew — just from the panic of his voice — the health department was here!

Hank pointed down the row of rooms, and I saw the inspectors making the rounds with my parents.

"Just a minute!" I called back. "I'll be right there! I just need to make a very important call!"

Racing into the front office, I threw my backpack down. Hands shaking, I dug out the card for the editor in chief and dialed her direct number.

"Katherine? I mean, Ms. Addison," I asked. "It's Mia Tang here. Remember the inspection I was telling about? It's happening. Right now."

"I'll send someone over," she said.

. . .

Forty-five minutes later, an *Anaheim Times* reporter showed up.

Rachel Allen took careful notes as the health department official, Mr. Moretti, gave us his glowing report.

"Excellent job," Mr. Moretti complimented my dad and

Mrs. Davis. "I give you guys an A-plus for guest room cleanliness."

Dad and Mrs. Davis high-fived each other.

"Thank you so much," Dad said to the inspector. "It feels so good to hear you say that."

"Here at the Calivista, we take room cleaning very seriously," Hank assured him. "In fact, I can't imagine who complained about us."

I coughed. That would be me.

"Will you be inspecting any other motels today, Mr. Moretti?" I asked.

"As a matter of fact, I'm going to the Magna right now. We received a complaint about them too."

"If you don't mind, Mr. Moretti," Rachel the reporter cut in, "I'd love to go over there with you. The cleanliness of our local motels is a public issue that's *very* important to our readers."

My grin must have been extra wide because Hank put two and two together.

"You. Are. A. Genius," he whispered, then gave me a wink.

• • •

The next day, we woke up to the front-page news in the *Anaheim Times*:

Local Independently Owned Calivista Motel Beats National Chain the Magna in Cleanliness!

As it turned out, besides not wiping down bathroom countertops, the health department also found that the Magna never washed the guests' bedspreads — they only put a new sheet under them. The health department slapped a $1,000 fine on the Magna. All the weeklies and my parents whooped with joy when they heard the news.

"Can't believe you thought of this, Mia!" Hank slapped his leg, laughing, as my dad got on the phone with all the investors. "It was BRILLIANT!"

Fred turned on the TV and the radio. "I wouldn't be surprised if this gets on the evening news!"

I tilted my head with a smile. "Whoever said a piece of paper can't compete against a commercial?"

. . .

Just when I thought the week couldn't get any better, at school I received another note, this time with better options than Jason's.

Dear Mia,
     I missed you too! I'd love to come over to the motel to unstick things. I have a big test coming up next weekend, but I'm free after that. Should I come over after school?
     YES   NO

                                        Love,
                                        Lupe

I immediately circled YES!!!

CHAPTER 43

The motel cleanliness story ended up airing on *five* different TV channels! Our investors were delighted that I'd found a *free* way to get even with the Magna. But as excited as I was about the coverage, I was even *more* excited about Lupe coming over.

It was hard to be patient that week, so I distracted myself with a trip to the middle school library to research my piece on how Anaheim was changing. I was determined to impress Katherine with my expanded seven-hundred-word column and get it published in her paper!

"Hi, Mrs. Stevens," I greeted our librarian. "How do I find out which local shops have recently closed or changed owners here in town?"

Mrs. Stevens put a finger to her chin, thinking.

"That's a really great question," she said. "I've been noticing it myself. The coffee shop I used to go to, over on Coast and Lincoln, Maria's Coffee and Pastries? It's now a Dunkin' Donuts."

I opened my notebook and started taking notes.

"I think the best way to research this would be to compare the local business directory this year with one from a few years ago," Mrs. Stevens went on, leading me to a set of files with business directories. Her long brown hair, tied up in a ponytail, swung as she walked.

"What is this for?" she asked as she pulled out the directories and handed them to me.

"It's for a column I'm writing for the *Anaheim Times*," I told her, feeling very grown up.

She raised her eyebrows, impressed. "Well, you know what I would do? I would also look up who owns the properties at the county clerk's office."

In my notebook, I wrote *County clerk's office.*

"It's over in Santa Ana," Mrs. Stevens added. "Not too far from here."

"Thanks!" I said, jotting that down too. What a difference it made having a professional librarian at my school.

I sat down and started working, reading the directories all through break and lunch, writing a long list of businesses that had changed hands.

> Maria's Coffee and Pastries
> Lincoln Street Minimart
> Lorenzo's Car Repair
> Joe's Air Conditioning and Heating
> Deja's Hair Salon
> Magnolia Ice Cream and Frozen Yogurt
> Crescent Avenue Gas
> La Palma Office Supplies
> Carmela Rosa's Bakery

A few were close to school. I couldn't wait to stop by to talk to the staff!

CHAPTER 44

The next week, my cousin Shen called me early one morning before school.

"Mia! I read your latest column in the paper!"

I groaned. "Ugh, don't mention it. I know everyone thinks I'm boy crazy."

"What? Everyone loved it," he said. "The girls kept talking about it during lunch."

"They did?" I asked, perking up.

"I've wondered myself, how do you know if you like someone?" Shen said. "So—how are things going with you and Da-Shawn?"

"Good!" I told him about the Spring Dance, which was coming up that Friday.

He had a million questions—what was a dance? Who was going to be there? I tried to answer him, but truth be told, it was my first time too.

"I wish *we* had dances," Shen said with a sigh. "Hey! Maybe if you write about it in your next column, our teachers will like the sound of it and let us have one!"

It was a great idea—but when I thought about the fan mail I might receive for that, my heart sank. Fingers curled around the phone cord, I told my cousin about the letters calling me *qing fu*.

"That's ridiculous!" Shen erupted. "I'm so sorry. But you can't listen to them. They're just a small fraction of people. The rest of us love your columns. We might not all be writing to you, but we eagerly await what you have to say."

"Thank you, Shen," I said. "That really means a lot."

"And?"

I laughed. "And I promise I'll write about the dance!"

• • •

In class, Da-Shawn and I turned in our project to Ms. Swann. It was a story told from dual perspectives: a boy who started at a new school and a girl whose best friend recently moved to another school, and how they each didn't think they'd find new friends.

Then it was time to move back to my old seat. I was sad to leave Da-Shawn.

As I set my stuff down at my old desk, Jason pulled his headphones tightly over his ears. I still hadn't returned his note. I knew he was probably annoyed, but I really didn't know which box to tick.

Instead, I studied my list of businesses and decided I'd stop by Magnolia Ice Cream and Frozen Yogurt first. I'd been in Magnolia Ice Cream once before, with Hank. The owner, an Indian woman, had given us an extra cup and spoon so we could share one scoop.

That afternoon, I walked to the Magnolia shop—and found a Baskin-Robbins instead. Inside, a woman with a nametag that said "Michelle" smiled from behind the counter. "Would you like a free sample of one of our flavors?" she asked.

"No, thanks," I said. "But can I ask you something? Do you know what happened to the Magnolia Ice Cream and Frozen Yogurt shop?"

"No, sorry," Michelle said. "I just started working here."

A tall, skinny guy with a name tag that said *Tony: Manager* came over and said, "You mean Mrs. Sanker's shop? I used to work for her in the summer! She was a great boss."

"And where is she now?" I asked.

Tony shrugged. "After the sale, I think she tried applying here as a manager. But . . . corporate had other plans."

"Corporate," Michelle repeated, rolling her eyes.

"Why'd she sell to them?" I asked, jotting all this down in my notebook.

"I think she needed the money," Tony said. "Her son was going off to college, and the rents in this area were going up."

"And they didn't let her stay on?" I asked.

Tony shook his head. "No, unfortunately. . . . They didn't even want any of her flavors. She had this really great flavor—what was it again?" Tony closed his eyes, trying to remember. "Oh, yeah. Salted caramel rice pudding ice cream . . ."

As Tony described the delicious salty-sweet ice cream Mrs. Sanker lovingly made from scratch every morning, my mouth watered. It reminded me of Jason's miso butterscotch ice cream that he made last year for the school cookout. I bet he would like Mrs. Sanker's recipes.

"People used to line up outside the door for it," Tony went on. "And she'd always make an extra batch for the homeless."

That was kind of her—and reminded me that I'd noticed the homeless population seemed to be going up recently. I scribbled a note in my notebook to check out local real estate prices, for businesses like the Magnolia shop *and* apartments.

Tony sighed, gazing out the window. "I hope Mrs. Sanker is out there making her rice pudding ice cream somewhere. It'd be a shame if she never made it again."

He took one of the tiny spoons and scooped a sample for me.

"Don't get me wrong. Our ice cream is pretty good," Tony said as he handed me the spoon. I put my notebook and pen down so I could take it. "But . . . hers was *out of this world*."

CHAPTER 45

On Friday, Mr. Cooper called as I was getting ready for the dance.

"Are you sitting down?" he asked. "I just talked to the Vacation Resorts people and they're willing to increase their offer to *three times* what we paid for the motel!"

"Three times?!" I asked, practically falling off my stool. I did the math in my head . . . practically a million dollars!

"I know! I told all the investors and everyone is *thrilled*! And the best news of all—they're offering a very generous severance package for your family, Hank, and José," Mr. Cooper said. "They know how much work you've put in, so they're willing to give you guys thirty thousand dollars each. Can you pass along the news to your parents?"

My mouth formed an O. It was a huge amount of money, more than a year's pay.

"And they're also willing to give all the weeklies twenty thousand each to help with relocation," Mr. Cooper went on. "Isn't that amazing?"

"*Wow*," I muttered, then told Mr. Cooper I'd let everyone know and hung up the phone. I'd bet Mr. Yao never thought he'd be able to get a million dollars for the motel, not to mention such generous severance packages.

Still, the word *severance* sat heavy in my head as I went to my closet and looked for a dress. What were Hank and my dad going to do after the sale? We could probably live off of Mom's income for a while, but where would we live? Was $30,000 plus the profit enough to buy a house?

I thought about going out and asking Hank and my parents, but decided I'd wait till tomorrow. Billy Bob wasn't back from work yet. We should all make a decision together.

Searching through my closet, I wondered if Lupe was going to be at the dance, and what she thought about the sale offer.

The Garcia family had put in $10,000, more than all of us. Three times $10,000 was $30,000, plus José's $30,000 severance, made $60,000 — enough to pay for college. And at the rate Lupe was going, she would need it soon.

Still, it would mean that our time at the front desk was *truly* over. I wiped a lone tear from my cheek and told myself to just think about tonight — to put on a nice dress and go to my first dance with the boy I liked.

Except none of my dresses fit! They were all too tight. I finally settled on a white shirt and a long, pale pink skirt my mom had gotten me. It went all the way down to the floor, reminding me of Katherine the editor in chief's skirt, and of how I couldn't wait to turn in my expanded column to her. The interview at Magnolia Ice Cream had been so helpful. I just needed to visit a couple more shops and go to the county clerk's office next week.

I looked at the columns on my desk, my eyes pausing on the one I wrote about liking Da-Shawn. I wondered if I should establish a few ground rules when we were at the dance, like no kissing. I liked him, but I wasn't sure if I was ready for *that* again.

There was a gentle knock on my door.

"Mia, you ready to go?" Dad asked.

I quickly stuck my Da-Shawn column, a pen, and my reporter's notebook into my purse as Dad walked in.

"Wow," he said as I spun around in my pink skirt. His eyes were all shiny as he smiled back at me. "My little girl is all grown up."

"Oh, Dad," I said, blushing.

Mom came in to give me a hug.

"You look beautiful, sweetheart."

As I walked out the door, Hank and the weeklies came rushing out of their rooms to see me off. Hank snapped Polaroids and Mrs. T and Mrs. Q put flowers in my hair and gushed about my beautiful skirt. I blinked back tears, unable to stop thinking about the Vacation Resorts offer and the possibility of us all moving away. I couldn't imagine not living with the weeklies and supporting one another every day.

In the car, I clutched my purse, quiet and tense.

"What's wrong?" Dad asked.

I shook my head and looked out the window, trying not to say. But Dad kept asking me until he finally got it out of me. When he heard the new Vacation Resorts offer, he pulled the car over and sat there, stunned.

"Are you serious?"

I nodded. "I know it's a lot of money," I said. "But what would we do afterward? And the weeklies . . . what's going to happen to them? After the sale, they'll all be gone. . . ."

A tear fell, and then another. My dad put his hand over mine.

"First of all, we don't have to accept it," he said.

"But Mr. Cooper's already told all the investors!"

"So what?" Dad said. "We'll figure it out." He shook his head and started the car again. "Please don't think about any of this tonight. Tonight, just have fun." He patted my hand. "It's your first American dance!"

When we pulled up in front of the school he turned to me. "You excited?"

I nodded.

"You're going to have so much fun!" Dad said.

I spotted Da-Shawn across the parking lot, getting out of his mom's car. Da-Shawn had on a gray blazer that looked silver in the moonlight. I smiled.

I rolled down the window and called, "Da-Shawn! Come meet my dad!"

"No, no, no," Dad protested, looking down at his tattered T-shirt and pants. "I'm not dressed appropriately. I'm still in my towel-washing clothes!"

"What are you talking about? You look fine. And besides, you could be wearing a *lampshade* and I'd still want people to meet you."

"Really, a lampshade?" Dad asked, chuckling.

"Okay, maybe not a lampshade." I rolled my eyes.

"You sure? Because I could go back to the motel and get one," Dad teased.

I laughed as Da-Shawn walked over. Dad got out of the car and shook Da-Shawn's hand.

"Hi, Da-Shawn. It's so good to meet you," Dad said.

As they talked, I spotted Jason getting out of his mom's car. I craned my neck to see who he was with.

Then my jaw dropped.

Jason's date was Bethany Brett!

CHAPTER 46

I gawked at Jason walking into the dance with Bethany Brett. I guess when I didn't reply to his note, Jason ticked off his own box for me. But still! Bethany Brett?? Her navy sequin dress glittered like a pinball machine, the total opposite of my plain pink skirt.

"Should we go in?" Da-Shawn asked at the door. I nodded.

When we walked inside the gym, I gasped. It was beautiful! Our teachers had decorated the huge room with strands of golden lights that hung from the ceiling like icicles. In the middle, a disco ball shined a kaleidoscope of colors onto the floor.

"This is amazing!" I cried.

Ms. Swann, who was standing near Da-Shawn and me, smiled.

Da-Shawn took a disposable camera out of his pocket and snapped a picture. "For the school paper," he explained.

I smiled and got out my pen and reporter's notepad. For the next twenty minutes, I went around interviewing the girls. I asked them if they'd ever turned down a guy for a dance, and if so, what had happened. I was surprised how many of the girls said they'd asked out a guy and then were labeled "boy crazy," or worse.

Bethany Brett walked over as I finished interviewing an eighth grader. I wasn't *that* interested in what Bethany had to say, but I made myself push my personal biases aside.

"What do you think?" I asked her.

"In my opinion, a girl should wait until a guy asks them out. That's what I did," she said, nodding at Jason over by the fruit punch table. "I waited and waited. And then Jason Yao *begged* me to come with him."

"Good to know," I said, closing my notebook.

I walked over to Da-Shawn, who asked if I'd gotten everything I needed for my piece. "I think so," I said.

"In that case . . ." He smiled and held out his hand. "Mia, do you want to dance?"

I blushed as I put my reporter's notebook away in my purse. "Sure!"

I didn't really know *how* to dance, but it seemed so magical to be standing underneath the icicle lights. As "One Sweet Day" by Mariah Carey and Boyz II Men played, Da-Shawn put his arm around my waist.

I followed his lead and soon got the hang of it. "One Sweet Day" was a slow song about missing someone, and as we swayed to the music, I thought about Shen. I hoped the teachers at his school would let him have a dance too. I was definitely going to write about mine for my next *Gazette* article. I didn't care what my readers called me. I was starting to realize that labels were like soda cans — they get thrown around a lot, but if you crush them with your feet, they don't take up any space at all.

The song ended and a familiar singer belted — *"Everybody dance now!"*

My eyes lit up.

"I love this song!" I told Da-Shawn.

As the music blared, I nodded my head to the beat and got ready to do Hank's dance!

Da-Shawn laughed and cleared a space for me as I did all the moves Hank had taught us in Beijing. One by one, the other kids started coming onto the dance floor too. Before I knew it, everybody was doing it! Clapping their hands, moving their hips, hopping from the left to the right. Even Bethany Brett was doing it! I was leading the entire school in a group dance!

The only person who wasn't dancing was Jason. He remained stubbornly glued to the fruit punch table, scowling. When the song ended, I walked over to him.

"Hey," I said, pouring myself some punch. "How come you're not dancing?"

He shrugged, staring at the pyramid of cupcakes next to a sign that said *Carmela Rosa's Bakery*. He lifted his cup of fruit punch to his mouth.

"What do you care?" he asked. "It's not like you're going to dance with me."

I turned to leave, but Jason grabbed my arm, accidentally spilling punch onto the table.

I immediately reached out with my napkin to clean up the puddle.

Jason leaned over so he could look me in the eye. "He doesn't even know you, Mia," he said. "Not like me."

I shook my head. I was so tired of him always putting his feelings first! What about *my* feelings? I threw the soggy napkin in the trash and turned to him.

"If you knew me so well, Jason, you wouldn't be acting this way!"

He glared, and I could feel the anger welling inside him, like a wave in the ocean about to break.

"Acting what way?"

Then he dropped his cup of fruit punch onto the floor — on purpose. I froze. Jason did *not* just do that.

"Stop it!" I ordered, reaching for more napkins.

Jason ignored me. He just picked up a new cup and started pouring more fruit punch for himself.

"You can't lose control like this," I shouted at him. "What about what you said in the letter? About having control so you can be a good chef?"

"Yeah, well, that's *never* going to happen," he said.

He held out his cup as if he was going to drop more punch on the floor. "*Jason!*" I screamed.

Heads turned as the music stopped. All the other kids stopped dancing and looked over at us. Out of the corner of my eye, I saw Da-Shawn walking over to us.

"I'm sorry, am I embarrassing you?" Jason asked.

A crowd gathered. I put my hands to my head, trying to figure out what to do.

Suddenly, I heard Bethany Brett's voice. "I did *not* come with him, I swear."

Jason's face turned beet red. Clenching his jaw, he reached over, put both his hands on the gigantic fruit punch bowl, and tried to lift it. This time *everyone* shrieked, "NOOO, JASON!" The punch wobbled in the bowl.

"Young man!" Mrs. Beadle said sharply. "If you spill that punch, you are going to be in a *megaton* of trouble!"

Mrs. Beadle only used *megaton* when she meant business, but Jason didn't care. With an extra burst of strength, he lifted the punch bowl and furiously hurled it onto the floor. The glass shattered, and a tidal wave of sticky fruit juice cascaded onto the dance floor.

"AHHHHH!!!!" we all shouted.

I jumped back too late. My pink skirt was bright red and sopping wet.

. . .

Da-Shawn found me sitting on a bench outside school, still dripping.

It was impossible to continue dancing after Jason's outburst. Even after Mrs. Beadle and Ms. Swann dragged him away, there were too many shards of punch-bowl glass to clean up. So the dance ended early, and all the kids scattered. I lost Da-Shawn in the crowd and went to call my dad. Now I was waiting for him to pick me up.

"There you are," Da-Shawn said. He took a seat next to me and studied my face. "You okay?"

I shook my head, my shoulders slumped forward. I didn't know how to explain the complicated feelings coiling inside me. The worry that what happened with Jason was somehow my fault. Maybe if I had just "gotten over it," he wouldn't have ruined the dance.

But why was it *my* job to make sure he behaved?

"I'm just sad," I said.

"He was probably just having a bad day," Da-Shawn offered. When I didn't say anything, he added, "I don't know Jason that well. Actually, it's weird. He's always staring at me in class."

"That's because he thinks I like you," I muttered.

Da-Shawn got all quiet. Slowly, I pulled out the crumpled-up column from my purse. Now was as good a time as any to tell him.

As Da-Shawn read my words, I waited with my heart in my throat. When he was finally finished, he looked at me in the moonlight.

"Wow, Mia. This is so flattering."

I held my breath.

"But, Mia, I don't feel this way about you," Da-Shawn said.

"Oh."

I plunged my eyes down into my empty hands, wishing I had never given him my column.

"You're a really great friend," Da-Shawn continued. "But I just don't get that same tingly feeling in my stomach when I'm around you. I'm sorry."

I nodded awkwardly. My mind started sifting through every single thing he'd said to me and every single thing I'd said to him, like a scientist. How could I have gotten it so wrong?

"But you said yes to coming to the dance with me," I said.

"Because I thought we were going as friends."

There was a long pause. I listened to the doors of my friends' parents' cars opening and closing, wishing my dad would hurry up and get here.

"You know what I *do* get?" Da-Shawn asked.

"What?"

"The . . . what did you call it? Here — the 'flutter of excitement of working with another talented writer.'"

It was nice of him to say, even though I still felt totally crummy. "Thanks," I said.

I blinked furiously in the starry night. For a second, the sadness felt almost unbearable.

Then Da-Shawn turned to me, unfolded my column, and pointed to the words *I don't want to lose what we have — I need all the friends I have at school right now.*

"You won't," he said quietly.

And I smiled.

CHAPTER 47

All day Saturday, the Calivista phone rang off the hook, leaving me no time to wallow in my Da-Shawn rejection. One by one, our investors called in.

"A million dollars, Mia!" they cheered.

"I can finally pay off the second mortgage on my house!" Mr. Lewis declared.

"It'll be a big help toward my mom's medical bills!" Mrs. Miller said.

I heard the joy in their voices. But I also saw the uncertainty in the weeklies' eyes as they came into the office to discuss *their* future.

"Twenty thousand bucks is a lot of relocation money. Enough to cover a year's rent," Billy Bob said.

"But not in Anaheim," Hank pointed out. "Prices have gone up so much, I'll have to live somewhere else."

My heart sank to the pit of my stomach.

"Maybe we could get a job managing another motel in the area," Dad said to Hank.

"They're all chains now," José said. "We'd have to apply through their headquarters."

"What if we applied for *this* job?" Hank asked. "I may not have boutique hotel experience, but I can learn!"

"So can I!" I added, then bit my lip. Vacation Resorts probably wouldn't hire me because of my age.

Still, we all decided to send the Vacation Resorts people our résumés and apply for our jobs. The severance package was generous and all, but as my dad once said, *It's better to have a fishing rod than a bunch of fish!*

As José packed up his cable tools to go home, I followed him outside and asked how Lupe's test went.

"Pretty good!" he said.

"So she's free after school?" I asked. I picked up the pool skimmer and started fishing out the leaves that kept blowing over from the Magna — they seemed to be using their leaf blowers to send everything over our fence.

José chuckled. "I think she mentioned something about coming over on Wednesday."

I swished the net in the water and smiled. Right now I'd take all the good news I could get!

. . .

Jason wasn't in school that Monday. There was a rumor circulating that he was suspended, possibly expelled, for what he did at the dance. When I heard the word *expelled*, I thought, *Oh, no.*

"Expelled, really?" I asked Ms. Swann.

"This isn't a discussion for my classroom," Ms. Swann said, and everyone turned back to their books. I sat at my desk, chewing my lip.

I was so distracted I almost jumped when Da-Shawn walked over and whispered, "Hi, Mia!"

I smiled and handed him what I'd written for the school paper that weekend.

To my surprise, Da-Shawn exchanged my story for one of his. "Here's mine on the dance!"

My eyes widened at the opening paragraph:

In an epic display of jealousy and rage, Jason Yao knocked over an entire glass bowl of fruit punch at the Spring Dance, sending a tsunami of fruit punch onto the gym floor as little pieces of glass flew everywhere and the dance came to a halting stop!

"You sure it's a good idea to open with this?" I asked.

"Of course! It's *so* good!" Da-Shawn said, kneeling down by my desk. "Don't you love how dramatic that opening line is?"

It was dramatic all right. And no doubt it would cement Jason Yao in everyone's mind as an enraged plague sore (as Lupe would say) forever. But was that really the best thing to print?

"I dunno," I said slowly. "The editor at the *Anaheim Times* told me that good journalism is less about drama, and more about analysis." I reached into my backpack and handed Da-Shawn the journalism ethics pamphlet.

"Da-Shawn, time to return to your seat," Ms. Swann said.

He nodded and took the pamphlet from me. "Thanks, Mia. I'll think about that."

I smiled. I knew I was too personally involved to make that call, but I hoped after reading the pamphlet, Da-Shawn would reconsider his paragraph. I knew I would have made different choices to my columns if I'd read it earlier.

• • •

After school, I headed to Carmela Rosa's Bakery. I'd asked Ms. Swann for their new address after seeing their sign at the dance. I found the shop tucked behind a dentist's office, way in the back, barely visible from the street.

Two ladies sat by the window, and they leaped up as I walked in.

"Welcome!" one of the women greeted me. "You looking for cakes? Cookies?"

"I'm Carmela," the other woman said warmly. "We've got freshly baked brownies! Would you like to try some?"

"Sure!" I nodded eagerly. I *loved* brownies. She handed me a chunky piece. "Mmmmm . . ." I closed my eyes as I bit into it. These were so much better than the ones over at Purple Star, where Fred usually went. "Wait till I tell my friend Fred about this place!"

"Please do, we need all the business we can get," Carmela begged. "Not a lot of people know about us."

"The location doesn't help." The other woman pointed to the dentist's office. "People don't exactly want to eat sweets after a cavity filling."

I felt around my mouth with my tongue. Even though we now had health insurance, we still didn't have dental insurance. I didn't even *know* how many cavities I had.

"We were at Euclid and Ball before. *That* was great," Carmela said.

"Euclid and Ball . . . isn't that where Purple Star is?" I asked.

Carmela nodded. "Yup!" she said. "They bought us out."

"Course we didn't know it was them at the time," her partner added. She dropped her voice and added, "These large corporations, they got so many confusing names. . . ."

"They offered us a good price, so Tanya and I said, what the heck." Carmela shook her head as she rearranged the unsold cupcakes in the display fridge. "Little did we know it would take us a *year* to find another place."

"A whole year?" I asked.

Carmela nodded.

"What's that thing the real estate guys are always saying? Location, location, location?" Tanya asked.

I nodded, having heard it many times from going to open houses with my mom.

"What they don't tell you is how the good locations are all taken up by the big guys," Tanya said.

I took my notebook out and asked if I could take notes and ask them more questions. When I was done, I thanked the women for their time, paid for the brownie, and promised to tell as many people as I could about their shop.

Walking home, I thought about how difficult it must have been for Carmela and Tanya, trying for a whole year to find another shop. I still remembered when my mom lost her restaurant job. We had to eat day-old bread and pick the mold off with our fingers.

I couldn't imagine going back to *that*. But now I wondered if the American dream was like a park slide. You climbed and climbed and climbed, but boy, was it easy to slide back down.

We just *had* to get Vacation Resorts to let us keep working at the Calivista!

CHAPTER 48

That night, Mr. Cooper called to say that Vacation Resorts had gotten our résumés.

"And?" I asked. I immediately waved over Hank and my dad to pick up the other line.

"And I'm sorry to say they don't want you or Hank to stay on," he said. "They *are* open to your dad and José applying to be a part of the on-site property team. But you might not get assigned to the Calivista."

"Why not Hank?" I asked. I understood why they wouldn't want to take me on; I was just a kid. But Hank had the longest résumé and most experience of all of us.

"They said they don't feel like Hank's the right fit for the kind of front desk *experience* they want their customers to have."

"What's that supposed to mean?" Hank asked.

"Oh, hi, Hank. You're not high-end enough," Mr. Cooper said bluntly. "They want to go after an upscale clientele."

Wow. It was Kyle the school photographer all over again.

"How much is the starting salary for the on-site positions?" Dad asked.

"I think it starts at $4.25 an hour," Mr. Cooper said. "I can have them fax over a brochure."

"Minimum wage?" I shrieked. "You've got to be kidding me!"

"Hey. They're not trying to win Employer of the Year here. They have a responsibility to their shareholders to maximize profit and keep overhead as low as possible," Mr. Cooper said. "Which is the way it should be."

"That's real *low* all right," Hank muttered.

"Anyway, think about it. It's still a very attractive offer. Remember — nearly a million dollars for all the investors, plus severance packages for staff and relocation for your weeklies," he said. "We have until Monday to give them our answer."

Later, I lay awake in bed, listening to my parents' conversation through the thin walls. Mom had finally decided to tell Dad what her new job had been like so far. Not the shiny, polished version, but the real version.

"Why didn't you tell me earlier?" Dad asked.

"I didn't want you to be worried about me . . . and I guess I didn't want to admit I was having problems," Mom said. "You worked so hard so that I could have this job. So I could be on the main road."

"But we're a team, remember? You've got to tell me these things."

"I know."

"I'm sorry you've been going through that," Dad said gently. "For what it's worth, I think you're a wonderful teacher." There was a pause before he added, "Maybe if we sold the motel, you can take some of the profit and study to be a full-time teacher."

"But what if it doesn't get any easier? You want to put all our eggs in one basket?"

Dad didn't hesitate. "If the basket is as amazing as my talented wife, then yes," he said.

I drifted off to sleep thinking of Dad's words. I was glad Mom had finally told him the truth. I'd once written that nothing was harder than going through something alone. And I was glad Dad responded so supportively.

Still, I wished we didn't have to sell our beloved motel. There had to be another way. . . .

CHAPTER 49

Lupe was waiting for me at the motel when I got home from school the next day. We squealed and hugged and then hurried to my room to talk.

"How was your test?" I asked. I sat at my desk, which luckily I'd cleaned before going to school that morning, putting all my columns in my drawer.

"I'm *so* glad it's over," she said with a sigh.

"Me too," I said, then added quickly, "I mean—I'm glad you were able to come over. We have so much to catch up on!"

"I heard about the offer!" Lupe said.

"What do you think?"

"It's a *lot* of money," she said, plopping down on a chair. "I'd be lying if I said we weren't tempted."

I nodded, completely understanding. "It would help with college."

"It's not just college that's expensive—it's getting *to* college," Lupe said. "You know how the high school counselor says I should do all kinds of activities if I want to have a real shot at Stanford or Yale. I don't know how I'm going to juggle it all. Or how my parents are going to pay for everything. . . ."

I nodded as I listened. It all made sense. And yet.

"But what about after we sell?" I asked. "Where would my parents and I even live? What would I do?"

I was so proud to be the Calivista's front desk manager. I loved getting up in the morning and counting the keys of all the rooms that had been rented the previous night. I couldn't imagine it not being a part of my identity.

Plus, this place felt like the last critical piece holding me and Lupe together. What would happen to us without it?

"You'd have more time to do more writing," Lupe suggested.

I sucked in a breath. Should I finally tell her about my column?

Before I could decide, though, Lupe said, "Hey, you got anything to drink?"

"Sure!" I jumped up to get us cream sodas from the vending machine, telling myself that as soon as I got back, I would come clean with her. I would muster up the courage and just say it.

All the weeklies were crowded around the vending machine, debating the motel sale.

"Can't believe they're not offering you and Hank a job," Billy Bob said.

"And what's with only giving your dad minimum wage?" Mrs. T added.

Fred shook his head. "It's not right."

Hank walked over, adding, "It's just so typical of this country. And it's never going to change. Maybe I should just take the money and move to China. Give opening my restaurant another shot."

"What?" I blurted.

"I'm sick of constantly trying to fight for what I deserve," Hank said. "It's just so exhausting."

I put a hand on Hank's arm. I totally understood. But going to the other side of the world was not the answer! I ran back inside the manager's quarters to find Lupe. Hopefully the two of us could talk Hank into staying.

She was at my desk, reading. It took me a second to see that my drawer was open — she was reading my *column*!

"What are you doing?"

"I was looking for a calculator, and I saw all these newspapers," Lupe said, turning to me. She held one up. "What is this?"

"I can explain," I started to say, but she cut me off.

"'It's like she doesn't even care about our motel anymore. It's like all of a sudden she thinks she's too good for the motel.'" Lupe narrowed her eyes at me. "You *wrote* about me??"

The color drained from my face, and I took a step back, fear blocking my throat.

Lupe's hands shook with fury as she reached for another piece of paper and continued reading. "'She's so selfish! Even if she comes back, you should never forgive her. Stay away from Lupe!'"

"I didn't write that one," I said quickly. "It was a letter from a fan."

With tears in her eyes, Lupe shook her head at me.

"I can't believe you wrote about me to all of China!" she said. "I thought you were my friend!"

With that, she threw all the columns at me and walked out of my room.

CHAPTER 50

I didn't come out of my room the rest of the day. I ended up falling asleep, curled up in a ball of regret. When I woke up the next morning, my eyes landed on the columns Lupe had thrown at me. Once upon a time, I considered them my finest writing. Now they sat like crinkled leaves, reminding me of how low I'd let myself go to get something published. To feel successful. And how much I had hurt my best friend.

I wanted to burn them all.

Dad knocked on my door. "Mia? You up?"

"Yeah."

"Did you still want me to take you to the county clerk's office after school?"

"No," I muttered. I had done quite enough damage with my words.

Outside I heard Dad and Mom talking about the offer. I got up to open my door a crack, listening.

"I wrote to Mr. Chen," Dad said.

"Mr. Chen?" Mom asked. "Why?"

"Well, you know how Hank's talking about going back to China? It got me thinking. Maybe after the sale, I could get my old job back. You wouldn't believe how much the salary's gone up. I bet if we invested in China's booming real estate market —"

"Wait, what? You want to go back?" Mom practically shouted. "But what about me?!"

"No, listen," Dad said. "You and Mia wouldn't have to leave. I could send you guys money every month! You could finally live in a house. With a white picket fence, like you always wanted."

"I don't want a white picket fence!" Mom said. "I want my husband."

"It kills me not to be able to help you. But if I went back to China and invested smartly, maybe it would help take some of the pressure off!"

"No!" I shouted, storming out of my room and running up to Dad, falling, and clinging to his feet.

Mom and Dad looked down at me in surprise. "Mia! I didn't know you were listening," Dad said.

First Lupe, then Hank, now Dad? *No.*

"I'm just thinking about the future," Dad said in a softer voice. "We have to be smart. What's going to happen when you get into a fancy college?"

"I won't," I promised. "I won't get into a fancy college. I'll only apply to bad ones." He pulled me up, and I cried into his shirt as he stroked my hair, trying to get me to stop, saying his shirt was dirty from cleaning rooms. But I didn't care.

I was *not* losing my dad.

CHAPTER 51

Jason was still not back at school. I was starting to really worry, so I called his house.

He answered on the third ring.

"Where've you been?" I asked.

"Home," he said. "I . . . uh . . . I got suspended."

I was afraid of that, though I was glad it wasn't worse, like him being expelled.

"I'm sorry I lost control," Jason said quietly.

Wow. The apology was so unexpected, I was speechless.

"My parents are thinking of transferring me to a private school," he added.

"Why?" I asked.

"I dunno. They think maybe I'll be happier there. Be less distracted."

In the background I heard Mr. Yao barking, "Is that Mia? Hang up the phone! None of this would have happened if it weren't for her!"

I couldn't believe Mr. Yao was blaming this all on me.

Then again, I could *totally* believe it.

"Can we talk about this in person?" I asked Jason. "Before you decide to move schools?"

"Why?" Jason asked.

Before I could answer, Mr. Yao's voice was shouting over the phone. "Good-bye, Mia Tang," he said, and hung up on me.

I stared at the phone in disbelief. Heat rose up my arm to my neck as I fought back tears. I wanted Jason to respect me—I didn't want him to *leave*. He was my friend, and one of the few people I knew who understood how hard it was to be a creator trying to go after a dream. Like how I went after my column so hard and wrote all those pieces . . .

I was still clutching the front desk phone, stunned, when José came in looking for my dad.

"How's Lupe?" I asked him, wiping my eyes and putting down the receiver.

He dug around in his messenger bag. "Actually, she told me to give you this," he said, pulling out an envelope.

I hopped down from the stool and took the letter into my room. Closing the door, I sat down on my bed and opened it.

> Dear Mia,
> If you're going to write about me, you should get your facts right. Here's what the last few weeks have really been like for me.
> Lupe

Enclosed was a column.

> High School
> BY Lupe Garcia
> My high school classmates look at me and see a middle schooler. A girl they think is too smart for

her own good, probably a total know-it-all. "Who does she think she is?" they whisper behind my back. They think I can't hear them, but I do. I hear every snicker, joke, and name they call me.

And yet, I soldier on. Day after day.

Because here's what they don't see. They don't see my mom, whose hands are like sandpaper from washing dishes at the local taqueria. On her nights off, she babysits for wealthy white people so they can go on their weekly date night. They don't see my dad, who gets up at the crack of dawn to slip his business card into folks' mailboxes, in case he soon finds himself out of a job at the motel.

Neither of my parents finished high school. My dad was two credits away from graduating when he had to help my sick abuelo with the farm. My mom only made it to fifth grade. When I go to college, I'll be the first person in my family to get a higher education.

For a long time, that wasn't a <u>when</u> — it was a big <u>if</u>. I didn't know if I'd be allowed to stay in this country, so I didn't let myself dream that far. But now that we officially have papers, I am grabbing the opportunity to go to college by the neck. Because education is the best vehicle for social mobility. It's the only way to jump tracks — from the bad roller coaster to the good one.

In fifteen years, I want people to look at me differently. I want them to see Dr. Lupe Garcia. Congresswoman Lupe Garcia. Or Judge Lupe Garcia. Which is why I'll take the stares and the eye rolls today. I'll take them from my bullies and I'll even take them from my friends. Though I don't want to have to take them from my friends. I hope my friends understand...it's not me choosing school over them. It's me choosing a bright future over a hard one.

Tears dripped down my face as I read. How could I have gotten it so wrong? I grabbed a pen.

Dear Lupe,

I'm so sorry I hurt you with my words. It was wrong. I'm also sorry for a million other things, which I hope you'll give me a chance to say in person. Meet me after school by the benches?

My deepest apologies.

Love,
Mia

CHAPTER 52

Before José left, I handed him my note for Lupe, along with a thick stack of all my columns. Though some of them were completely embarrassing, I wanted her to know what had been going on with me these last few months.

Then I mailed a set to Jason, adding an apology for everything I'd written about him. Maybe after he read what I wrote, he'd know why his losing control affected me so much — not because I hated him and wanted him to move away, but because I liked and respected our friendship.

Dad came in as I was finishing up. "Don't forget, there's a share-holder meeting on Friday after school," he said. "Vacation Resorts wants our answer on Monday."

"Where's it going to be?" I asked.

"Mr. Cooper rented out a conference room in Fullerton," Dad said. He ran his fingertips across the keys hanging under the desk. "What-ever happens, I want you to know that I'm proud of you. You've done a fine good job managing the front desk. A fine good job."

I nodded, biting my inner cheek.

· · ·

On Thursday, I sat by the benches after school, waiting for Lupe and Jason. As the minutes ticked by and everyone streamed out of the building, I started to lose hope. But then I looked up and saw two figures holding envelopes walking toward me.

"You guys came!" I exclaimed.

Lupe nodded. "Thanks for sending us the letters," she said.

I jumped up and hugged them both.

"I'm so sorry for what I wrote in those columns," I said to Lupe. "It was so wrong and selfish of me. I just got carried away. . . ."

"We *all* got carried away," Jason said. "I'm sorry I kissed you without asking. Your columns, they really made me understand. I feel awful."

I felt a weight lift from my shoulders. While it didn't undo the kiss, Jason's apology was a step toward healing our relationship. A big step.

"Thanks," I said. "Now you know."

"I know I have impulse control issues," he said. "It's something my teacher at the cooking academy has pointed out to me before, and I'm working on it. I just . . . I don't know what happened. I didn't think."

"Yeah, I know. . . . But it was my first kiss too. I should have gotten to decide when and where it happened."

"Of course you should!" he agreed. "And you should get to decide who you share it with," he added in a small voice.

"Yes . . . that too," I agreed.

"But, Mia, I need you in my life," Jason said gently, sitting down next to me. "These last few weeks have been so hard for me."

Slowly, he told me and Lupe about his new teachers at his elite cooking school, and how they'd been giving him a hard time about cooking Chinese food, calling his station greasy, smelly, and dirty.

We were both shocked.

"That's terrible!" I said, shaking my head. It broke my heart to think that Jason's mean teachers were stomping all over his dream of being a chef.

"Despicable," Lupe added. "I'd like to go over there and have a word with those bull's-pizzle stock-fish!"

I giggled.

"Thanks," Jason sighed. "It's good to hear that. I was starting to really doubt myself. . . ."

"The last few weeks haven't been easy for me either," Lupe confessed. "The high school kids are pretty ruthless too. They tease me all the time, and then they still copy off my work!"

"That's it," Jason said. "Want me to go and crash their dance?"

"No!" Lupe and I both said together.

I suddenly remembered something. "You know what you should do?" I said, smiling. "You should write down all the wrong answers, and then at the last minute, change them all back."

Lupe gave me an odd look.

"Just something one of my fans wrote me," I explained with a shrug. "But speaking of fan mail . . ." I reached out a hand to Lupe. "I'm so sorry for all the stuff they wrote. And all the stuff *I* wrote about you."

"It's okay," Lupe said.

"I broke all the rules of journalism ethics, and what's worse, I broke all the rules of friendship!" I put my head down. "I think I'll stop writing for the paper for a while."

"No, no." Lupe shook her head. "Don't do that."

"You can't stop writing," Jason agreed. "You're a great writer.

You just gotta tell *us* how you feel, and not just your fans."

I nodded. For someone who'd been suspended from school, Jason was surprisingly wise.

"Well, can I send my editor what *you* wrote?" I asked Lupe. I thought about the journalism pamphlet and how it was important to get all sides of a story. "I really think the readers should know the whole story. I got it *so* wrong."

Lupe thought for a moment, then smiled. "I suppose so. I'd like that."

Jason turned to me. "By the way, I can't believe you get *fan mail*."

"Yeah, well, it's not always nice." My face fell a little as I told my friends about the last batch I got. The word *qing fu* still stung sometimes.

"Haters gotta hate," Lupe said. "Right, Jason?"

Jason nodded.

As we put our hands together and made a pact to ignore the haters, I peered hopefully up at Lupe. "It'll be a lot easier to ignore them if we have each other," I muttered softly.

Lupe leaned in and touched her forehead to mine. "I'll be around more, I promise. I'm going to balance my studies with my friends from now on," she said. "I realize now how important that is."

My heart did a somersault.

"And I'm going to try to balance my studies with my cooking," Jason added. "Though I don't know how on earth I'm going to finish all my assignments for Mrs. Beadle. . . ."

"I can help you with that!" I volunteered. "And I'm also going to go to your next cooking competition. When is it?"

Jason grinned. "Next week! It'd mean so much if you came."

"I'll be there."

Jason jumped back and chopped the air with his hands like he was cooking.

I giggled, watching him for a second before I asked, "Does that mean . . . you're still going to private school?"

"Not if I can help it," he said. Then he reached over to give me and Lupe a hug—but stopped. "May I give you guys a hug?"

"Yes," Lupe said, and I smiled and nodded.

The three of us held one another, and I felt the friendship river flowing again. It filled me with joy.

CHAPTER 53

Back at the motel, I found my dad in the laundry room.

"Can you still drive me to the county clerk's office?" I asked him. It was the last place I needed to visit to write my column for Ms. Addison.

"Sure thing, sweetheart," he said, putting down the towels he'd been folding.

While he went to grab his keys, I walked out to the parking lot and gazed up at the motel. I tried to imagine it as a luxury boutique hotel — the kind that people paid $100 a night to stay in.

"Whatcha looking at?" Hank asked, walking over.

"Just trying to imagine what the Vacation Resorts people want to do to this place," I said, closing one eye.

Hank turned and followed my gaze. "They're gonna want to put in a restaurant. Right there," he said, pointing, "by the pool. Maybe a bar. The whole nine yards."

"I can't even imagine," I muttered, shaking my head, and I was *really* good at imagining. It wasn't that I couldn't see it — it was that the Calivista was good the way it was. Maybe it could use a fresh coat of paint or two, and we could fix up some of the rooms, do away with the bunk beds. But a *luxury* hotel??

Hank ruffled my hair affectionately, and I leaned against him, noticing that my head nearly reached his shoulders.

"You still thinking of going to China?" I asked.

"Maybe. We'll see how things go after the sale."

"*If* there's a sale," I said.

Hank didn't say anything.

"I wish things didn't have to change," I whispered.

"Me too." Hank sighed. "But sometimes things gotta change to survive."

Was that true? Was selling the Calivista the best thing we could do for it, if we wanted it to survive?

"Mia, you ready to go?" Dad called, walking out with the keys.

I waved to Hank and skipped over to the car.

As Dad drove, I turned and asked timidly, "Are you still thinking of going back to China, Dad?"

He shrugged. "It would only be for a little while, after the sale. I'd use some of the money from the sale to help your *lao lao*. Maybe invest our severance in an apartment of our own in Beijing. Then when you go off to college, we can sell it," he said. "You'll be needing college money soon."

"I can earn my own college money!" I insisted. "I make fifty yuan for each of my columns. And I'll bet Ms. Addison will pay me even more at the *Anaheim Times*."

Dad smiled. "I know you're earning money, sweetheart, but it's my responsibility to see to it that you don't have to," he said.

"But after you invest the money . . . are you still thinking of getting a job there with Mr. Chen?"

Dad didn't reply. We stopped at a red light, and he stared at the plastic golden Chinese coin charms that hung from the rearview mirror.

I put my hand over his on the gearshift.

"I won't let you go," I said, pretending to hold his hand hostage.

My dad joked, "C'mon, you don't want your dad being a motel maid forever, do you? You want all your fancy college friends knowing that?"

"Dad, the only person who cares about that is you," I told him.

He looked at me, the corners of his eyes shiny.

"You say that now, but one day you're going to grow up . . ." he whispered.

"And I'll say it then too," I promised.

His chin quivered.

"And besides, it's *cleaning professional*."

Dad let out a laugh.

"We'll make the money *here*. Together." I interlaced my fingers with his. "I'll help you. I'm your lucky penny, remember?"

My dad moved our hands up and kissed my knuckles, smiling as we pulled into the county clerk's office.

• • •

I waited in line at the Public Records counter, flipping through the various brochures. According to one of them, you could look up who owned which property by their name or address.

When it was finally my turn, the woman behind the counter asked me how she could help me. I gave her the list of businesses I was researching.

"Just a minute," she said, and went to get the paperwork.

Ten minutes later, she returned a big stack of files. I thanked her and took a seat. The reports were fascinating. They told me the names of the company that bought the property and also how much they bought it for.

Just out of curiosity, I got back in line and did a search on the Lagoon Inn and the Topaz next door. I wondered how much they got for it when they sold to Magna.

"Looks like they were purchased for seven hundred and fifty thousand and one-point-two million dollars," the woman said. "By a company called Vacation Resorts."

"Did you say Vacation Resorts??" I asked.

My dad looked up as the files in my hand landed with a *THUD* on the floor.

. . .

As it turned out, Vacation Resorts was actually owned by Mega Magna Hotels! Armed with the information that we were about to sell to our worst enemy, my dad and I raced back to the Calivista, and I ran from the car to call Lupe while Dad gathered the weeklies.

"Those sneaky suits!" Hank shouted when he heard. "I can't believe they tried tricking us with a different name!"

I remembered what Carmela and Tanya had said when Purple Star Bakery tried to buy them. *Course, we didn't know it was Purple Star at the time. . . .*

"They probably want to put us together with the Magna . . ." Fred said, his eyes wide.

"And own the whole street!" Billy Bob finished the thought.

It was just like what Hank predicted would happen! After they cut prices, they'd wipe out the competition. Once they owned practically all the hotels in Anaheim, there was no telling what they were going to charge!

"What are we going to do?" Mrs. T asked, her hands shaking as she held her glittery cat-eye glasses in her hands.

· 277 ·

"We're going to have to convince the investors not to sell," I said.

Lupe nodded. "On it," she said, grabbing a notebook from her backpack. I looked over at her, very moved by her support, and her sacrifice.

When the weeklies went back to their rooms and it was just the two of us again, I asked, "What about your pricey extracurriculars?"

"I'll figure out another way to pay for them," she said. "Besides, it's better for my dad to have a stable job."

"*We'll* figure out another way to pay for them," I corrected.

Lupe smiled and slipped her hand in mine. Together, we went to the front desk. As Lupe worked on how to persuade the investors, I put the finishing touches on my column for the *Anaheim Times*. One way or another, we had to stop the sale!

CHAPTER 54

All eyes were on Mr. Cooper at the shareholder meeting. I spotted Auntie Ling, Uncle Zhang, Mr. Lewis, Mr. Abayan, and many other familiar faces. I wanted to yell out what I'd uncovered, but I made myself wait.

"Thank you all for coming," Mr. Cooper said. "As you know, we're all gathered here to decide on an exciting purchase offer from Vacation Resorts of one million dollars."

The investors cheered. I glanced at Lupe and Hank and mouthed, *Ready?*

They nodded. *Ready.*

I cleared my throat. "We have some new information," I said loudly.

Lupe and I got up and unfolded our speeches from our pockets.

"Hi, everyone," I said. "I'm Mia Tang."

"And I'm Lupe Garcia," Lupe said. "And as you know, we run the front desk of the Calivista along with my dad, José, and Hank Caleb, our director of marketing."

Hank, José, and my parents waved.

The investors gave us all a big round of applause. It was so kind and unexpected, it took me a second to recover from the wave of love and get back to my speech.

"We had a terrific last year," I managed to go on, "despite very hard circumstances with the economy and the election. There was a time last year when business was hurting, way worse than it is now. Do you remember that?"

Mr. Lewis and Ms. Miller nodded.

"But we got through it because my friend here, Lupe, had the brilliant idea to change course and turn the guest rooms into low-budget bunk rooms."

Everyone clapped again, and Lupe smiled.

"And that worked well for a while," she said. "We had a great spring. A tremendous summer season. And the *best* fall and winter ever recorded. Why? Because we treated everyone like family. We cared for our customers. We made every single person feel at home." She paused. "That's the difference between us and the Magna."

"Hate the Magna!" someone called out.

Then Hank got up. "The Magna represents everything we're not," he said. "Owned by Mega Magna Hotels, they took over our neighbors, the Topaz and the Lagoon, stole our business model *and* our cleaning personnel, and undercut our prices."

Mr. Abayan shook his head. "Awful!"

"And they tried to blind us with their ridiculous pool light!" Dad reminded everyone.

"As if that wasn't enough," Hank went on, "they ran ads spreading lies about us. Lies which Mia *disproved* though her smart, quick thinking." Hank and I smiled at each other.

José got up next. "Their goal is simple. To crumble us," he said, smashing his fist into his palm, "so they can own the entire street."

"But now our problems are solved!" Mr. Lewis cut in. "We're getting bought out by Vacation Resorts!"

"Not so fast," I said. "The other day, I went to the county clerk's office and did some research. And guess what I found out? Vacation Resorts is *owned* by Magna Hotels!"

There was a collective wave of gasps around the room.

"They're one and the same!" Lupe added.

"Calm down, everybody!" Mr. Cooper called. "So what?"

Of all the people in the room, I noticed, Mr. Cooper seemed the least surprised by this news.

"The offer remains the same," he said. "It's a good offer! We need to team up with the big guys to survive!"

"No, we don't!" I cried. "We already *beat* the big guys! We got Mrs. Davis to come work for us again, didn't we?"

"We sure did!" Dad said.

"We've been getting more business," Hank added. "And we hit back at their TV ads — hard! We don't need their money to beat them; we already beat them!"

Everyone around the room cheered. Mr. Abayan got up from his seat and declared, "They can take their money and shove it. No sale! Not after all the horrible things they've done!"

"But, guys," Mr. Cooper yelped, "the horrible things are just going to continue. If we sell, we don't have to deal with any of it anymore! We can all just cash our checks and walk away."

Fred frowned, his eyes cutting into Mr. Cooper's. "*You* can walk away."

Mrs. Q patted Fred's hand supportively. "The Calivista is our home. Don't you care what happens?" she asked Mr. Cooper.

"I'll tell you what's going to happen," I said. "After we sell, Magna is going to have a monopoly. They're going to hike the prices up and squeeze customers for every last penny!"

I thrust my fist in the air and squeezed. The immigrant investors took in a sharp breath.

"You guys are not thinking rationally," Mr. Cooper protested. "This is a once-in-a-lifetime opportunity. I wouldn't have brought it to you if I didn't think Magna was offering something—"

I pointed at him. "So you *knew*!"

Mr. Cooper's face flushed. "I . . . No. I mean," he mumbled. "I suspected."

"And you didn't think to tell us?" Hank exclaimed.

"Look, I'm a businessman. I make *business* decisions, not emotional ones." Mr. Cooper glared at me and Lupe. "We bought the property at a low price, and now it's time to sell at a high price. This is how business works! Who cares who we sell to?"

He looked around the room at all the investors. All of them were frowning.

"*We* care," Mr. Bhagawati answered.

"I think you guys are making a big mistake," Mr. Cooper said, getting up to leave. "But do whatever you want. *I'm* still selling *my* shares to Magna."

He stormed out, and I jumped up from the table and ran after him. I finally caught up just as he was unlocking his car.

"Please don't do this," I begged. "Don't sell your shares."

"Mia," he sighed, putting his keys down for a second. "You know, when I first met you, I thought, *There's a future CEO.*"

I blinked in surprise.

"But the more I got to know you, the more I realized, you are way too emotional," he said, climbing into his car. "In business, you can make popular decisions, or you can make profitable ones. Not both."

That's not true, I wanted to shout. That was just what people like Mr. Cooper and Mr. Yao told themselves so they could sleep better at night.

But Mr. Cooper was already driving away, so I walked back into the conference room. There was panic on our investors' faces. Mr. Cooper was our biggest investor, owning nearly 20 percent of the Calivista. If he sold his shares, it would mean Magna would own a whole chunk of our business!

CHAPTER 55

"They can't do anything with twenty percent," Mom insisted when we got home. The three of us were huddled in the living room of the manager's quarters. "Magna would need fifty percent or more in order to tell us what to do. Let's just hope nobody else sells to Magna." She looked at Dad.

"I'm not selling to them!" he protested.

"You're the one who wanted to go back to China," Mom said.

"I did," he admitted. "But after talking to Mia and listening to everyone talk today about how much this place means to them, I realized . . ." He looked over at me. "There are some things more important than money." Dad smiled. "Thanks for reminding me, lucky penny."

I gave him a hug.

"I'm glad," Mom said, walking over and putting a hand on Dad's back.

"It does mean it'll be a while till we can buy a house with a white picket fence," Dad told her.

"Will everyone stop obsessing over the white picket fence?" Mom said. "I don't even like fences! I'd much prefer my partner by my side."

"Even if that partner can't do a thing to help fix your problems at work?" Dad asked.

"I don't need you to fix my problems. I don't need silk scarves or fancy date nights. All I need from you is to listen to my problems. To encourage me when I've had a setback and celebrate with me when I've had a breakthrough. That's all."

Tears gleamed in Dad's eyes as he promised her, "I can do that."

I smiled.

"But what about Lao Lao's apartment?" Dad asked.

Mom shrugged. "We're just going to have to tell Juli we need more time."

"Why don't you try talking to Lao Lao and Lao Ye first?" I suggested.

Mom pursed her lips, like that would be way too awkward. It brought me straight back to sitting in the frigid car in the middle of winter in front of the fake Jason house, while my mom fretted about losing her face.

But the chill of that memory had thawed. Now I said gently, "Just because something's embarrassing doesn't mean we shouldn't talk about it." Mom lifted her eyes to meet mine. "And just because we talk about it doesn't mean we'll lose face," I went on, reaching up and patting my plump cheeks. "We still have plenty of face."

A little smile escaped from my mom's mouth.

That night, as my parents practiced what they were going to say to my grandparents on the phone, I went out back to find Hank. He was in Billy Bob's room, setting up a game of Monopoly with the weeklies.

"Good news!" I told them. "My mom says that so long as nobody else sells to Magna, they can't tell us what to do!"

"Well, they're not buying any of *my* shares!" Billy Bob said. Mrs. T, Fred, and Mrs. Q agreed.

"Or mine!" Hank added.

"But what about China? Giving your restaurant another try?" I asked him.

"Ahh, that can wait," Hank said, waving his Monopoly piece with his hand. He was always the iron, and I was always the hat. "We're a family. We have to stick together."

"Hear, hear!" Mrs. T seconded, sitting down at the board.

Hank smiled, handing me the hat. "It may be tough in this country, but today I realized I have powerful allies all around me, young and brave."

I took my place at the foot of the bed and rolled the dice. His words meant more to me than he would ever know.

That night, as we settled in for another game of Monopoly, we decided to reinvent the rules. No longer did we charge people the crazy-high rates it said on the cards, even if we owned all the hotels on the street. Instead, we charged people a fair rate. A *human* rate.

"We should rename the game Fairopoly," I suggested.

"I like that, Fairopoly!" Hank beamed.

The weeklies cheered, and Billy Bob put his racecar in the air. "That's how we win against Magna!"

CHAPTER 56

My mom's chirpy voice woke me up the next morning. She was talking on the phone with my grandmother. Quietly, I reached for my extension so I could listen in.

"Thanks so much for letting me know," my grandmother was saying. "Don't worry about chipping in for my apartment—I don't even want to move."

"Are you sure?" Mom asked.

"I've been trying to tell your sister, I *like* where I am," Lao Lao insisted. "This is my neighborhood. The people at the park are my friends! So you just focus on what you gotta do. We'll be fine."

"Thanks, Mom," my mother said. "I'd love to contribute some money, though, to get you guys indoor plumbing."

"Me too!" I blurted. "I have some column money!"

Lao Lao laughed. "Thank you, that's very kind."

"I'll make sure Aunt Juli gets you the best toilet," I added. "I know a *lot* about toilets!"

"I'm sure you do." Lao Lao chuckled. "And Ying? Don't ever hesitate to let us know if things are hard for you out there. We're family. That's what we're here for . . . the good times and the bad."

My mom thanked my grandmother, and they said good-bye. Then she walked into my room and sat down on my bed.

"You were right, Mia. Just because something's embarrassing doesn't mean we shouldn't talk about it."

I smiled, proud of my mom.

Suddenly, a loud sound like chanting came through the window. Our heads jolted up. "What's going on?" I asked.

"Come quick!" Dad called from the front office. "Something's happening at the Magna!"

We all grabbed our jackets and ran outside. In front of the Magna, there was a huge crowd of people! I recognized Carmela and Tanya from the bakery as well as Mr. Abayan and Mr. Bhagawati and some other people. Carmela and Tanya were carrying signs that said *Support Small Businesses!* and *Shop Indie, Stay Indie!* And everyone was shouting together.

I ran over to Carmela and Tanya. "What's going on?" I asked.

Carmela beamed at me. "There's our famous reporter!" She took a copy of the *Anaheim Times* out of her bag and showed it to me.

My column! On the front page!

"How to Fight Big Business with Big Heart" by Mia Tang.

"Oh my God!" I screamed, jumping into the air.

In minutes, people were coming up to me to shake my hand.

"Congratulations! We loved your piece!" they said. "We couldn't agree more!"

"And we're going to do everything we can not to let Magna get its greedy, grabby hands on the beloved Calivista!" a woman added. "We'll camp out here day and night if we have to!"

I joined Carmela, Tanya, Mr. Abayan, Mr. Bhagawati, and the other residents that day to chant "Support small businesses!" Cars stopped along the side of the road and even more people marched around the Magna parking lot with us. It wasn't long before the reporters and TV cameras came too.

. . .

That night, we appeared again on the evening news. Lupe came over, and we all gathered around the TV.

"Look! It's Mia!" Lupe pointed.

I leaned against my best friend as we watched my interview. I talked — on camera! — about the plight of our small motel, urging folks to support independent businesses. Behind me, you could see the Magna staff in the background trying to chase the chanting residents away with a broom.

The weeklies erupted into laughter as the camera zoomed in on the Magna staff.

"Good luck getting customers now!" Hank said.

Lupe turned and gave me a high five. "You were amazing," she said.

I smiled. "Thanks for encouraging me to finish my column."

When the segment ended, I turned the TV down and let Lupe have my room so she could finish the rest of her homework without distractions.

Later that night, as Lupe was about to go home, the phone rang.

It was Mr. Cooper calling!

CHAPTER 57

"Well, I hope you're happy," Mr. Cooper complained. "Thanks to the little stunt you pulled, Magna Hotels has officially withdrawn their offer."

YESSSSS!!! I can't believe it worked!

"They said it's too much of a PR risk," he sighed. "They won't even buy my shares. . . ."

"That's great news!" I couldn't help shouting.

Mr. Cooper scoffed. "It's *terrible* news," he barked. "With an attitude like that you'll never make it in business, Mia."

I nearly burst out laughing. "Oh, I think I've already made it, Mr. Cooper. I got an entire corporation to back down with just my words!"

As soon as I got off the phone, I ran to tell my parents the good news. I found my mom by the vending machine.

"Tomorrow I'm going to bring a cream soda for my new student," Mom said as she pushed the button. "She's a new immigrant from Cambodia. She says I'm her favorite math teacher, even though I'm just a substitute."

"That's wonderful!" I said. Then I told her about Mr. Cooper's call, and we did a little happy dance together, right there by the vending machine.

My dad saw us and walked over from the laundry room, holding a pair of slacks and a freshly ironed shirt. "What's going on?"

"Magna withdrew the offer!" Mom cried. "They got too much heat after Mia's piece, so they backed off!" She pointed at his slacks and shirt. "You going somewhere special?"

"As a matter of fact, I am. To your school. I thought tomorrow I'd come and watch you teach—if that's allowed," Dad said shyly. "Hank and Mrs. Davis said they could man the fort by themselves. What do you say?"

Mom set her soda down and wrapped her arms around Dad.

"I say that beats all the date nights in the world," she said, kissing him on the cheek.

As my parents walked back to the manager's quarters, I skipped away to tell the weeklies the happy news.

. . .

The next morning at school, I ran up to Jason. He was back from suspension and giving out handwritten apology notes to all the teachers for the mess he'd made at the dance.

To my surprise, he handed me one too.

"Sorry I ruined your first date with Da-Shawn," he said.

"It's okay," I said, taking the note from him. "It wasn't really a date. . . . We're just friends."

I must have looked a little disappointed, because Jason said quickly, "Hey, that can be pretty cool too."

I smiled. It could indeed.

"Hey, Jason?" I asked. There was something that had been weighing on my mind.

"Yeah?"

"I'm sorry for what I said back in fifth grade. About how I would rather like a rock than you." I looked down. "That was unkind."

Jason sucked in a breath, like never in a million years did he think I would ever apologize for that. And I probably wouldn't have, until I experienced firsthand what it was like to be rejected. Now I understood how tender the wound was. And how deep words could cut.

"Thanks for saying that. It means a lot to me," he finally said.

Together, we walked to class. "So, are you excited about your cooking competition after school?" I put a hand over my rumbling belly. "I know I am!"

Jason chuckled. "First I gotta get this stack of homework done." He sighed, pointing to all the papers in his backpack.

"Don't worry, I've got you," I said, patting his shoulder.

Over snack break and lunch, I tutored Jason, chipping away at his pile of overdue work until there was only a very thin stack left.

He grinned as he finished the last worksheet all by himself and packed up his stuff.

Mrs. Stevens, the librarian, waved at me as we walked out.

"I *loved* your piece in the paper this weekend," Mrs. Stevens said. "I hope you guys don't sell to Magna Hotels. It would be such a shame."

"Actually, we're staying put!" I told her.

"Oh, I'm so glad!" she said. "I told my cousin to stay at your motel when she comes and visits me next month!"

"Thanks so much. We'll take good care of her," I promised. "And thanks for your tip on the county clerk's office — it saved the motel!"

"Happy to help!" Mrs. Stevens replied.

• • •

Mrs. Yao looked warily at me as I climbed into her car after school.

"Are you sure it's a good idea for Mia to come?" she asked Jason. "This is a big competition for you. I don't want you getting all distracted."

"No, I want Mia there," he said, climbing in to sit beside me. "She's not the reason I got suspended. I am. But I'm going to do better from now on." He opened up his empty backpack to show his mom. "Look, I finished all my homework."

"Wow," Mrs. Yao said. She gazed at me in the rearview mirror as she started up the car. "Well, all right, then."

Jason made sure to give me plenty of space in the back seat. As we drove, Mrs. Yao asked him what he was going to make. Jason said he was thinking maybe a lychee salad wonton cup appetizer.

"What? I thought we talked about this! You weren't going to make Chinese food!" Mrs. Yao complained. "It's hard enough getting those snobby judges to take him seriously," she explained, meeting my eyes in the rearview. "If he makes Chinese food, he'll never get high marks."

Jason sighed. "They *are* pretty snobby."

"Really?" I said.

He nodded. "The whole industry's like that."

He told me about a food critic in New York who actually wrote that a restaurant was pretty clean "for a Chinese restaurant." The critic proceeded to trash the Chinese eateries in the country, writing that they were "all so gross."

I pulled out my columnist notebook when I heard that and wrote down *POSSIBLE TOPIC: RESTAURANT DISCRIMINATION* in big letters.

"Which is why you should open a high-end French restaurant one day," Jason's mom told him. "Everyone respects white-people food!"

The words cut even deeper coming from another Asian American person. I waited until Mrs. Yao had parked and was out of the car before turning to Jason.

"Don't listen to your mom," I told him. "You should make whatever you want."

"I dunno . . ." he said. "I'm going up against all these kids whose parents are famous restaurateurs."

Jason gazed nervously out the window at a huge group of white kids with whisks and pristine aprons, all marching into the convention center. Then he looked down at his own apron, which had splotches of soy sauce on it.

"Remember at the photo shoot, when they asked us to move to the back?" I asked.

Jason nodded.

"Don't move yourself to the back."

Jason rubbed at one of the soy sauce stains. "But what if they don't like what I cook?" he asked in a whisper.

"You told me once that you cooked for yourself first, not for anyone else," I reminded him, thinking of the first time I came over to his house.

He smiled. "Guess I did say that . . ."

"You didn't just say it—you *did* it and it was *delicious*. Cook from your heart, Jason Yao!"

. . .

An hour later, Mrs. Yao and I craned our necks from our seats in the audience, trying to see what Jason was making. The clock on the wall read five minutes left. Jason was running back and forth from the oven to the chopping board. Mrs. Yao was so nervous I had to hold her hand. She gripped it like a steering wheel, muttering, "C'mon, c'mon, c'mon," under her breath.

The timer went off. All the chefs, including Jason, put their whisks down. The celebrity judges — famous chefs from restaurants all over Los Angeles — stopped by each station, and I watched as each contestant held on to the counter to keep from fainting.

"Good texture!" they said to Pierre, who had made *merveilleux*, a Belgian dessert.

Pierre looked positively radiant as he offered the judges some more of his meringue and chocolate cream pastries, but the judges declined. They were onto the next station. On and on they judged, mincing no words, until they finally got to Jason.

Mrs. Yao dug her nails into my hand. "Here we go," she said.

"This is interesting. What do we have here?" one of the judges asked Jason, peering down at what looked like little crispy golden cups.

"These are wonton wrappers," he said.

"Wonton wrappers?" Mrs. Yao wailed. "Oh God, I can't watch this!" She put the hand that wasn't clutching mine over her eyes.

I scooted to the edge of my seat, trying to see Jason's appetizers. It looked like he'd filled the wrappers with shiny lychee squares. I smiled. He'd made his lychee salad wonton cups after all!

One of the judges, a celebrity chef named Lucille Amato, reached down and tasted one.

"Mmm . . . this is really interesting," she said. "The lychee is cool and refreshing and the wonton is so crispy and flavorful."

The other judges had a taste too and nodded.

Lucille turned to Jason. "The texture reminds me of a tortilla chip. Is that what you were going for?"

Jason shook his head. Bravely, he said, "Actually, I was going for wonton soup, the kind my mom used to make when I got home from school."

He looked out into the audience and smiled at his mom. The audience let out an *awwww*.

Mrs. Yao lowered her hand. "Did he just say . . . ?" she asked. She let go of me and beamed back at her son, tears glistening in her eyes. It didn't matter who else was in the room; the food brought them together.

"It's time to declare the winner," the emcee announced. All the anxious parents held their breaths — and I held mine.

"And the winner of the Los Angeles Junior Culinary Competition is . . . Jason Yao!"

Mrs. Yao and I jumped up and clapped so thunderously, some of the parents sitting next to us glared at us. But we didn't care. I ran to Jason.

"Congratulations!!" I cried.

"Thanks!" he said, beaming. "You were right. It feels good to be front and center!"

I smiled — it sure did.

Jason took one of his wonton wrappers and held it to my mouth. "Now try this."

The lychee melted in my mouth as I bit down on the crunchy wonton crust. No wonder the judges picked Jason as the winner — this was out of this world!

Lucille, the judge, came over and congratulated Jason. "Keep cooking from your heart — it really shows."

We started jumping up and down when she left, pausing every few seconds so I could pop another wonton into my mouth.

"I can't stop eating these," I said to Jason. "I wish we could take some home for the weeklies — and give some to the customers! Then we'll *really* get more business!"

Jason laughed. "Maybe we should start selling them!" he joked.

Suddenly, I stopped jumping. "That's a great idea!" I shouted, my eyes widening. Why didn't I think of that before?

We didn't need to go all the way to China to start a restaurant — we could do it right here at the Calivista!

CHAPTER 58

I stood in the entryway of East Meets West, our newly opened bistro at the Calivista, waiting for Jason. There were customers all around me, waiting to get a seat at the packed red-and-white bar counter. Several of them were reading Lupe's column in the *China Kids Gazette*, which was framed and hanging on the wall of the bistro. Others were reading my pieces for the school newspaper and my article on restaurant discrimination. Inspired by what Jason told me in the car on the way to the cooking competition, I'd done some digging, and Jason was right — elite restaurant reviewers did discriminate against Chinese restaurants, sometimes to the point of openly making fun of our food! All summer, I worked hard on my piece, filling it with research and analysis. This time, Ms. Addison was so blown away, she recommended I submit it to the *New York Times*.

The day that I got published in the *New York Times* was one of the happiest days of my life. But what *really* made me proud was the letter next to all my writing, from my very favorite fan.

Dear Mia,

I have been reading your columns for many, many months now. Your writing fills me up on long, lonely days, when it's just me in my siheyuan. On those days, I close my eyes and imagine I am halfway across the world with you, at the Calivista Motel, just five miles from Disneyland!

I know life's not always easy for you and your parents. But you are making a difference in the community with your voice. Thank you for always writing honestly about your problems and trying to find a way to solve others' problems too. It makes me proud to have given you all those Popsicles.

You're obviously learning a lot in America, not just about school but about life.

Love,

Popsicle Grandpa (Mr. Pang)

"You ready to go?" Lupe came in and asked.

I looked over from Popsicle Grandpa's letter and nodded.

"Just waiting for Jason," I said. I glanced over at him, taking out the last batch of lychee wonton cups as Hank worked at the grill.

"Two saltine burgers, well done!" Hank hollered. Mrs. Q took the burgers from him and put them on a plate with a side of Jason's five-spice sweet potato fries.

I breathed in the heavenly smell. It was *such* a great idea to open up the restaurant. Ever since we opened, it had been the talk of the town. The bank even gave us another loan, which we used to repaint the motel, take out the bunk beds, and expand East Meets West. It was just like Hank envisioned, and it was run by *us*.

"Save us some mint chocolate chip cupcakes for when we get back?" Lupe asked Carmela and Tanya.

"And some ice cream!" I smiled at Mrs. Sanker.

The ladies nodded. "You got it!" they said.

They weren't just cooks at the bistro—they were also owners of the Calivista now! After we came up with the idea of opening up a restaurant, I went to Mr. Cooper to see if he wanted to sell his shares to our new partners. He didn't like the idea of East Meets West, so he dumped his shares. Too bad, because business has been through the roof!

"Have a great time at Disneyland!" Hank said.

Lupe, Jason, and I grabbed one another's hands. I couldn't believe it. We were finally, *finally* going to Disneyland.

"Don't forget to pick us up by the gate tonight," I reminded Hank. He was taking us home because my dad was going with my mom to a faculty dinner tonight.

"Be there at ten! Right after the fireworks."

We gave him a thumbs-up as Jason took off his apron and we ran out the door.

"C'mon, let's go!!!" he exclaimed.

• • •

My dad stopped the car and dug into his pocket, pulling out four twenty-dollar bills. "Get yourselves a little something from the gift shop," he said.

"No, no, no," Lupe, Jason, and I all said at the same time.

"I've got my column money," I said, pulling out two crisp twenty-dollar bills from my own pocket. My grandfather had just wired me my last five columns' fees, minus the renovation money I'd contributed to their new bathroom.

"And I've got my front desk money," Lupe said, beaming. I was so glad she was manning the front desk with me after school again on Tuesdays and Thursdays.

"I have my bistro money right here!" Jason announced, pulling out a thick wad of cash. Lupe and I both stared. "Tips," Jason explained.

Dad chuckled. "Glad to hear it," he said. He turned and handed me Hank's Polaroid as we got out of the car. "Now go! Have fun! Take lots of pictures!"

"We will!" Lupe waved as she got out.

I lingered at the car for a second, peering at my dad. "You nervous about meeting Mom's coworkers tonight?" I asked. It was his first time going out with all of my mom's colleagues.

"A little nervous . . ." he admitted.

"You'll be great," I said.

Dad smiled. "Maybe I'll wear a lampshade!"

I giggled as I got out of the car, waving as he pulled away.

"C'mon!" Jason shouted, laughing as we raced toward the entrance. "A Whole New World" was playing over the loudspeakers. The air smelled of cotton candy and possibility. I closed my eyes and thought about all the long years I'd waited for this moment, how many times I worried it was almost never going to happen. And now here it was!!!

"You ready????" Jason asked me as Lupe waved our Disneyland tickets in her hand.

"READY!!!" I cried.

GIRLS GO CRAZY FOR RESPECT
By Mia Tang
Staff Writer
Anaheim Junior High School Times

At the Spring Dance, "Respect" was the name of the song that all the girls wanted to hear.

"We're tired of getting funny looks when we ask a boy out to a dance," Rena Escobar, grade 7, said. "Why shouldn't we be the one to ask?"

When it comes to the delicate subject of asking out a crush or telling a crush they liked them, many girls reported being labeled hurtful names or getting teased. Girls also reported being called upsetting names when a boy asked them out and they declined.

"We're 'mean' if a boy asks us out and we say no. And we're 'boy crazy' when we ask a boy out—it's like we can't win," says Fiona Smith, grade 8.

According to the Department of Education, 24% of girls and 20% of boys suffer from bullying. Bullying can include name-calling, harassment, taunting, teasing, excluding them from activities, spreading rumors about them, telling other kids not to be friends with them, and physical aggression, such as hitting, tripping, pinching, and breaking someone's things.

All this is at a huge cost to students' mental health. Studies show that when a student is bullied, they are impacted emotionally, mentally, and academically.

"We're tired of all the labels. The only 'crazy' I want to be called is respect-crazy!" said Lupe Garcia, grade 7.

That is exactly what many universities are prescribing. Researchers at Princeton, Rutgers, and Yale universities found that when kids call out bullies for their bad behavior, incidents of bullying go down at those schools.

So next time you see bullying, don't turn the other cheek. Speak up! You could make a huge difference in your school!

THREE FRIENDS GO TO DISNEYLAND
AT LONG LAST!
By Mia Tang, Lupe Garcia, and Jason Yao
Contributing Writers
Anaheim Junior High School Times

**Editor's note: The writers of
this piece interviewed themselves
for this story. And while normally,
this would go against journalistic
guidelines, we'll allow it for this
special story.

On Saturday, Anaheim Junior High
students Mia Tang, Lupe Garcia,
and Jason Yao visited Disneyland
together for the first time.
Even though they've lived next to
Disneyland for most of their lives,
the seventh graders had never had
the chance to experience the Magic
Kingdom together.

"We always wanted to go but
there was never a good time. We
were always busy or working," said
Mia, who runs the front desk of the
local independent Calivista Motel
with her best friend, Lupe Garcia.

The busy managers found time to celebrate three years of friendship. Along with their friend, local celebrity chef Jason Yao, they went on Space Mountain, the Jungle Cruise, the Submarine Voyage, Splash Mountain, and more! The verdict?

"It was everything I hoped it would be," said Mia.

"The fireworks were incredible!" Lupe agreed.

"*And* the Mickey Mouse ice cream sandwiches were pretty good," Jason added.

When asked which was their favorite ride, Mia replied, "My favorite ride was It's a Small World, because it made me think of my relatives back in China."

Lupe nodded. "Same here—it made me think of my aunts and uncles in Mexico."

Both girls' parents came to the United States in pursuit of the American dream. Now the kids are forging their own paths . . . one dream at a time!

AUTHOR'S NOTE

Me at eleven years old, right after we landed at Beijing Capital International Airport on our first trip back to China.

When I was eleven years old, my parents took me back to China to visit my relatives. I hadn't been back, or seen my cousins, aunts, and uncles, in the five years since we'd moved to the United States. I was so nervous when I got off the plane. I didn't know whether my cousins would still recognize me. Had they spent this whole time missing me, like I had them? Or had they been too busy having fun without me?

As it turned out, my cousins were as thrilled to see me as I was to see them. They remarked on how tall I was and how I could speak mouthfuls of a foreign language. I felt like an astronaut who had come back from the moon!

I wasn't the only thing that had changed. My jaw dropped when I walked out of Beijing Capital International Airport. Instead of bikes everywhere, the streets were full of cars. Tall buildings were going up all over the city, replacing some of the *siheyuans* I knew and loved. And everyone was super excited about this new restaurant, McDonald's. My cousins thought it was the fanciest restaurant in the world! Boy, did I have stories for them . . .

That Christmas, my cousins crowded around me, listening to my stories about America. My grandfather, a retired high school English teacher, caught an earful and encouraged me to write them down. So I did. I'll never forget the day my grandfather read one of my stories. He leaped from his bed — Charlie Bucket–grandfather style! — and ran to the nearest post office. He was mailing it off to the editor of a newspaper for middle school kids in China!

I thought my grandfather might have eaten one too many of the Jelly Bellies I had brought over from the US, but to my surprise, the editor wrote back — he wanted to publish my story! Thus began my long career as a young, international columnist!

We flew back home and I continued writing for that paper, about my friends, my customers at the motel, my teachers, my parents — you name it, I wrote about it! I wrote about the multiculturalism of the US (sadly, the colorism depicted in the story still exists in China). The columns were wildly popular in China, in part because at that time, there was very little information about life in America and everyone was curious.

Soon, I was writing for three different newspapers — all while trying to finish my homework, checking in on the weeklies, and learning the flute so I could stay in my marching band (which allowed me to avoid PE).

I didn't tell any of my friends at school what I was doing. That's because some of the time (okay, a *lot* of the time), I wrote about them, and about the different situations and problems we got into. I knew it probably wasn't a good idea, but I needed material! And I figured my writing was being published across the world, so they'd never read it. It was my secret.

Until one day I was out sick. And a stack of fan mail arrived for me at my school.

My classmates stared curiously at the stack on my desk, addressed to Author Kelly Yang. My disbelieving friends decided to peek inside. *Uh-oh!*

The next day, I had a *lot* of explaining to do.

After apologizing profusely to all my friends, and vowing never to write about them again without their permission, I was able to share my secret. Just like Mia, I had to learn my first lesson on journalistic integrity. And it was an important one.

I continued writing for newspapers throughout middle school and beyond. Eventually, my columns in China were compiled into two books, *Diary of a Young American Girl*, published when I was twelve, and *Kelly Yang Experiences America*, published when I was eighteen. It was surreal and scary being a memoirist at such a young age, opening myself up on the page and allowing myself to be vulnerable. Like Mia, I often struggled with fan mail, especially because so many of my stories were deeply personal. It was hard at times receiving critiques of not just my writing but also my life and my decisions, especially as I was still trying to figure them out.

In 2003, over Christmas, I went on a book tour in China where I met ten thousand kids, many of whom had grown up reading my stories. Meeting my fans for the first time was the most emotional, incredible experience of my life. I saw firsthand the impact of my writing, in not only bringing the world closer together . . . but each other closer together.

It is my biggest hope that I can give this power to readers of the Front Desk series — that through my books, children will be similarly empowered to use their pens and voices to effect change, just as Mia does. As an assault survivor, I also hope that *Room to Dream* opens a window for important conversations with children about consent. And gives kids the tools to advocate for themselves and their choices, from an early age.

Some of my early stories:

Reading My Way Home

By Kelly Yang, age 12

At first my writing aspirations started with just a simple program at a library in Anaheim, California, where I attended grades 3 and 4. I would summarize the book I had read and the librarian, whom I envied because he was the only one who beat the number of hours I stayed at the library, would give me a pencil, a sticker, or if I was really lucky, a brand-new book. Not only did this program awaken more of my reading eagerness, it also guided me to better organize my thoughts as a young writer.

When simply summarizing a book was no longer a challenge for me, I raised the level and started to write my own stories. Drifting in and out of every creative story bursting inside my head, I would stay up all night to weave sentence after sentence, as though they were pieces of a quilt. While my other classmates took vacations to Florida and Europe, I spent my summer comfortably at home as my pen unfolded each story. When I started to win essay contests, it dawned on me that when the librarians nourished me with books, they were also watering the writing seed inside of me, which then grew to become a blossoming flower with petals of spectacular stories.

A great deal of gratitude is owed to the librarians in this nation who have provided me with crucial steps along my way to becoming a writer. And whenever I walk into a favorite library and smell the scent of aging books, it doesn't matter what the library looks like — it could have torn wallpaper and worn-out carpet — no other place could make me feel more at home.

Attention, Everybody!

Every day in my math class, everyone is always bored. Some people sleep, other people eat breakfast, others daydream. No matter what you do, nobody listens to our teacher. To solve this problem, our smart math teacher finally came up with a solution.

Mr. French decided that since everybody likes candy, the only way to get our attention was to give us candy. So, he came up with a brilliant idea. He put a bunch of candy inside a big plastic ball that anyone can open. In class, as he taught in front of us, he asked us math questions. Anytime someone answered one question right, Mr. French would throw the ball at the student and the student could grab some of the candy inside. Then, the student would have

With John Simon, my favorite librarian at Anaheim Library, holding up one of my columns.

to throw the ball to the next student and they would grab some candy and so forth.

The idea made us all sit up and pay attention for a while, but soon, everybody went to sleep. We had all eaten too much candy! The only person who was still eating was a kid named Mo. He ate so much candy that finally Mr. French just looked at him and said, "I'm sorry, Mo, but I don't have enough money to keep feeding you. You're going to have to get this question wrong."

<u>I am Chinese-American</u>

I am Chinese-American. I grew up in America, but was born in China. I recall my life in both countries quite vividly.

I remember spending time with my family in China when I was little, eating dumplings on Lunar New Year's Eve, riding on my parents' bicycles on the way home, and yes, I even remember using those "clean" public bathrooms China is infamous for.

When I was six, I moved to America for "a better life." My parents stressed that the education system in America could provide a finer academic atmosphere, and with that, we boarded the plane. Growing up with American friends, I acted like any other American girl and I was proud to be an American. I remember eating hot dogs and hamburgers with pride at baseball games with my dad, shedding tears of joy when the US Women's Figure Skating Champions Michelle Kwan and Tara Lipinski took home the gold, and enjoying total freedom in a country that provides this to me.

But I did not forget that I am also Chinese. I grew up with a sense of pride for both my native country and my new home country. I consider my life a unique mixture of both cultures, like most immigrants in the US. I don't feel entirely of one culture or another, but both America and China make me who I am.

ACKNOWLEDGMENTS

Thank you to my agent, Tina Dubois, for always giving me the room to dream, and supporting those dreams every step of the way. This book would not have been possible without you. Thanks for always believing so hard in me.

To my editor, Amanda Maciel, thank you for guiding this story and traveling with me across the world. We edited most of this story during the pandemic. It was so special to be able to journey with you through these pages. I am honored to have you as my editor.

Warmest thanks to my greater Scholastic family: Talia Seidenfeld, David Levithan, Lauren Donovan, Taylan Salvati, Ellie Berger, Erin Berger, Rachel Feld, Lizette Serrano, Emily Heddleson, and Danielle Yadao. Thanks for supporting me, Mia, and the entire Calivista crew!

My deepest thanks to Maike Plenzke and Maeve Norton for bringing my girl Mia to life; your artistic talents never cease to astound me. To my dear friend John Schumacher, thank you for spreading book joy wherever you go and for supporting the Front Desk series. Many thanks as well to Audra Boltion Ortiz, for spreading the word about *Three Keys*.

To my greater ICM team: Alicia Gordon, Ava Greenfield, John Burnham, Tamara Kawar, and Roxane Edouard—thank you for bringing my stories to the world. To my lawyer, Richard Thompson, thank you for working tirelessly on my deals. Much love to Olivia Milch, Ian Bryce, Alan Gasmer, Peter Jaysen, Wayne Wang, Janet Wu, Caroline Mak, and Naketha Mattocks: Thanks for going on this wild journey with me!

Sincere thanks to my publishers around the globe—Knights Of, Walker Books, Kim Dong Publishing, Dipper, Omnibook Press, Porteghaal, Éditions Albin Michel, Grupo SM, and Kodansha.

To my family, particularly my mom, who helped translate so many of my early stories. Love you, Mom, so, so much. Thank you, Dad, for never thinking any of my dreams were too out there to realize. To my husband, Steve, and my kids, Eliot, Tilden, and Nina: You guys are my everything. Thanks for cheering Mommy on. Eliot, thanks for reading an early draft of *Room to Dream* and encouraging me.

Thank you to all the librarians and independent booksellers who have supported me and placed my books in kids' hands. I am where I am today because of you.

Finally, I would like to thank all the readers. It is the greatest honor of my life to be able to write for you, and I hope my stories bring you joy, hope, and laughter.

Author photo by Denise Pontak

KELLY YANG

is the author of the *New York Times* bestselling novels *Three Keys* and *Front Desk*, which also won the 2019 Asian/Pacific American Award for Literature and was chosen as a Best Book of the Year by multiple organizations, including NPR, the *Washington Post*, and the New York Public Library. She's also the author of the young adult novel *Parachutes*. Her family immigrated to the United States from China to California when she was young, and she grew up in circumstances very similar to those of Mia Tang. After leaving the motels and attending college at the age of thirteen, she graduated from UC Berkeley and Harvard Law School. She is the founder of the Kelly Yang Project, a leading writing and debating program for children in Asia and the United States, and has written for the *South China Morning Post*, the *New York Times*, the *Washington Post*, and the *Atlantic*. To learn more about her and the Front Desk books, visit frontdeskthebook.com.